THE GREEK SUMMER

*To Charley and Pam
Best wishes
JP Miller*

THE GREEK SUMMER

A Novel

John Douglas Miller

iUniverse, Inc.
New York Lincoln Shanghai

THE GREEK SUMMER
A Novel

All Rights Reserved © 2003 by John Douglas Miller

No part of this book may be reproduced or transmitted in any form or by any means, graphic, electronic, or mechanical, including photocopying, recording, taping, or by any information storage retrieval system, without the written permission of the publisher.

iUniverse, Inc.

For information address:
iUniverse, Inc.
2021 Pine Lake Road, Suite 100
Lincoln, NE 68512
www.iuniverse.com

ISBN: 0-595-29767-6 (pbk)
ISBN: 0-595-66049-5 (cloth)

Printed in the United States of America

This is the West, sir. When the legend
Becomes fact, print the legend.

    Editor of *The Shinbone Star,* in
    The Man Who Shot Liberty Valance

Contents

Chapter 1:	The Earthquake	1
Chapter 2:	Dramatis Personae	12
Chapter 3:	Earthquake's Box	24
Chapter 4:	The Ring of Guy-jeez	34
Chapter 5:	Enter: Apollo Lykeios	44
Chapter 6:	Up Jumped the Pantheon	55
Chapter 7:	Dionysian Frenzy	66
Chapter 8:	The Symposium	79
Chapter 9:	Living the Good Life	90
Chapter 10:	Kings of the Earth	102
Chapter 11:	The Good Guys Versus the Bad Guys	113
Chapter 12:	Epistole Adelphon	124
Chapter 13:	Zoe Mou, Sas Agapo	136
Chapter 14:	The Lords of the Ring	147
Chapter 15:	A Cock for Asclepius	159
Chapter 16:	The Young Philadelphians	170
Chapter 17:	To the Chief, Ave Atque Vale	180
Chapter 18:	The Party	192

Chapter 19: Breaking Up is Hard to Do 204
Chapter 20: Deja Vu, All Over Again 215

Chapter 1

The Earthquake

The rain came early that day, about mid-morning, a soft rain that whispered through the leaves and pitted the dark lake water. The day wore on; the rain continued. I could barely make out the houses across the lake. I sat in the study, reading a bit, and finally gave up to a strange, wistful sadness, lay the book aside, and stared out at the rain, the gauzy outline of houses, the dark lake water. If I had any concrete thoughts, I don't know what they were. I spent most of the day in the study, and most of the time in the study I spent looking out at the rain. I couldn't shake off the feeling that something strange was about to happen; not something bad, and not something good, but something strange.

Nothing strange happened. The rain finally died away to a mist. Darkness came, and the houses across the lake glowed like smudges of yellow paint. I got up and went to bed.

At two-thirty a.m., the bedside phone screamed in my ear and jerked me awake. Here it comes, I thought as I rolled to my left side, propped myself on one elbow, and picked up the receiver. Here comes the strange thing that in a more reasonable universe would have happened before I had achieved something of a sound sleep.

"Miller?" said a familiar voice. "Miller, did I wake you up?"

"No, Bowman," I replied. "Why would I be sleeping at such a time as this?"

"Twelve-thirty."

"Twelve-thirty on your end of the continent. It's two-thirty here. Come to think of it, even in Malibu most reasonable people are in bed asleep by this time."

"Earthquake O'Toole died," he said.

"You don't say. I didn't know he was still alive."

"He's not."

"Yeah, but I thought he died years ago. I haven't heard from him since he called with that crazy scheme for bilking welfare money out of the government."

"He didn't just die. He was murdered. Beaten to death with a blunt instrument. They found him near the railroad tracks down in San Ysidro."

"Oh, my God…"

I don't know how long after invoking the name of God I sat there dumb with the receiver pressed against my ear, but it was long enough that he finally said, "Are you still there?"

"Yeah. Let me call you back."

"Why? Are your kidneys still causing you trouble?"

"I want to get out of bed and make some coffee," I said. "By the way, how did you find out about Earthquake?"

"The county coroner called me. I started to call you earlier, but…"

"Why did the coroner call you? Never mind. I'll call you back as soon as I can get up and get my head in gear. I spent all day fighting a feeling of impending doom. I hope I'm dreaming all this."

"I hope you are too, because that means I'm asleep and none of it really happened."

This last comment reminded me of a conversation Bowman and I had forty years before, when we were drinking beer on the beach at La Jolla, talking solipsism and slobbering toward drunken euphoria. "Maybe none of this is really happening," he said. "Maybe it's all a dream, and I'll wake up in Brookville and run down to Mrs. Hopkins' second grade class."

No such luck, Bowman.

Mumbling to myself, I got up, pulled on this old, ratty bathrobe, went into the bathroom to splash cold water on my face, then paused to look at myself. I was about as old and ratty as my bathrobe. But it wasn't always so; forty years ago when we were lifeguards together—Bowman and Earthquake O'Toole and I—why I fancied myself a magnificent specimen. But that was then, and this was now, and Bowman and I were aging Americans, while the Earthquake, or what was left of what had been the Earthquake, lay on a coroner's slab in San Diego.

I brewed coffee and called Bowman back.

"Surprise," he said, cynical as always. "You weren't dreaming, and I'm about as pissed off as I've ever been in my life."

"I thought you sounded a little miffed when you called," I answered. "But I don't get it. You're mad because someone killed the Earthquake. There have been several times I thought you were gonna kill him yourself."

"Oh, it's not the killing that's got me going. Wait till you hear the whole story. The coroner didn't just call me out of the goodness of his heart, like I was the next of kin or gave a damn what happened to the Earthquake, that fat little son-of-a-bitch…"

"Of course not," I said. "He called because you've been included in the Earthquake's will."

There was a pause.

"How did you know?"

"I thought I was making a joke," I said.

"Well, the joke's on me," he said. "The Earthquake left a holographic will and named me as his executor."

"What would he be leaving to anyone? The last I heard he didn't have a dime to his name."

"Are holographic wills legal?" Bowman asked.

"They are in Oklahoma. Texas, too. I don't know about California. But they probably are. But I still don't know what he could be leaving to anyone, or why anyone would have to be his executor. Do you suppose he had some money stashed away?"

"If he did he sure wouldn't be leaving it to me," Bowman said. "The last time I saw him I threw him bodily out of the house. Told him if I ever saw him again I'd shoot him sure as hell."

"But strange things can happen," I said. "He did leave a will, and he did name you as his executor."

"So what? Does that mean I have to do it? Maybe I'll just turn the job down. Is the state of California coming after me because I refused to play nursemaid to that idiot one last time?"

"Now hang on, Bowman," I said. "Think about it a minute. Maybe the Earthquake was a skid row bum, but occasionally those guys surprise you. Why, I heard of a case right here. Some guy died up in Tulsa. I mean literally in the gutter. And it turned out he had something like half-a-million scattered out in banks all over the country. And he left it all to some goofy charity that cares for homeless dogs because his cousins wouldn't have anything to do with him."

"So what are you saying, Miller?"

"I'm saying, Bowman, that it wouldn't do you any harm to contact the county officials in San Diego and at least talk to them. That's all. Then you can blow the whole thing off. Or maybe you wind up a wealthy man. He might even have left me something. In fact, he might have left me his entire estate. I never threw him out of the house and threatened to shoot him."

"Why, you miserable bastard," said Bowman.

This conversation took place very early on Tuesday morning. The following evening, at the civilized hour of eight o'clock, Bowman called again.

"All right," he said, "on your advice, and against my better judgment, I called the county."

"And you learned?"

"Not much. They're sending me a Xeroxed copy…not of the will, but of the letter he left naming me executor."

"No indication of what his estate amounts to?"

"Nary a word. The county has some other documents, and I'm supposed to meet with a court appointed attorney to sign some papers, then we open and read the will. I still have a good mind to tell them to kiss my ass. Every time I think of that fat little bastard saddling me with this, I get madder. It's like revenge for me throwing him out that time."

"Look, Bowman," I said, "what better thing do you have to do than take a trip down to San Diego? Plan it as a mini-vacation. Go to some of the old places. Go out to La Jolla and throw beer cans into the cove."

"Well, since you put it that way," he said, "what better thing do you have to do than to go with me?"

"What do you mean?"

"Just what I said. You've got nothing to do. Fly out here tomorrow. Next day, we'll drive down."

"I can't…"

"If you don't go, I don't go," he said. "Period!"

He was right, of course. I had nothing better to do. And he was right about something else, something unspoken but that was just as surely knocking around inside his skull as it was in mine: we were both eaten up with curiosity about Earthquake O'Toole's estate, what was in his will, and why he would have named Bowman his executor. Whatever he had intended, the Earthquake had hooked two fish with his final haul, for by this time there was no way we could have been kept from making the trip to San Diego to get a look into the sealed documents that held the final bequest and wishes of a bum neither of us had seen in over thirty years. The next day I boarded a Delta flight in Oklahoma City, bound for

Los Angeles International, off on one of the screwiest wild goose chases of my career. For me, however, the goose laid a genuine golden egg, but not in the way I expected.

I took a book with me to read on the plane. I always do this, but I never get any substantive reading done. This trip was no exception. The flight to Dallas for the Los Angeles connection was only forty minutes. There was no time to settle in and read on that one. Then, on the Los Angeles flight, I was seated beside a talkative young lady coming home from SMU for the summer, and she was engaging enough as a conversationalist that she made me forget that talkative strangers on planes usually annoy me. In fact, she turned out to be just what I needed because she asked the sorts of questions I needed to answer for myself, and my answers to her evoked the memory of a summer long ago, the summer of 1960.

She was bright and pretty, and her name was Peggy Gaines. I guessed she was about the age of my granddaughter, and I also guessed she was probably a freshman, and certainly no more than a sophomore. She turned out to be a junior, and, of all things, a philosophy major. This, in fact, is what started our conversation.

"*The Republic*," she said, pointing to the book I had on my lap but hadn't yet opened.

"Just brushing up on some stuff," I said. "Trying to remember what was going on in my head when I was about your age."

"You read Plato when you were my age?"

"Oh, I read at him. I'm not sure how much of him I understood. Enough that I majored in philosophy."

She smiled. "That's my major," she said.

"Well, then you know these fellows—the Greeks."

"Not very well. I've only read part of *The Republic*. You know how professors are, a little here and a little there."

"Actually, I do," I told her. "I taught philosophy for thirty years. I've assigned plenty of bits and pieces in my day. But I retired. Now I'm trying to put the bits and pieces together."

"So what was going on in your head? When you were my age, you know?"

I laughed. "I'm not sure. When I was your age, I was a lifeguard at a swimming pool in San Diego. If I remember, all I had in my head were images of girls in two-piece swimsuits."

"Then why did you read *The Republic*?"

"It was sort of an accident. One of the other lifeguards, a fellow named Bowman, was taking a course in philosophy, and we sort of fell into discussions about what he was having to read. All that summer we sat in the sun and partied and discussed philosophy. Bowman and I call it the Greek Summer."

"You and Bowman are still friends then."

"Yes, we are. We've been best friends ever since then. I'll tell you something else. See this book?" I tapped the closed volume on my lap. "This is the very book we were reading and discussing. I've kept it all these years."

"Gosh, that's neat," she said. "I hope I have some of the same friends when I'm your age."

"I hope so, too. You probably will."

"Where is Bowman now?"

"He lives in Malibu. He's like me, retired teacher. Single. I'm on my way out to see him."

"Wow. I'll bet you two have fun when you get together. What year was that—when you were lifeguards?"

"Nineteen-sixty."

"Forty-one years ago. In forty-one years I'll be sixty years old."

"I'm sixty-one," I said. "Bowman is sixty-three. And we do have lots of fun when we get together. But I'm not sure how much fun we'll have this trip."

"Oh," she said. "Trouble, huh?"

"Nothing unusual," I told her. "One of the facts of old age is that people start to die. One of our buddies from the swimming pool is dead, and we have to settle his affairs. The Earthquake."

"Huh?"

I laughed. "Earthquake O'Toole was his name. Well, I guess it wasn't his real name, but I don't know what his real name was. Maybe I never knew it. We called him the Earthquake because he reminded us of a cartoon character in *Li'l Abner*."

"What's that?"

"A long dead cartoon strip that was very popular at the time. Things do change, don't they?"

"Boy, they sure do," she said.

"I guess that's why I brought *The Republic* along. I'm trying to remember what we were doing and thinking back then. I know it had a lot to do with philosophy, but I'm sort of seeing through a glass, darkly."

We talked on in this vein until she nodded off to sleep (I have talked many students to sleep over the years) and left me with my unopened book, staring out the window at clouds, thinking about Bowman, Earthquake O'Toole, and the Greek Summer. Ironically, the first time I met Bowman, we were sent off together to get the Earthquake out of trouble; now here we were again, as this unwilling association drew to its close, off to get the Earthquake out of the last trouble he would ever know—if he knew anything now. Ah, the joy of lapsing into metaphysical speculation!

When we landed at L.A. International, Peggy Gaines, representing irrepressible youth, bounded up, refreshed and eager while I, representative of the older generation, was exhausted.

Bowman met me at the gate. He was exhausted, too, and still angry.

"What's the plan?" I asked. We were walking toward the escalators that would take us down to the baggage claim area.

"Do you have any bags?"

"Only what I'm carrying. You know me. Travel light."

"Okay. We roll."

"Roll where? I need some sleep, man. I'm beat."

"I am, too. Hardly slept at all. But the attorney meets us at nine in the morning, and I'm not up to fighting the early interstate traffic down to San Diego. We'll make San Diego in two hours and get a good night's sleep before our legal encounter."

"You mean before *your* legal encounter," I said. "Remember, I'm only an interested bystander."

"Keep it up, Miller. I, the executor, will have you declared mentally incompetent and assign your part of the estate to one of your cousins in Texas."

The trip to San Diego ought to have been time for the two of us to fill in all the gaps in our memories of Earthquake O'Toole, but it turned out to be another of those exercises in selective recollection Bowman and I have engaged in over the years. One of us remembered one thing, and the other remembered something else, and neither of us could agree exactly on what any of us had done or said. We particularly couldn't agree on the enigmatic Earthquake. He was like the Cartesian ego which David Hume refused to accept as a concrete entity: as we pursued him, he collapsed into a million colored fragments of impressions: dust in the wind. And what remained, apparently eternal to our minds? The pool, bronzed bodies, and the Greek philosophers bouncing ideas off one another like participants in a game of intellectual dodge ball.

"Why did Earthquake gravitate to our circle?" I asked.

"The booze and the girls, I guess. The booze at least. None of the girls wanted anything to do with him."

"He didn't get into the philosophy, did he? I don't remember him ever reading a book."

"But he came to the Symposium," Bowman said.

"The what?"

"Remember, that's what the Amazon called our get-togethers. The Symposium."

"Yeah," I said. "I forgot about that. O'Toole came to those?"

"Yeah. Just sort of laid around."

After a bit, Bowman said, "The Amazon. Boy, there was an argumentative bitch."

"I wonder what happened to her," I said.

"Probably became a counselor at Bennington—or one of those places."

So it continued, all the way down the coast, through Del Mar and La Jolla, the haunts of our youth, and into the dazzling glare of nighttime San Diego. We found a motel, and after a couple of jolts of Glen Livet 12, we slept, really slept. As I have already said, we were both exhausted.

Things looked much better the next morning, at least to my refreshed and rested eyes, and I had to admit that Bowman had been right about driving down the night before. We showered, shaved, packed up, and checked out of the motel. Then we went into the restaurant for coffee and breakfast. Mainly coffee. Amazing, isn't it, how one reaches a point in which life seems to consist in struggling to stay awake and fighting to go to sleep. Just then, we were struggling out of our sleep cycle.

I suggested Bowman call the county coroner while I drank more coffee.

"Don't need the coroner," he said. "We have to get to the law office of this guy...a..." He fished up his wallet, opened it, took out a business card, and read. "Paul Baxter, attorney at law."

I can assure anyone who is interested that the attorney functions under a name other than the one I have given him. He came across, to me, as the sort of fellow who cheated on his bar exam, and I wouldn't have hired him to go into court on a traffic violation. But he had this case, through some county process that I never quite understood, and we were obliged to deal with him if we wanted to get a look inside the will of Earthquake O'Toole.

"Paul Baxter," Bowman later said. "A name that will live in infamy." He said this because Baxter, a court appointed attorney being paid by the tax payers to take care of business, had the temerity to send each of us a bill for his services several months later. Bowman responded with one of the most hilarious letters I have ever read. But I digress.

"Gentlemen," he began, once we were seated in his rather plush office. "Gentlemen," he leaned back in his leather-upholstered swivel chair. "By the way, sir, who are you?"

"Me?" I pointed to myself.

"Yes. I know Mr. Bowman, here, and he has shown me proof of his identity. But who are you?"

"I'm..."

"He's a close friend of the deceased," Bowman said, "and I have reason to believe he is included in the will."

"Yes," Paul Baxter said, "but who are you?"

"Doug Miller," I said. "John Douglas Miller, to be exact."

"Ah, Miller," said the attorney. "As a matter of fact, you *are* included in the will. You two are the only ones named." Grinning, he shook his head. "This is unusual business," he said. "Oh, not that I haven't been involved in settling up matters for a bum or two in my day..."

"Which I've been wondering about myself," said Bowman. "What sort of estate could the Earthquake..."

"Who?"

"Earthquake O'Toole."

"How quaint," he said, and drummed his fingers on his desk. "How charming. The Earthquake. According to the coroner he looks as if he was on the business end of an earthquake. Do either of you gentlemen actually know the given name of Mr. O'Toole?"

"You know," I told him, "we were talking about that on the way down here. Before Bowman got the letter from the county, I'm not sure we ever knew his real name."

Paul Baxter, Esquire, never losing the lopsided grin he'd had on ever since we came in, shook his head again and said, "Another oddity of the O'Toole case. The two heirs don't even know the name of their benefactor. Well, to answer Mr. Bowman's question, the estate of Mr. O'Toole is contained in that cardboard box over there." He nodded toward the corner of the room.

The box, battered and held together with masking tape, sat on a small table. It was perhaps a yard long and a foot and a half wide and high. It looked as if it had been sat on, hard, by someone who weighed at least as much as Earthquake.

Paul Baxter, Esquire cleared his throat. "When the body of the late Mr. O'Toole was found, a subsequent search of his domicile was conducted. I understand it was a real dump, something over in Lemon Grove that should have been condemned prior to the gold rush. Anyway, that box was found, and nothing more. Oh, except the letter, a copy of which you have received, Mr. Bowman, and an envelope containing Mr. O'Toole's will. Shall I read it?"

"I can't wait," Bowman said.

Paul Baxter, Esquire smiled. "I, Percival Gregory O'Toole, being of sound mind, leave all of my property of any kind to my friend Bruce Bowman. Except for my copy of Plato's *Republic*, which I leave to my friend Doug Miller."

Bowman and I sat there for a moment, waiting for something more. But there was nothing more. In fact, Paul Baxter, Esquire, told us there was nothing more.

"There's nothing more, gentlemen. I doubt you expected much when you came, so you can't be disappointed. My secretary, has some papers for you to sign, a release, etcetera, etcetera, and you may take the estate of the late Mr. O'Toole and be on your way."

"Where's my book?" I asked him.

"Your what?"

"The book left to me by the late Mr. Percival O'Toole. Where is it?"

He shrugged and said, "I suppose it's in the box. If not, I have no idea."

"Open the box," I said. "Before I sign any release, I want to be sure that I've got my book."

We all got up and crossed the room to the table, which held the misshapen box. Paul Baxter, Esquire, took a penknife from his pocket, opened it, and cut the tape. Immediately, a musty smell of unwashed clothing rushed up at us. Baxter folded back the box's flaps, then gestured toward its contents as if to say, "Lo and behold." But, in fact, he said nothing, only shook his head again.

Bowman began pawing through it.

"I'd be careful if I were you," I told him. "The egg plant that ate Chicago could be in there."

"No," he said, "but you can quit worrying. Here's your book. And junk, junk, junk..."

We decided against driving back to Malibu; for reasons I can't quite explain, we wanted to hang around the San Diego area. I had described the proposed enterprise to Bowman as a mini-vacation, and this is exactly what it turned out to be, for both of us. We hadn't been together in San Diego for many years, and here we were reliving, prompted by the strange and unasked for contribution of Earthquake (excuse me, Percival Gregory) O'Toole, the halcyon days of our golden youth. We tossed the box in the trunk of Bowman's car and took off, back to the beaches of La Jolla, where we found as reasonable a motel as we could, invested in two pairs of swimming trunks and a case of beer, and set out to walk the sands that had once been as familiar to us as our own backyards. We were young Greeks again, and it was the Greek summer of 1960…as long as we avoided looking into mirrors.

Chapter 2

Dramatis Personae

This part is actually supposed to go at the first of a drama, but this is not the first part, and my story is not exactly a drama. I mention this to show that I know what I'm doing, and not because I really care. There was a time when I cared, but that day is long past, and now I just please myself in what I do, and in what I write and think. It's a nice chapter heading, if I do say so.

This is a true story, with this disclaimer. It has a few stretchers. I stole that line from Mr. Samuel Clemens, who put it in the mouth of Huckleberry Finn, and I'm sure Clemens and Finn forgive me. It's a good line, and it expresses exactly what I wish to convey: why—as the fellow says—reinvent the wheel? But let's tighten it up a bit: this is *mostly* a true story (I stole that line from *Butch Cassidy and the Sundance Kid*) about events that occurred in the spring and summer of 1960 to a group of young men just beginning to figure out what it means to be a human.

Ah, I heard that!

No, this is not a standard coming of age tale. In my estimation, too many of those have already been done, and most of them have been done rather poorly. This is a story of young men, in the most unlikely of circumstances, groping toward intellectual enlightenment, something none of them knew existed until they encountered an old Greek who wandered barefoot in Athens some 350 years before the birth of Christ. His name was Socrates. And just as he impacted the lives of young Greeks in that early time, he impacted the young Greeks that we were. Except we weren't Greeks. We were the standard mixture of young males that came out of middle-America in the days prior to Vietnam, civil rights demonstrations, drugs, and sexual liberation. We were Irish, Scot, German, and many things in between.

I guess this could be called an intellectual coming of age.

Now, as to the characters. When I say this is a true story, I mean just that. But with the exception of Bruce Bowman and myself, not one of the people in this book ever actually existed. So don't go looking for Earthquake O'Toole, for you won't find him. He, like all the others, is a composite of several people Bowman and I knew in the Greek Summer, and many of the events are composed of several events (and some didn't happen at all), and most of the dialogue is reconstructed from my admittedly rusty memory. All that said, I return to my earlier statement: this is mostly a true story.

And the characters were:

Myself: nineteen years old at the time and a product of the East Texas cotton fields, who was moved to Oklahoma when very young because my father couldn't support a family in the world of waking reality as a small cotton farmer. I was educated in the school system of Oklahoma City, had gone to Oklahoma State University at Stillwater, and had dropped out to avoid flunking out. With this stellar background, I went out into the world to seek my fortune.

Bruce Bowman. He was twenty-one and came from a little town in southern Ohio named Brookville. His father worked in Dayton, and Bowman was a typical product of the Midwest. He was an Eagle Scout, graduated from Brookville High School in 1956 with little to distinguish him except that for years he held the high school record for the discus throw. He went off to Bowling Green University in the fall of 1956, dropped out to avoid flunking out, and went out into the world to seek his fortune.

Percival Gregory O'Toole, AKA the Earthquake. He was not a college dropout. In fact, he never dropped in. He read, eclectically, and had a smattering of knowledge about many things, but no real depth in any area so far as I ever knew. How he wound up as a lifeguard was always a matter of wonder to me, for he looked like nothing so much as a pear: all gut and hips, with narrow shoulders, small feet, and hands that Bowman used to describe as little garden rakes. All things considered, however, he was much more interesting than Bowman and I could have ever hoped to be, which is probably why we allowed him to hang around. He opened a world for us that we, the products of stable, Middle American homes, rarely saw. His home life was lamentable, and, in fact, all but nonexistent. He was actually raised by a maternal uncle, educated in the parochial schools of St. Louis, whipped into a semi-civilized state, literally as well as figuratively, by nuns who brooked little nonsense, and was kicked out into the world to seek his fortune. He was street-wise, opportunistic, and, at the same time, apt to commit blunders in human relations that a six-year-old child would have easily avoided. Where it not for this strange misfit, dubbed the Earthquake because of the blank look he assumed when not being directly spoken to, there would be little for me to write about, for he became the foil against which Bowman and I tested our infantile flights of philosophical fantasy. For years, every time Bowman and I got together and began reminiscing about the Greek Summer, it wouldn't be long before one of us would say, "Do you remember when the Earthquake…" and so on.

The Amazon. Her name was Betty Ann Greybow, but we called her the Amazon for reasons I will later explain. Her younger sister, Mary Alice Greybow (Maggie, to us), was sort of sweet on me, and I liked her, too, to tell the truth. The Amazon was a physical education major at a university in Washington State, and was home for the summer. She was also a water safety instructor. She got a summer job at the pool with us. She was tall, tanned, blond, and good-looking, and she once humiliated Earthquake by beating him arm wrestling. "She cheated," he said, without bothering to explain how. He needn't have tried to cover for himself, because the Amazon was strong enough that Bowman and I could hardly beat her. When she blew the whistle and said, "Hey, kid, you with the blue suede shoes, outta the pool," people moved, blue suede shoes and all. I have always thought that the Amazon began by looking down her nose at us, and wound up being in love with us—with Bowman, at any rate.

The others. No list of characters would be complete without some reference to that crowd of invisible, but very present, individuals that swarmed around us that summer. Socrates was there, and Plato, and Glaucon, Thrasymachus and Crito. Jack London was a part of the gathering. In fact his book *Martin Eden* had as much to do with our awakened interest in philosophy as did the college course Bowman was taking. Friedrich Nietzsche showed up regularly, as did Ayn Rand, or, perhaps more accurately, John Galt and Francisco d'Anconia. And winking at us from behind every tree was Dionysus, inviting us to leave the Apollonian world of the philosophers and to come over and revel with him. We were awash in the golden light of the past. Winds came to us from Ionia, across the wine-dark sea of Homer, and brought exotic smells and the tones of lute and aulos. Ah, to be young, and to discover that you actually possess a mind.

The supernumeraries. There are lots of these in my little drama, such as Paul Baxter, Esquire. They neither require, nor do they deserve, a paragraph of their own, but I'll give them this brief one to show how decent I can be.

The scene. This entire drama was played out against the backdrop of an olympic-sized pool, and the beaches of southern California. In my memory, we are never far from water, never under skies that are not awash in sunlight or swarming with a million stars. We are never far from the sound of thundering surf and wind stirring in palm trees. The smells of suntan lotion and chlorine are mingled with those of exotic flowers. The public address system at the pool is wired into a radio, and in between announcements ("Billy Smith, your mother wants you to call home."), Bobby Darin is singing "Somewhere beyond the sea…"

I am not sure how much I actually believe in accidents, but on the other hand, I am not sure how much I actually believe in fate, which is a non-philosophical way of saying that I am caught up in the same metaphysical riddle the Greeks struggled to solve but never actually did. Was Oedipus forced by some overriding cosmic necessity to live out the prophecy of the oracle? More to the point, did we all just flounder our way to the pool that summer, or were we guided by something or someone greater than ourselves? I know what happened, in simple, naturalistic terms, but I have always suspected there was more to it than can be accounted for by simple naturalism.

We joined the Navy.

Why would anyone join the Navy? I've heard a variety of reasons given, usually when the boys were drinking and moaning collectively about their disliking for the circumstances in which they found themselves. One was trying to get away from a woman, and another was trying to get away from an irate husband, and one wanted to see the world, and one was at loose ends and facing the threat of being drafted into the Army, and one had been fascinated by the books of Jack London. One said he joined because he had always liked the uniform. This always seemed to me a singularly stupid reason for signing up for a government sponsored cruise, but several women I have known, including my deceased wife, disagreed. "Sailors are so cute," she always said, and I would respond with something to the effect that their behavior was generally anything but cute.

Bowman, the Earthquake and I were from the loose ends school. We joined because we had nothing better to do at the time, and crawling around in mud with the Army didn't appeal to us. Then accident, or fate (take your pick), moved us on life's great chessboard to Naval Air Station Miramar, north of San Diego on Highway 395. Bowman and Earthquake had reasons for being assigned there that made some sense: they were both what we called airdales, aviation electronics techs. I was a mere seaman, blackshoe navy, and should by any logical expectation have been riding a destroyer in the Taiwan Strait; but logic does not always guide government decisions, and for reasons only a metaphysician could love, I wound up with orders that sent me from boot camp to Miramar where I was assigned to Special Services.

The swimming pool, operating under the Special Services aegis, was nominally a combat training pool. But how many pilots can be dumped in full flight gear into a pool to see how well they can get out and get their life rafts inflated? It actually served as a free summer diversion for sailors and their dependents, a military version of the sort of place that exists in any community of any size and draws sun worshippers and fun seekers by the hundreds. And they came, sailors and non-sailors, young and old, beautiful and ugly, to dive from the boards, and to plunge into the water, or to just lay around and look beautiful.

Those California girls were simply gorgeous.

Now at this olympic-size pool there were lifeguard towers, one at the middle of the pool and one on the shallow end, and the lifeguard towers had to be manned by lifeguards who actually could swim, and who could actually go into the pool and save someone if the situation called for it. So the call went out across the base for those who had the requisite abilities to show up for a swimming test and for possible temporary transfer to Special Services. Bowman and I were naturals. Both of us had been Boy Scouts and had swimming and lifesaving merit badges. I was already attached to Special Services. The Earthquake floundered in through some strange process, probably the same one that arranged for my orders to Miramar. And there were others, including the Amazon, so that we had ten lifeguards divided into two sections, each section covering the pool for three days with three days off. The pool was closed on Mondays. At any given time, there were three lifeguards on duty, one on each of the two towers and one walking the pool perimeter. Two would be resting, which usually meant lying in the sun and talking to the girls. Of course, the pool was such a great place that even on days off we generally went there and hung around the girls. In the years since, a large number of which I spent as a philosophy professor, I have often told my male students that they do not truly grasp the meaning of dying and going to heaven unless they have been lifeguards in California.

But the Earthquake almost didn't make it.

This brings me to a point to which I alluded earlier: it is ironic how Bowman and I first met when we were called on to get Earthquake out of a mess, and at the end, with Earthquake stretched out on a slab at the morgue, we came together again to get him out of a mess.

I suppose I should say something more definite about Chief Crouch, although at the first of this chapter I merely lumped him together with the unnamed supernumeraries. He was assigned to the pool as the section chief, which is interesting because he couldn't swim across the pool, did not possess lifeguard credentials, hated the sun, didn't much like people, and tolerated the Navy only because he was close to retirement after a twenty year stretch that began prior to the Japanese attack on Pearl Harbor. We got him because no one else wanted him. Chief Crouch, you see, had a definite drinking problem, a thing not totally unknown to sailors. He, like Bowman and Earthquake, was an electronics technician of some species, but because his hands frequently shook, and because he was subject to seeing double, no pilot wanted him on the line dealing with aircraft one of them might actually have to get in and fly. So he was assigned to us. How much trouble could he cause, after all, as long as he did nothing more than sit under a palm tree at the swimming pool?

Even the proverbial drunken sailor must occasionally have to make a decision, however, and on the day in early May when I first reported to the pool, Chief Crouch was confronted with just such a necessity. Actually, his decision had already been made for him; he just wasn't sure how to carry it out. I found him sitting at a table beside the pool.

"Chief Crouch?"

He was staring deeply into his coffee cup as if something of great importance rested on the very bottom.

"Huh," he said, jerking up like a child caught at something naughty.

"I'm Miller. I'm a lifeguard."

He regarded me with a degree of suspicion, blood shot eyes rolling about beneath his chief's hat. "You ain't Earthquake O'Toole?"

"No. Miller. Doug Miller."

"Yeah, that's what I was afraid of."

"Is something wrong? I'm supposed to report…"

"Yeah, I've got you on the list. I just thought maybe you was O'Toole. Well, I guess what I heard is true. Hey, you over there," he called to a sailor walking about near the deep end of the pool. "Yeah, you. Come over here."[1]

It was Bowman, the very first time I'd ever laid eyes on him. He sauntered over at a leisurely pace.

"Bowman, this is Miller."

We shook hands.

"Do you know this guy Earthquake O'Toole?"

"Yeah," Bowman said. "I know him."

"Earthquake," said the chief. "What the hell kind of name is that?"

Bowman laughed. I stood there looking, I'm sure, like some kind of fool, because I was wondering exactly the same thing.

"I got word this morning that O'Toole is in jail. Just one damn thing after another." He looked at us as if he wanted us to respond, but since we didn't know what response was appropriate, we simply stood waiting.

"Don't you get it?" he finally said.

"Yeah," Bowman said. "The Earthquake's in jail. What's to get?"

"Tomorrow the pool opens. Your section is on. And I ain't got a full supply of...whatever you guys are. Each section is supposed to have five. You've only got four as it is—and one of you is locked up, an enemy of society."

Bowman was always quicker on the draw than I was when it came to spotting an opportunity for a day off.

"You want us to go get him?" he said.

"Us who," the chief asked.

"Me and..." He looked at me.

"Miller," I said.

"Yeah," he said. "Me and Miller. We'll go in and bring him back, won't we?"

"Well, yeah," I said. "I guess so."

"I thought maybe they would just turn him loose. Thought Miller was him. How are you gonna bring him back?"

---

1. I am not sure that footnotes ought to be a part of a novel, but I'm putting one in anyway. I need to say something about profanity, and what I have to say needn't take up space in the story I'm telling. Sailors are ancient practitioners of the art of profanity. They hardly ever speak a sentence that is not laced with crude references to body functions and the sex act. I could easily recreate the speech of the sailors, but beyond an occasional "hell" or "damn" I choose not to. Be assured, however, that Chief Crouch was at this point turning the air blue.

"I'm waiting to hear the answer to this myself," I said.

"We'll just go in and bail him out," Bowman said. "What's he in for. I'll bet he got drunk and insulted a cop."

"He's in the San Diego city jail," Chief Crouch said. "He got drunk and insulted a cop. How did you know?"

Bowman smiled and shrugged.

"Anyway, what are you gonna bail him out with? You got any money? What's the fine for drunkenness and insulting an officer of the law?" The chief had difficulty getting this last sentence out, mangling the word officer in the process.

"No, I don't have any money," Bowman said. "Do you?"

"Me?" I said, pointing to myself. "I stay broke. I'm always broke."

"How much does it cost to bail out a drunk?" Chief Crouch asked his coffee cup.

"Hell, Chief," said Bowman, "you should know if anyone does."

"Fifty bucks," said the chief. And then, suddenly realizing he might have been insulted, "What's that crack supposed to mean?"

"Nothing," Bowman said. "I just figure you've been around the block a few times. Anyway, give us fifty dollars..."

"Payday was last week," said Chief Crouch, looking both hurt and bewildered. "Where the hell would I get fifty dollars?"

But Chief Crouch was not lacking in the ability to mooch, an art form that has long been the salvation of veteran drunks. He called the other lifeguards together, explained the situation, almost broke down and cried at one point, and succeeded in raising the necessary funds, promising all the while that O'Toole would pay back every penny with interest or he, Crouch, would see him dangled from whatever we had that could serve as a yardarm.

So off we went, Bowman and I, disguised as civilians[2], to get Earthquake O'Toole out of the hands of the constabulary. We were not exactly professional in our approach, and it took us half the morning to find out where Earthquake was. But by the pure, blind luck that sometimes guides the footsteps of imbeciles, we managed to time our arrival in the municipal court perfectly. Last night's detainees were in the process of being arraigned before a judge that reminded me a great deal of Chief Crouch. There were pimps, prostitutes, a host of drunks, one fellow accused of beating up his wife, three homosexuals (one of them in

---

2. Another footnote is necessary. Military personnel stationed ashore were not required at that time to dress in uniform when they were on liberty. I don't know whether or not this policy is still in effect.

drag). And there was Earthquake O'Toole, looking as ratty as any of them. His shirt was torn down the front. He was missing one shoe.

"There's our boy," Bowman whispered to me. We were seated about half way back in the courtroom.

"That's O'Toole?"

"Yeah."

"Holy mackerel! If I'm ever drowning, I hope he's not the one who comes to pull me out."

Bowman laughed.

"Is he a friend of yours?"

"Not really," Bowman said. "Only an acquaintance."

The judge was working his way through the mob with an efficiency that suggested experienced indifference. It went something like this:

"What's the charge? Drunk and disorderly. How do you plead? Guilty, Your Honor. Five days or fifty dollars. I'm a little short of cash, Your Honor, but I can…Five days. Lock him up."

Bowman and I realized at some point that Earthquake didn't even know we were there, ready and able to pay his fine and take him home. We were wondering how to get his attention without disrupting the proceedings of a judge that didn't appear to like disruptions. We needn't have bothered. O'Toole had no intention of making things easy on himself.

"O'Toole," the bailiff said. "Percival."

"Here."

"Stand up," said the bailiff.

He rose, head drawn in. I found as I got to know him that he always looked that way. He had no neck to speak of. His hair, orange as a carrot, was clipped down to his skull like that of a concentration camp inmate. His lower lip was thrust out and he had this pugnacious stance—at least from my angle of view—as if he were saying, "I am set upon by a host of enemies, and I know not why."

"What's the charge."

"Drunk and soliciting."

"Soliciting what?" the judge asked. "A prostitute?"

"He was panhandling on the street, Your Honor."

"I was bumming money to get a drink," O'Toole announced.

"Shut up!" the judge barked. "You speak when spoken to."

"Well if you wanna know…"

The judge slammed down his gavel. "One more word out of you, and I'll find you in contempt of court. Now, I'm about to ask you a question, and I want a simple answer. How do you plead?"

"Well, I..."

"Guilty or not guilty?"

"Not guilty, of course."

"Bind him over for trial," said the judge. "Day after tomorrow at nine o'clock."

"What do I do in the meantime?" O'Toole wanted to know.

"We've got nice municipal accommodations, son. Same cell you just came out of. Unless you want to post bail."

"How much is the bail."

"One hundred dollars."

"Everyone else got fifty."

"That was their fine. You're posting bail. Show up for trial, and I'll give you your money back, less your fine if you're found guilty."

Earthquake O'Toole was angry, but his anger was nothing compared to Bowman's. "Why that ignorant, stupid little son-of-a-bitch," he shouted to the heavens as we stood on the sidewalk outside the municipal court. "All he had to do was keep his mouth shut and pay his fine and he was home free. But no, he has to assert his rights. Voltaire. Thomas Jefferson. He takes a simple fifty-dollar fine, and with a few stupid sentences, doubles it to one hundred. And us hustling up the money to get him out. Well, he'll rot in there before I ever lift another finger to help him again."

And so on...and so forth...

"Bowman," I finally said, "what difference does it make? Let him do two more days in jail and..."

"I'll tell you the difference it makes, Miller. Think about it, boy. We need five lifeguards. We only had four to begin with. Now we're down to three. That means we're gonna have to cover for that fat, bald-headed little puke for the next two days while he sits up there in his cell asserting his rights. He'd better be glad he's in jail, because if he were down here right now, I'd strangle him with my bare hands."

We rode a bus back to Miramar, and Bowman calmed down enough to tell me what he knew about Earthquake O'Toole, and what he thought I needed to know. My first question was where he got the name Earthquake. We were riding in the back of the bus, bumping along, inhaling the exhaust fumes and swatting at flies that seemed to inhabit all public buses in those distant days when air conditioning was non-existent.

"That big, dumb wrestler in *Li'l Abner,* Earthquake McGoon," Bowman said. "Keep your eye on O'Toole. When he's just sitting around and not actually engaged in any sort of conversation, he gets this empty look. I mean empty. Like no one's at home."

"He couldn't be all that stupid," I said. "He's an aviation electronic tech."

"No. I guess he's not stupid. But he's not exactly smart either. He was down on the line working on a radar out of an F-3, and he shorted the thing out, blew it up like a firecracker. So the chief ran him off and sent him down to the mail room."

"Okay. So he's stupid," I said.

"Well," Bowman said, "maybe not. He's stupid like a fox. He never did like electronics. He got into it because it's an open rate and he wanted third-class pay. But he didn't want to have to do anything. He's as lazy as a bloated tick. We always thought he deliberately blew the radar up to get off the line and down in the mailroom. Anyhow, stupid...no. But he's always looking for an angle. You know the type."

"Yeah, but I can't figure out how he got sent over to the pool. He looks to me like he'd drown in a heartbeat."

"Looks to me like he'd float like an inner tube," Bowman said. "But who knows. I guess he passed the lifeguard test. But he's not exactly the standard picture of the lifeguard."

I laughed. "You look like you're in pretty good shape."

"Thanks. So do you."

We rode awhile in silence.

"I lift weights pretty regularly," Bowman said. "You wanna come over to the gym with me sometime?"

"Yeah," I said, "I'd like that. How about tonight?"

"Can't do it tonight. Got a night class at San Diego J.C. Taking a course in philosophy. But we're finishing up the semester in about a week."

"I took a course in philosophy at college," I told him. "Intro to philosophy 1113. Made a C in it. Boy, that stuff is hard. But I'll tell you what, it really fascinated me. I kind of thought I'd major in it."

"So why didn't you?"

"I was failing political science, history, college algebra. Thought it was time for me to move on."

"Yeah," he said. "I'd say so. That's kind of what happened to me. Only I was passing history. I was failing this stupid course in personal hygiene."

"You gotta be kidding me."

"Nope. I couldn't seem to get out of bed and get to class on time. Anyway, I'm taking some courses now. Sooner or later I'll get out of this chicken outfit, and I'd like to do something other than flip hamburgers."

"What do you want to do?" I asked.

"I don't know," he said. "Maybe I'll be a philosopher."

I knew, that day on the bus, that our relationship, Bowman's and mine, was going to be something more than temporary. You get that feeling sometimes about someone, almost like you've known them for years when in fact you only just met them. As for O'Toole, it never occurred to me that I would have any connection at all with him after the summer was over, and very little while the summer was going on. Bowman was my type; O'Toole was not. As it turned out, I was right in one of the cases and wrong in the other; my friendship with Bowman was for life, and my connection to O'Toole went on, and on, and on. He was the proverbial cat that keeps coming back.

Chapter 3

▼

Earthquake's Box

Wow, what an awesome feeling! I am the skipper of a time machine, taking quantum strides across years and galaxies, restrained only by my imagination, or lack thereof. In the last chapter, I was forty years back and almost two thousand miles to the west. Now I have returned to the present, but I'm still almost two thousand miles to the west, at the Cove in La Jolla.

The Cove is not the sort of place in which Bowman and I would normally stay the night, though we are, by this stage of life, what are sometimes called comfortable. We got where we are by working hard and not spending money in overnight stays at places like the Cove. I am a Motel Six man myself. But this trip was different than most, and sensing that we would probably never travel back this way again—at least not under these conditions—we decided to live it up. We got a room in a plush place overlooking the ocean, had our luggage, including Earthquake O'Toole's box, brought up by uniformed bell hops, and settled in to determine the extent of Bowman's new holdings.

We should have gone through the box back in the law office, but Paul Baxter, Esquire made us feel unwanted; and who can blame him? What normal person wants his place of business cluttered up by the heirs of a skid row bum? He probably expected one of us to vomit on the floor, or maybe to go into d.t.'s and start seeing pink snakes or something. So I can understand the counselor's urgency to get us out the door and get on to more profitable ventures; but, my capacity to understand and my capacity to forgive are apparently not wired up to the same generator. As for Bowman, I'm not sure he even made an effort to understand.

"To lawyer Baxter," he said, raising a glass of beer in a toast. "I hope the bugs crawl all over him tonight. And if it's not the bugs, I hope it's the snakes."

I was seated in a leather-covered chair, Bowman was seated on the couch, and O'Toole's box was on a coffee table between us.

"Here, here," I said, raising my glass in response. "Let's agree that lawyer Baxter ought to be stricken with a mysterious affliction of hives. But enough of these pleasantries. Open up the box, Bowman. Even you should be somewhat curious about what you've been left."

"All right. Here goes. Boy, this is like entering King Solomon's mines. For the first time, I know how Allan Quatermain and Henry Curtis must have felt."

Imagine, however, that Haggard got it wrong, and that upon entering the cavern where the treasure was supposed to be, Quatermain and Curtis found themselves wading hip deep in the great universal garbage dump.

Two-thirds of the box's contents was clothing, and I mean clothing of the worst kind. There was a pair of wing-tipped shoes, beaten and scuffed as if someone had deliberately taken a file and a nine-pound hammer to them. There were holes in both soles, a heal was badly worn on one and missing altogether from the other.

"Dumpster," Bowman said.

"We need a trash bag," I said. "I have a feeling that most of your inheritance is bound for the dumpster."

There were underwear and socks, both replete with holes. In fact, it was hard to find one sock that matched another. Bowman and I looked at one another.

"Dumpster," we both said.

A used toothbrush…

"A used toothbrush," said Bowman. "Who in his right mind would will somebody a used toothbrush?"

"My lad," I told him, "in all the time I've known you, the one thing I've never heard you accuse O'Toole of is sanity."

Three pairs of pants rapidly went the way of the trash bag, and then, incongruously, Bowman hauled out a very fine trenchcoat.

"I'll take that," I said. "That is, if you're just going to toss it."

"Hell no," he said. "You've got your book. This is mine, bequeathed to me by Percival Gregory O'Toole. A man deserves something for his troubles."

A necktie stained with…who knows what?

A hat that a horse pulling a milk wagon would be ashamed to be seen in.

Several rubber bands. "Brother, I'm sure glad to get these," Bowman said.

A bag of marbles.

"A steely, two cat's eyes, three aggies," Bowman said. "You want 'em."

"Sure," I said. "Why not."

A stained jockstrap with not a vestige of elasticity.

Bowman held it up between thumb and forefinger, as if it were infected, which it might have been. He let it fall to the floor, and sat there with an expression between pain and bewilderment, as if he'd been hit hard, squarely between the eyes, with a club. I couldn't tell if he was serious or just putting me on. He began to shake his head slowly from side to side.

"I've been suckered again," he said. "For the last time, that Irish reprobate has stung me good. Why was I expecting something more?" He reached for his beer, finished it off in one long swallow, and slammed the glass down on the coffee table.

He had voiced what both of us had been thinking from the very first, exploding what was, in retrospect, the most colossal of pipe dreams. Did we really believe we would find a stack of money in the box? Or the map to a lost diamond mine? Or a deposit book for a Swiss bank account?

"Well, as Tullulah Bankhead said, 'I think there's less to this than meets the eye.'"

Bowman didn't appreciate my humor. He swung his feet around and stretched out on the couch, folded his hands on his chest and stared up at the ceiling.

"It's not the stuff in the box that bothers me," he said after about five minutes of silence. "It's that I'm stupid enough to get taken again. And this time, there's nothing I can do about it. Earthquake O'Toole has checked in at that Great Flophouse in the sky, beyond the wrath of Bowman. But not beyond the wrath of God," he suddenly shouted, bounding up and shaking his fist. "Do you hear me up there, Earthquake? Or down there? Or wherever you are? I hope you're having delirium tremens for the next thousand years, you miserable, disaffiliated slug."

Then it all became too funny, and we both began laughing, and laughed until tears ran down our cheeks and I, for one, literally ached. Here we sat, two hot shot college boys, hustled one last time by a shanty Mick without a dime to his name.

"Six-hundred dollars for a round trip plane ticket," I howled between fits of laughter. "A hundred dollars a night for a motel room in La Jolla. And for what? A used jock strap and a bag of marbles."

"Don't forget the shoes and toothbrush," Bowman shouted.

"What the hell," I gasped. "Nothing ventured, nothing gained. At least I got a book out of the deal and you got a trenchcoat. Remember the boys in *Treasure of the Sierra Madre* at the end when the wind blows the gold dust away?"

"Yeah, Tim Holt and Walter Huston. Laughing like crazy men. Well, open another beer. Let's drink up, sleep it off, and head for home in the morning."

"Guess we can throw all this junk back in the box and take it down to the dumpster," I said. "I can't stand the smell of it any longer.

"There's some more stuff in there," Bowman said.

"More? Well, are you gonna look at it?"

"Nah," Bowman said. "The jock strap sort of did me in. You go ahead and look. If you find a key to a safe deposit box, let me know."

This set us off again, laughing like Tim Holt and Walter Huston, and as both of us laughed, I went digging, taking things out of the box and tossing them onto the coffee table. We were past the clothing now, down to those items of no obvious utility, those types of things we all accumulate because for some reason they have meaning to us.

"Here's a beat up copy of *Martin Eden*," I said, "and one junior varsity letter. I wonder what he got it for."

"Football, I guess," Bowman said. "Certainly not for the high hurdles."

"One...well I'll swear. It's a Star Scout badge. I never knew he was a Scout."

"Neither did I," said Bowman. "But it kinda figures."

"What's that?"

"Look at it like this. Did the Earthquake ever actually finish anything he started? Whatever it was, it always wound up half-baked. So he was junior varsity. He was a Star Scout. Lots of guys got to Star, but not many made Eagle."

"Look at this," I said.

It was a picture of a girl, probably from high school, probably a class photo.

"Not bad," I said.

Bowman wrinkled his nose. "Not good," he said. "Not my type."

"Not my type either," I said, "but several cuts above what I would expect from the Earthquake. Here's a message written on the back: To Percy, best wishes, Amy. Dated May, 1955."

"He kept that all these years," said Bowman.

"Here's some stuff rubber-banded together," I said. "Some letters. And a loose-leaf notebook. That's it. End of the story. No more of O'Toole's life to be pawed over."

"All right," Bowman said. "Get into the letters. Maybe one of them contains a map to King Solomon's mines."

"Okay, here goes. Here we have a letter with a five-cent airmail stamp on the envelope. Man, how long since we've used those? Postmark looks like 1961."

"At least that long then," Bowman said.

I extracted the letter from the envelope, unfolded it, and read: "Dear Percy: I got your letter last week. I almost didn't answer it. I am flattered that you feel about me the way you do, but I can't imagine how you got the idea that you were ever anything to me but a friend. I am marrying Chuck Kramer next month. Yours truly, Amy."

"The old dear john treatment, huh?"

"It's not much of a dear john," I said. "Sounds to me like O'Toole had some kind of school boy crush on Amy, and she didn't reciprocate."

"Want another beer?" Bowman asked. He got himself up and in motion toward the small refrigerator in the kitchenette.

"Don't mind if I do," I said. "The life of Percival G. O'Toole is becoming depressing. Not that it was ever much to rejoice over. Hey, Bowman, here's one to you."

"No kidding." He was opening bottles and pouring beer.

"It's in a sealed envelope. Quote: to Bruce Bowman, to be opened in event of my death. And it's got a written date on it. Good grief! This is dated June 5, 1967."

Bowman was on his way back with two glasses of beer. He stopped in the middle of the room and stood for a moment, looking at nothing in particular. "You know," he said, "that's just about the time I threw him out of my place in Alhambra and told him I never wanted to see him again."

He got into motion, handed me a glass, and resumed his place on the couch.

"What happened there anyway? Didn't that have something to do with a baseball game?"

"Ostensibly, yeah," Bowman replied. "But that was just the straw that broke the camel's back. I was already up to here with Earthquake O'Toole. So were you."

"Yeah. So what happened?"

"The Dodgers were at home. I think Drysdale was pitching. Anyway, the Earthquake was supposed to get tickets and meet me at the ballpark. He didn't show up. Didn't call. Not so much as a by your leave. So about a week later he shows up at my place with that goofy little grin of his and not a hint of an apology. Brother, that did it. I didn't actually throw him out; I never let him in. Told him if I ever saw him again it would be too soon, and slammed the door in his face."

We sat there, sipping beer, both of us looking at the sealed envelope I held, as if the obvious next step of opening the envelope was one that was anything but obvious.

"Man, this guy becomes more and more of an enigma," I said. "He must have gone straight home that very day and written this."

"Open it," Bowman said.

"It's addressed to you."

"Open it."

I tore the envelope open, a rather unceremonious gesture for something this weighty, and took out one page of paper torn from a loose-leaf notebook. I unfolded it.

"Dear Bowman," I read. "If you are reading this it is because I am dead. Mill is probably there with you." I swallowed. "He always called me Mill, didn't he."

"We all did—back then."

"Mill is probably there with you," I read again. "You two guys were always together." I paused and looked up at Bowman, who was looking at me.

"This is getting weird," he said. "It's like he set up a hustle over thirty years ago, and that he knew exactly what we were going to do. I always said he was stupid like a fox."

I read on. "I want you to know that you guys were the best friends I ever had. In fact, I think you were the only friends I ever had. I just never was able to fit in anywhere. I always admired you guys. You in particular, Bowman. You had discipline. I never did have. I was never able to set goals and work toward them. I know I never will amount to a hill of beans. Those days at the pool were the best of my life. You guys probably thought I didn't get anything out of the Symposium…"

Another period of silence. This was a hard letter to read. Bowman had sat his beer on the coffee table and was leaning forward, elbows on knees. "Fat, bald-headed little puke," he said, fighting to hide his emotion, fighting against O'Toole's ability to manipulate him even from beyond the grave.

"The Symposium," I muttered.

"The Symposium," Bowman replied."

"Yeah. Well, let's see…I didn't get anything out of the Symposium. But I really did read *The Republic*. Part of it anyhow. And part of *Martin Eden*. I thought Jack London was cool because he was like you guys."

"He never finished anything he started," Bowman said.

"You took the words right out of his mouth," I said, and went back to the Earthquake's letter. "I didn't finish either one. I never finished anything I started.

But I learned an awful lot from you guys. So I'm leaving all my stuff to you, Bowman. Except for *The Republic*. That's Mill's. I'd like for you to have me cremated. I want you to scatter my ashes at the Cove. And while you're down there, drink one for me. Your friend, the Earthquake."

I held the letter out and let it fall. It settled quietly to the coffee table. I exhaled. Bowman exhaled, finished off his beer, sank back into his prone position on the couch. He exhaled again and said, "Your friend, the Earthquake. I shouldn't let him do this to me, but I'm on a guilt trip."

"Yeah. We were his best friends. What do you know about that?"

I picked up the beaten copy of *Martin Eden* and began thumbing through it. He had underlined the author's name, Jack London, and had circled the verse at the beginning. I read:

> "Let me live out my years in heat of blood!
> "Let me lie drunken with the dreamer's wine!
> "Let me not see this soul-house built of mud
> "Go toppling to the dust a vacant shrine!"

Bowman jumped up from the couch. "All right, Miller," he said. "I'm guilt tripped into action." He crossed the room to the telephone.

"What are you gonna do?" I asked.

"Gonna call the county," he said. "Gonna see if we can have him cremated and scatter his ashes. It's the cremation of Sam McGee all over again. 'A pal's last need is a thing to heed, so I swore that I would not fail...'"

"You're showing your age, son. No one quotes Robert Service anymore."

He grunted. He had a phone directory and was ripping through it. "What am I doing?" he suddenly said. "I've paid my money. Let the motel get them for me." He picked up the receiver and punched in one number. "This is Bowman in room two-oh-two," he said. "I'd like for you to call the county coroner for me...that's right, the county coroner. Then transfer the call up here."

While this was going on, I was looking through the last unexamined item in Earthquake O'Toole's estate. It was a small loose leaf notebook, perhaps six by eight inches.

"Bowman, look at this," I said. "It's a diary of some sort. By damn!" I shouted, "it's a diary of the Greek Summer. Look at this first entry. May 20, 1960. Quote: I got out of jail today."

Bowman hung up the phone and crossed the room in giant strides, "Lemme see that thing," he said, then grabbed it just as I was about to turn to the next page.

"I got out of jail today," he read. "Met a guy named Miller, who is one of the lifeguards with us. And this girl named Betty Ann Greybow showed up. Boy, did I ever piss her off."

He quickly turned the pages and found that the diary took up about half the book; the second half hadn't been written in at all. The entries were dated from May 20 through September 5, my twentieth birthday, when the boys threw me a party which began in Escondido and staggered its way through San Diego to Tijuana. The final entry, in fact, had to do with my birthday party. Bowman read:

"We are throwing Mill a party tonight, at Charley Long's place in Escondido. He'll be twenty years old. Still too young to drink legally. When I think of all the beer we've bought for that guy this summer, I can't believe we're not in jail for contributing to the delinquency."

"Did you keep a diary that summer, Bowman?" I asked after he had closed the book and was sitting on the couch holding it in his right hand and slapping it into his left.

"Are you kidding?" he said. "When would I have had time?"

"Neither did I," I said. "Think about how often over the years you and I have sat around talking about the Greek Summer and trying to remember what happened. One of the most important events of our lives, and neither of us can even remember it clearly. But this guy kept a diary of it."

"Well," said Bowman, "if we had known at the time how important the Greek Summer was going to be, we probably would have kept diaries. But you never plan for this sort of thing. It just happens. Then it's over and done with, and it can never be duplicated."

He was right. It has only been in retrospect that either of us realized what the Greek Summer was to us, how critical it was to making us what we are today. At the time, we were only young sailors, glad to have a respite from military duties, and living the good life of California lifeguards; Jack London and the Athenian Greeks showed up without a proper introduction, and we didn't give them the reception they deserved. In fact, we treated them in a slightly cavalier fashion, as if they were nothing more than toys in a giant playpen, handed over to us for amusement at our leisure. I doubt any of them minded this. They were probably glad to be used in whatever way we chose to use them. Ah, like most youths, we were careless, frivolous, and tossed away our golden years like Ernest Dowson's roses. I have been faithful to thee, Cynara.

I was saying something like this, and Bowman had gone back to leafing through Earthquake's diary, when the telephone rang.

"Your call, sire," I said.

Bowman leaped up to answer it.

"Yes...Speaking...Do you still have Percival Gregory O'Toole down there? Yes...Oh, you are, huh? Well hold everything. I want him cremated. Who am I? . .I'm the executor of his will, and I have in hand a document in which he has expressed the desire to be cremated and to have his ashes scattered at La Jolla Cove. Well, sure, but...Look, I worked in a funeral home when I was an undergrad, and I know that cremation is cheaper than a burial...Not the way you do it, huh? Well, why take up space in a cemetery when you can do it like this? . . Oh, okay. Got it. Okay."

He hung up.

"So what's the verdict?" I asked.

"They're shipping him up to..." He named a prominent San Diego funeral home whose owners might not care to be mentioned within this context. Let's call it Heavenly Sunshine. "Sending him there for embalming and burial."

"When is he going?"

"He's on his way, brother."

"So your plan is...what?"

"Get in touch with them and get them to cremate him. Like right now. In fact, get up and let's get going. We'll be there about the time the meat wagon arrives."

The process turned out to be much simpler than either of us expected. The funeral home had a crematory, and a more accommodating bunch you never met in your life. They assured us that we had saved them a good deal of trouble, effort and expense, and in fact suggested that left to their own devices they would as soon take pauper customers out beyond the three-mile limit and bury them at sea. Our timing must have been perfect, for the funeral directors had no scheduled cremations for that day, and they got right to work. By three o'clock that afternoon we had the earthly remains of Earthquake O'Toole in a small, and not untasteful, plastic receptacle, and we were on our way back to La Jolla, feeling a little bit better about ourselves, a little less guilty about our treatment, over the years, of a misfit who thought of us as his best friends.

Back at the motel, we changed into bathing trunks and sandals, took beer, and the diary, and headed for La Jolla Cove, ready to make an evening of it in the way specified by Earthquake O'Toole. Our plan was to read through the diary, drink some beer, toss Earthquake into the waves, come back to the motel for a night's sleep, get up in the morning and be on our way. It was a good plan that failed of completion only because we drank ourselves into insensibility and didn't make it back to the motel until the next morning. Well, actually, the plan fell short in another area too—that of the disposal of the Earthquake's remains. More of that later. Hell, now that I remember it, the whole evening was a failure, if one measures success by the achievement of what one sets out to do.

But the first part went well; we did, in fact, reach the cove with beer, the Earthquake's ashes, and his diary.

The sun was halfway down the western sky by now, the sea was mumbling at the rocks, and gulls were crying, rising up on the landward wind.

Chapter 4

▼

The Ring of Guy-jeez[1]

May 23, 1960. I never knew Bowman very well. And I never knew this guy Miller at all. But I think both of them are a little bit crazy. They think I should have just paid my fine and forgotten the whole thing. Well there is more at stake here than fifty dollars. It's the principle of the thing.

—The Diary of Earthquake O'Toole

The diary entry suggests that Bowman and I cared whether or not the Earthquake paid his fine, went bail, or stayed in jail for the next fifty years. All we cared about, all any of the guys cared about, and all Chief Crouch cared about for cer-

---

1. I need to say something about this word. This is the name of the shepherd who Glaucon says found the remarkable ring that when worn properly rendered the wearer invisible. The story is contained in Book Two of *The Republic*. The word in Greek is *Guges*, but when translated into English the upsilon changes to a "y". Now, the Greeks had no soft "g" in their language, consequently both the first and second "g" were pronounced hard. Educated people uniformly know this, but at the time none of us were particularly well-educated, and we all pronounced the name "Guy-jeez" and thought we were doing fine.

tain, was that he be there to help us cover the pool. But he wasn't, which meant that the pool opened on schedule with only three lifeguards in our section, and our section the one on duty. We tried to get the port section (we were starboard) to switch with us, but they laughed and told us to get lost; they had all made other plans, none of which included covering for us just because it was our rotten luck to have drawn a man incarcerated for being drunk and bumming money on the streets of San Diego.

So we kicked off the swimming season two short, cursing O'Toole for his absence, but all things considered in magnificent form. Bowman and I had begun lifting weights together, and we were already acquiring the tans for which California lifeguards are noted, so we sat like lords upon our lofty towers, eyes hidden behind sun shades, blowing whistles now and then and saying things like, "Hey, buddy, no running in the pool area." Even with two bodies missing we had little to complain about: if you entered the Elysian Fields and found you had to sip some extra ambrosia because someone to whom it belonged didn't show up, would you complain?

On the third day after the pool opened, at eight o'clock sharp, the Earthquake walked in ready to go to work. The rest of us, that is Bowman, myself, a guy from upstate New York named Dennis Hopewell, and Chief Crouch, were already there, togged out in the uniform of the day (bathing suits and sunshades—except for the Chief), and enjoying the quiet that would give way to chaos when we opened the doors at ten. Chief Crouch was on the Earthquake immediately.

"Are you P.G. O'Toole?"

"Yeah," the Earthquake responded, and looked at him as if he wanted to add, "What's it to you?" But he let the mere, "Yeah," suffice.

"Well, I hope we're not inconveniencing you by asking you to actually do something."

"I was in jail."

"Really. What do you think I sent Miller and Bowman down to court for? They were supposed to get you out."

"Well, they didn't. I had to sit in that dump for two more—"

"They didn't get you out because you went and entered a not guilty plea, you stupid..." He trailed off into a terrific string of profanity. Even for a sailor, Chief Crouch achieved a level of eloquence in the profane that I rarely witnessed in another human being. When he got going he seldom used the same word twice. I didn't know there were so many foul words in the English language. Bowman, Hopewell and I stood listening in dumb amazement, while O'Toole stood there getting red in the face and bobbing back and forth like a Chinese doll.

"Okay," he said, when the Chief ran out of breath and started coughing. "Okay, I get the point. But," he giggled and shrugged, "better late than never."

This set Chief Crouch off on another cursing binge. "We covered for you by putting you on two days' leave," He said. "Now get over to personnel and sign your leave request, then get yourself back here and get a pair of swimming trunks on."

"You can't make me use my leave time if I don't want to."

"Would you rather be charged AWOL for two days? Would you, sea lawyer, huh? Just say the word, and I'll have you up before a summary court martial. I'll bust your fat ass back to recruit and toss you in the Thirty-Second Street brig for about ten days. And I guarantee when those Marine chasers get through with you, you'll wish you'd signed that leave request."

The Earthquake wheeled around without a word and left, heading, we correctly assumed, for personnel.

"All right, you boys get moving," said the Chief. "Chop, chop. Hose down the pool area. And make damn sure the women's head is clean."

I suppose I ought to have a go at describing the pool itself, and the area surrounding it, just to give some idea of the world we inhabited that summer; for apart from the time we spent asleep in the barracks, and our periodic forays to the beaches at La Jolla and Torrey Pines, the pool was our world, our very universe, our modern day Athens.

Very well. The pool was, as I have said, standard olympic-size, fifty meters long, running north and south, with low and high diving boards, two lifeguard towers, and a roped float barricade that separated the shallow and the deep ends. One of our duties was to keep the pool clean, chemicals in proper balance, water sparkling and inviting. In this, I must admit, we never came up short.

"With all those kids in there, the pool must be full of pee at the end of the day," Chief Crouch observed.

The greater pool area was surrounded by a concrete block wall about seven feet high. Most of the area within the enclosure was paved, but there were some unpaved areas that served as gardens for exotic plants that someone else (I'm not sure who) tended. The entire west side of the enclosure, an area about seventy-five by thirty feet, was planted in bermuda grass, mowed and tended by the same unknown individuals who took care of the gardens.

The main way into the pool area was through the dressing rooms, housed in a low, long, flat-roofed building of the same sort of concrete blocks that composed the enclosing wall. Swimmers came through the glass double doors into a common entrance area, then asserted their fundamental biological differences by going either to the right into the men's dressing room, or left to the women's. It was considered very poor form, even for sailors, to try to go into the women's dressing room. There were doors, of course, opening from each of the dressing rooms into the pool proper.

Out in the common entrance, an area about twenty by twenty feet, was a high counter, behind which sat someone with enough authority to herd swimmers in the desired directions. A telephone was there, public address system, and a radio tuned to a San Diego station that played rock and roll with a little Kingston Trio thrown in for the benefit of the folk music crowd. Country music was not played. Chief Crouch and I were the only ones who could tolerate it.

On the backside of the building, a snack bar served Cokes, hamburgers, what have you. And there were two small rooms, one on the building's south end, one on the north. In the southern room was an office with a desk, a coffeepot, and some chairs. This was Chief Crouch's normal hangout once the sun got high, say around ten o'clock. The chief was a night person, sort of like Dracula. Sunlight did him in. The northern room was ours. When we wanted to get out of the sun, which was seldom, we went in there. It was furnished with a cot, some chairs, and a dartboard someone brought in and hung up on one wall.

There it was, the world of the Greek Summer.

But I found something out that Summer about time and space, something I had never considered and that I have never forgotten: the size of the area you inhabit has nothing to do with the importance of the activities in which you engage. If there is a thing in this finite world that is not bound by time and space it is the human mind. Socrates rarely left the confines of the city of Athens, but mentally he ranged the far galaxies. Stone walls do not a prison make.

We are all, however, bound *physically* by time and space, including Earthquake O'Toole, which is why he had been in jail and had avoided an AWOL charge by requesting leave for the two days he was absent. At least, I assume that's what he did. He came back from personnel grumbling about injustice and how he was going to write his congressman, then, when pressed on the subject, admitted he had no idea who his congressman was. Bowman wouldn't let matters lie.

"You don't even know who the president is, do you O'Toole?"

"What do you think I am? Stupid? It's Roosevelt."

"Oh, and who is this guy Eisenhower who currently inhabits the White House?"

"Who cares? He's supreme potentate of Allied Forces in Europe, and he got put in the White House the way it's always done."

"And how's that?" Bowman asked.

We were lounging alongside the pool, waiting for the front doors to open. It promised to be another very hot day, without a cloud in the sky.

"Look," the Earthquake said, "you wanna know how anything gets done? I'll tell you. The guy with the biggest club calls the shots. Either that, or it's the guy who's the biggest crook who avoids getting caught. So Eisenhower beat the Germans. Now he's got me under his thumb. If he'd lost to the Germans, we'd all be speaking Kraut and goose stepping."

I had never heard anything quite like this in my life. Nothing the Earthquake had said actually made sense, but there was a suggestion of a hidden sort of logic to it that kept me listening, waiting for something more. He always affected me like this. It was as if he were about to say something of great importance at any moment, but somehow the moment never arrived.

"O'Toole," Bowman said. "That is about the dumbest thing I've ever heard." Bowman was flat on his back, sunshades in place, stripped but for his bathing trunks. He did not bother to turn and look at the Earthquake as he spoke. "You want us to believe that a big club is all you need to get through life."

"That's right, Bowman. What sort of dream world did you grow up in?" O'Toole was flat on his stomach, chin on hands. But he was not stripped. He had on a long-sleeved pullover. He, like many of the Irish, was very fair and would sunburn in the space of time it took to walk from the dressing room to the lifeguard tower.

"You know who he sounds like?" I said. "That guy in your book, Bowman. Thrasymachus. Justice is whatever the big man says it is."

"That was Glaucon," Bowman said.

"That was Thrasymachus," I told him. "Glaucon was the one who told the story about the shepherd and the ring. You do what you know you can get away with."

Hopewell was swatting flies with his hand. He probably thought he'd landed in an enclosure with a group of nuts.

"Both of 'em sound okay to me," said the Earthquake.

"That's because you've got the mind of a criminal," Bowman said.

"Just the same, I'd like to read that book. Sounds to me like some level-headed thinking."

"It's *The Republic*," Bowman said. "We're using it in this course down at school.

"I need to get a copy," the Earthquake said. "Who wrote it? Does he tell you how to beat the income tax thing?"

"Plato wrote it," I said.

"Mickey Mouse's dog?"

"That's Pluto," Bowman said. "Lord, what have I done to deserve this?"

"You enlisted," I said. And to the Earthquake: "The book is all about justice."

"Now that's all I'm after," he responded, and looked up as if posing for a law journal.

"You guys are too much," Hopewell finally said, and yawned.

"Picked up for being drunk and asking some respectable citizen for a little loose change. Then put in jail and fined. I ask you, is that justice. Do you think they'd throw Eisenhower in jail for panhandling? Hell no. He's got too big a club for them. This Thrash-whatchamacallem is exactly right. Me, they skin alive. They send Ike to Washington."

"This is hopeless," Bowman said, with little feeling, more to himself than to any of us.

"I'm still gonna get that book," the Earthquake said. "Where can I get it?"

"Any bookstore," I said. "I guess. Boy, think about it. Over two-thousand years on the bestseller list."

"Is it that old?" the Earthquake asked. "Hell, what the hell would he know about panhandling dimes?"

"It's philosophy, O'Toole," I said. "Plato was a Greek philosopher."

"You're wasting your time, Miller," Bowman said. "You're talking philosophy to a guy who was born without frontal lobes on his brain."

"Well, I may not know what philosophy is," the Earthquake said.

"But you know where the chow hall is, don't you, O'Toole?" Hopewell said, and yawned.

"Damn straight," said the Earthquake.

"What more could there be to life?" Hopewell said.

"Damn straight," said the Earthquake.

"Hopeless," Bowman said. "If you lobotomized him, there'd be nothing to cut loose."

"Read about a guy the other day," said Hopewell. "He was born without a brain, or something like that."

"Yeah, I remember that one," I said. "He had part of a brain, enough to make his body function. But all of the higher cognitive portions were gone."

"They said he had a brain like a lizard," Hopewell said. "They were studying him in some clinic."

"Hell," said Bowman. "They can come here and study O'Toole. All they have to bring is a little pocket change so he can get a beer when he wants one."

"Kiss my ass!"

We all laughed.

"You guys ever been in jail?" the Earthquake asked. "Huh? Have you? Ever been on the business end of our so-called justice system? Well let me tell you something. Those cottonpicking Greeks were exactly right. Justice is for the big man. Guys like me...Why, the judge wouldn't even let me explain anything."

"I was reading Bowman's book just yesterday," I said. "*The Republic*. This guy Glaucon had me going. I don't know how you answer a guy like that."

"What's he say?" Hopewell asked.

"Well, he told this story about a shepherd that finds a ring that makes him invisible. So what does he do? Moves into the palace, kills the king, seduces the queen, takes over the kingdom. The idea is that we can talk about justice all we want to, but when it comes right down to it, we all do what we think we can get away with."

"Damn straight," said the Earthquake.

"Yeah, I read that," Bowman said. "We talked about it in class."

"So what did the professor say?" I asked.

"Well...to tell the truth, I never did feel like he answered the question. I'm not sure Socrates did either. He goes off into this long discussion about the just society. But I've got to admit, like you said, Mill, this Glaucon had me going."

"Yeah," I said. "Like, what would you do if you knew you could get away with it?"

"God would know," Hopewell said.

"But say God didn't know. Maybe there's no God. No one knows, and you're not gonna get caught. You're invisible, and you walk into a bank vault..."

"Or into Marilyn Monroe's bedroom..." the Earthquake said.

"Yeah. Or wherever."

"Brother, you don't want to see me with one of those rings," said the Earthquake. "Wonder where I could get one."

"You're right, O'Toole," Bowman said. "I sure don't want to see you with a ring like that. Hell, none of us would have a thing we could call our own."

"Oh, is that so?"

"Yeah, that's so."

"Well, listen to mister hotshot morality here, fellows," said the Earthquake. "You want to tell me what you'd do with a ring like that if you had one?"

"Look out, Bowman," I said. "The lizard brain is about to put you into a tough corner."

"My whole problem with the Glaucon thing," Bowman said, "is that I don't see what it has to do with justice. So people do what they think they can get away with. That doesn't make it right."

"I don't know where Plato is going with this," I said. "But I think the whole question is whether or not there is such a thing as right, and such a thing as wrong—or is it just what you make up in your own head, or what you can get away with?"

"My point exactly," said the Earthquake.

"But what is your point?" I asked him. "Is there right and wrong or is there not?"

"Just like old Thrash…"

"Thrasymachus."

"Whatever. Just like he said. Whoever holds the biggest club tells everyone else what right and wrong is. It's always been that way, always gonna be that way."

"Hey, you guys get over here." It was Chief Crouch, standing just outside the door that led out of the common area, and with him stood a creature of amazing proportions, one who didn't look like any sailor we'd ever seen.

"Is she a Wave?" Hopewell whispered.

"When's the last time you saw a Wave who looked like that?" Bowman whispered back.

She was tall, muscular, busty, tanned, and she was dressed in a one-piece, black swim suit with a water safety instructor insignia on the right side, just above the beginning of her tanned thigh. She had on sunglasses, which is probably just as well, because I think her eyes would have revealed (assuming the eyes really are the windows of the soul) an attitude toward us that none of us would have liked.

"Meet the new addition to our staff," the Chief said. "Now that the errant Mr. O'Toole has deigned to grace us with his presence, we have a full compliment."

"Make a mistake, and they never forget it," said the Earthquake.

"This is Betty Ann Greybow, boys."

We all shook hands. There was no doubt about it, she was intent on showing us that she was our equal by gripping our hands as hard as she could. I'll admit that she was pretty strong.

The phone in the office rang, and the Chief went to answer it.

"Betty Ann Greybow," the Earthquake said. Then he giggled that silly little giggle which I would remember if I forgot everything else about him. "BAG," he said. "Betty Ann Greybow. Get it?"

We all laughed. She did not.

"Listen, buster," she said. "Call me Bag one more time, and I'll kick your butt so hard, you'll have to pull down your pants to brush your teeth."

The Earthquake stood his ground, but leaned backward and narrowed his eyes as if trying to stare her down. It didn't work. We couldn't see her eyes, hidden as they were by the dark glasses, but her grim, hard-drawn lips didn't quiver one iota, and her nostrils twitched like those of a fine thoroughbred.

The rest of us, of course, whooped and hollered.

"My kind of woman," Bowman shouted.

"I doubt it," Betty Ann replied, never changing her expression.

"Go ahead and kick his butt, Betty Ann," I said. "He's got it coming."

"Just be careful I don't have to kick yours," she said.

"But why would you want to?" I said. "Look at me. Gentleman, scholar, only slightly ostentatious, gracious to old ladies, kittens, puppies, the kind of guy you'd like to have move in next door and marry your daughter."

"Actually, all you guys look like nothing so much as a bunch of horny sailors," she said.

"Ah, don't say things like that, Betty Ann," Bowman said. "Why, the girls who come here think I look just like Troy Donohue."

"Oh, puh-leeez!" she said, and for the first time began to show traces of a smile.

"You don't have to talk to any of these bums, Betty Ann," Hopewell said. "You'll find me to be the most engaging conversationalist of the bunch."

"But you'll probably fall in love with me," Bowman said. "Women usually do."

The Chief came back and announced that Betty Ann Greybow was in charge of our section, a revelation that had little effect on everyone but the Earthquake.

"Now just a damn minute," he said. "She's a—"

She cut him off. "A woman. Huh, Fatso? Is that what you're about to say?"

"I was gonna say a civilian. And by the way, if I can't call you Bag, then you can't call me Fatso. Come to think of it, you can't call me Fatso even if I call you Bag."

"Oh, I can't?"

"That's right. Who died and made you boss?"

"No one died. The Chief just made me boss."

"You know," the Earthquake said, "we were just discussing people like you, just before you came in. You're just like old Thrashy…" He stopped and looked to me.

"Thrasymachus," I said.

"Plato's *Republic*," she said. "I guess you guys have a little more class than I gave you credit for."

"You're just like that guy, that guy Mill just said. Might makes right."

"Don't forget the shepherd's ring," said Bowman.

"That too," said the Earthquake.

"Okay," she said, and turned to the fat man with the belligerent scowl. "Now I'm not sure I got your name."

"Percival G. O'Toole," said Chief Crouch.

This really fractured her. She started laughing, and she couldn't get herself under control, and soon we were all laughing, except for the Earthquake.

"All right, Bag," he shouted.

"Why you smart little shit," she said, and got right in his face.

"All right," said the Chief. "That's enough. O'Toole, if I hear you call her Bag again, I'll have your ass."

"We call him Earthquake, ma'am," Hopewell said.

She smiled, showing a perfect set of white teeth in her deeply tanned face.

"Five 'til ten," the Chief said. "I hear the mob rattling the doors."

"Okay," Betty Ann said, "Miller, you man the tower at the middle of the pool. Bowman, shallow end. Earthquake, walk the perimeter. At eleven, Earthquake takes the middle, Miller shifts to the end, Hopewell takes the perimeter, Bowman is down. Etcetera. Everyone got it?"

"Yeah, yeah, whatever. Blah, blah, blah," said the Earthquake. "When do you get into the action."

"I'll rotate in at twelve."

The doors opened and in came the bathers, swimmers, sun worshippers, divers, kids who peed in the pool, girls who hung around the lifeguard towers and made sure we noticed them, which took little effort. Frankly, I found myself looking again and again at Betty Ann Greybow. She was a tall, muscular version of Katherine Ross (unknown to us at the time because *The Graduate* was eight years in the future), but she was all business and certainly out of my league. I was the baby of the bunch.

I'm not sure, looking back at it, who dubbed her the Amazon, or when she got dubbed, but something tells me it was Bowman, and it must have been on the first day she was there. She objected to Bag, for obvious reasons, but she took the Amazon as a compliment, and for the rest of the summer, that was her name. In fact, I had forgotten what her real name was. The Earthquake's diary reminded me.

Chapter 5

Enter: Apollo Lykeios

May 26, 1960. Bought a book today. What a waste of money. The Republic. I got it in a used bookstore. Mill wanted to go there, so I drove him down, and Bowman, too. Kind of a ratty place down by Balboa Square, about a block from where I got arrested for bumming money. Thought I'd read about the ring and justice. I couldn't make heads or tails of it, but the other guys think it's the greatest thing since sliced bread.

—The Diary of Earthquake O'Toole

This is as close as Earthquake ever came in his diary to getting to the heart of the Greek Summer as I remember it. He actually seems to have entered into the spirit of that time, briefly at least. As he indicates in his diary entry, he was the one who drove us from Miramar into downtown San Diego, where there was (as he also indicates) a ratty looking bookstore that dealt in anything used. The proprietor was the type one generally finds in such places—extremely well read and well-informed about literature, with an almost mystic love of the printed word in any form. He was small, bald headed, and bespectacled, and he was called Mr. Stuart. Bowman and I got to know him well that summer; he became our intellectual guide and mentor, and we followed his advice in reading, and hung on his every word. The Earthquake met him only once and seemed to consider that one meeting a waste of his time.

The shop was located on the ground floor of a corner building and took up a space perhaps thirty feet wide and fifty feet deep. It was dark and smelled of (what else?) old paper, a smell I have always found rather pleasant, like that of an alfalfa field ripe for harvest.

Bowman always said that Mr. Stuart looked like Rudyard Kipling. That was a good way of putting it. Indeed he did; and he was polite and sort of old-worldish.

"What can I help you with, gentlemen," he said when we walked into his shop for the first time.

"*The Republic*," I said. "Do you have any copies?"

"Of course," he said. "Right over in the philosophy section, there against the north wall. You like Plato, do you?"

"Well, maybe," I said. "Bowman…" I indicated my companion, "he took this course at San Diego J.C. on Plato, and they used *The Republic*. He sort of got me into it, and I've been reading his copy. Thought I'd get one of my own."

Mr. Stuart nodded.

"I want to find out about the ring that makes you invisible," said Earthquake.

Mr. Stuart looked at him and smiled, and I thought he could see through the Earthquake like a sheet of cellophane. The Earthquake must have thought so, too, because he giggled that silly little giggle of his and bit his lower lip.

"The ring of Gyges,"[1] Mr. Stuart said. "I was always a little troubled by that one. It's sort of scary to think what you might do if you knew you would never get caught."

"Wait a minute. What did you call that ring?"

"Gyges." He looked at the Earthquake and smiled.

"Us real Plato-readers call that Guy-jeez," said the Earthquake.

"It's Gyges, with a hard gee. But I'll say Guy-jeez if that pleases you. Come on. I'll show you where Plato is located."

We followed him across the room to where a shelf loomed up before us, and on it, floor to within a foot of the ceiling, were books of all sizes, colors, descriptions.

"I try to keep these alphabetized by author," Mr. Stuart said. "So Plato should be about right…Yes, here he is. And here are, well, five *Republics* that I see imme-

---

1. Poor Mr. Stuart. We thought he was so ignorant that he didn't know the name was pronounced Guy-jeez, and of course Bowman and I were too polite to correct him. The Earthquake was not.

diately. The two paperbacks are cheaper, of course. This one is in pretty poor condition, so I'll let it go for a quarter."

"How about this hardback?" I asked.

"Yes. That's Jowett. His translation is pretty much the standard. I'll let that one go for two dollars."

"Good enough," I said, and took down the book.

"I'll take the twenty-five cent paperback," said O'Toole.

"Now, I'll be glad to sell it to you," Mr. Stuart said. "But this is an abridgment."

"What's that?" O'Toole asked. "I didn't know they played cards back then."

Bowman groaned and rolled his eyes. "Frontal lobes..." he whispered.

"Give me credit for having some brains, Bowman. I'm making a joke, okay."

"It's a lame joke from a lame brain," Bowman replied.

Mr. Stuart was both patient and tolerant. "Abridgment means it's been edited and some of it left out," he said. "Look, this other paperback is complete, and it's only fifty cents."

"Give you thirty-five for it," said O'Toole.

Bowman groaned.

"Fifty cents," Mr. Stuart repeated and smiled.

"Okay," O'Toole said, and dragged it off the shelf.

Though none of us knew it at the time, this was the book O'Toole would leave to me in his will.

"Are you boys sailors?" Mr. Stuart asked.

"How did you know?" Bowman asked.

"I'm an old California man," he said. "I've seen lots of sailors in my day. Probably the haircuts. But you look like you spend all day in the sun. What ship are you on?"

"No ship," Bowman said. "We're at Miramar."

"We're lifeguards at the swimming pool," O'Toole said.

"You don't say," Mr. Stuart said, and he looked at the Earthquake as if he couldn't work out the equation: pear-shaped, freckled, skinhead equals lifeguard. He needn't have bothered trying; none of us could ever work it out either.

"I'm going back to college as soon as I get out of the Navy," Bowman said.

"Do you have a major in mind?" Mr. Stuart asked.

"Not really. But maybe philosophy."

"Let me recommend a book to you," he said. "Come over here."

He took us to another section of the shop, to a shelf he had labeled "American classics."

"Jack London," he said, and pointed to a book.

"Yeah," I said. "My old man was always talking about Jack London. *Call of the Wild. The Sea Wolf.* What's this one?" I meant the one to which Mr. Stuart was pointing.

"*Martin Eden*," he said. "Frankly, I always thought this was the best thing he ever did. It's about a sailor who educates himself and becomes a best selling author. It's full of philosophy. It'll open up a whole new world to you."

"I'll take it," I said.

"Give me one, too," said the Earthquake. The copy of *Martin Eden* that he bought, slightly newer but in worse condition than the 1913 Macmillan edition I picked up, is the one Earthquake would later leave to Bowman.

"I was born and raised in Oakland," Mr. Stuart said. "I knew Jack's daughter, Joan. Not well, but I knew her."

"Did you know Jack?" I asked.

"No. I was only six years old when he died. But everyone in Oakland knew Jack after a fashion. He was our guy. My father ran a fish market on the docks. Bought fish directly off the boats. He knew him a long time before he was a famous author."

"You don't say."

After we left the bookstore, we were faced with one of those decisions that was perhaps as serious as any other we would confront that summer—what shall we do now? The spring semester was over, and Bowman had skated through and earned a "C". Our lifeguard section was off duty. There were no movies playing that were sufficiently elevated to engage our interest (though Earthquake suggested we head to Tijuana for the porn flicks), so we took our books, two six-packs of beer, and drove to the beach.

I have always thought the California beaches are as fine as any in the world, and that the California coastline—especially as it runs from north of Malibu up to Monterey—is the most beautiful I have ever seen. But the California beaches are also some of the most crowded, and if one is not a people person, they are not particularly attractive. I mention this because Earthquake O'Toole by his own admission was not a people person, although he didn't put his feelings in exactly those terms. What he said was that when he got out of the Navy, he intended to become a beach bum; and then he said, almost as quickly as he had outlined his future for us, that the only problem was he didn't much like to go to the beach. Bowman and I loved the beach. It had everything a healthy youngster could desire—girls, girls and girls. The Earthquake liked girls fine, but they didn't like him, and he didn't like the sand, or the salt water, or, for reasons he never made clear, sea gulls. Why, then, did he wish to become a beach bum?

"I might find something out there. Maybe a bottle will wash up, and the ring of Guy-jeez will be in it, and I'll sneak up on your sorry ass, Bowman, and relieve you of your coin purse."

As for me, while I was and am a beach-going man, I was very poor company this day because of Jack London's book. I have rarely been so transfixed by a story as I was by that of the sailor become philosopher, Martin Eden, who left a ship's forecastle with barely enough education to read and write, and by his own efforts made himself into an intellectual giant. I hadn't even intended to read the book that day, and wasn't sure whether or not I would ever read it; but on the way down to the beach, I opened to page one while Bowman and O'Toole were arguing. They were in the front seat, with the Earthquake driving, and I was in the back. I heard Bowman say:

"Earthquake, watch what you're doing. You're gonna run over someone as sure as hell."

And the Earthquake responded, "You wanna drive, Bowman?"

And after that I didn't look up until I heard car doors slamming and realized we were at the beach. We headed for a bathhouse, with the Earthquake toting the beer, Bowman and I carrying towels and our swimming trunks, and me carrying *Martin Eden*. Our would-be beach bum didn't bother to change clothes, as he had no apparent interest in doing anything but drinking and arguing with Bowman. Bowman changed, immediately hit the water, and yelled for me to come on in. I looked up from my book long enough to see him talking to a girl who was standing about calf deep in the inrushing surf. I waved to him. The Earthquake said something about doing your reading at home, and why waste a day at the beach by sticking your nose in a book? I mumbled something in reply.

I read until it got too dark to read.

When I looked up the sun was hanging just above the Pacific, someone had built a fire out of driftwood, and someone else was strumming a guitar. People were around the fire singing Kingston Trio songs, and someone must have made a beer run, because there was no shortage.

"Hey, Mill," Bowman called. He was over at the fire beside a girl who looked a great deal like most of the other girls I'd seen that day, but might have been unique in the annals of femininity for all I knew.

"Hey, Mill, close that book and come on over."

"Well, we went one day," the guitar-player sang, and the others joined in.

I got up from beneath the palm I'd been leaning against, and I realized I felt a bit faint and had to steady myself against the tree's trunk. I was like a man waking out of sleep. I closed the book and crossed the sand to where the others were.

"So here we are," the guitar-player informed us, "in the Tijuana Jail. Ain't got no friends to go our bail."

The surf was breaking close to shore, and gulls were tossing on the wind.

"Ladies," Bowman said, to whichever ladies happened to be listening, "meet my buddy Miller, smartest damned guy I ever knew. Reads philosophy and poetry."

"You call him smart?" the Earthquake said. "He comes to the beach and spends the whole day sitting under a tree reading a book. Now that's what I call pretty dumb."

"On the other hand, ladies and gentlemen," I pointed to Earthquake O'Toole, "we see here the acme of the evolutionary process, the eternal seeker for wisdom and truth. Kindly stand up, O'Toole, and let this enlightened company have a look at you. You'll note that while he is well able to crawl upon his belly like a snake, he is also able to move about on all-fours, and even, occasionally and for limited periods, to achieve the upright posture suggestive of one of the great apes to whom he is distantly related."

A great laugh went up, in which even the Earthquake took part.

"Pretty damned good, Mill," he said.

"Did I tell you he's smart?" Bowman said. "Did I, huh?"

"You're kind of cute," said one of the girls.

"Don't get the wrong idea, honey," I said. "I'm not just a repository of fancy language. I can also drink and roll in the gutter."

She giggled. "So what are you reading?" she asked, nodding at the closed book I held in my right hand.

"South coast, the wild coast, is lonely..." sang the guitar player.

"This has got to be the best book I've ever read," I said. "*Martin Eden*, by Jack London."

"Yeah," someone said. "He wrote dog stories."

"This is no dog story," I said.

"I won my wife in a card game," sang the guitar player. "To hell with the lords o'er the sea."

Someone threw another piece of driftwood on the fire, sparks flew upward against the gathering darkness, and the landward wind moved the flames and caused orange light to pulse and dance on faces. Some people were singing along with the guitar player. Bowman and the girl he had taken up with were huddled together staring into the fire, while the Earthquake was opening another beer. He asked if I wanted one.

"Yeah," I said. "Listen, *Martin Eden* is about this sailor. Now this guy has been at sea since he was a little kid. It's all he knows. He can read and write, and he can probably add and subtract, but that's about all the education he has."

"Sounds like my kind of guy," one of the girls said.

"Working class," said a guy with a mop of unruly hair and wire-rim glasses. "London was always beating the drum for Karl Marx."

"So what happens to the sailor?" Bowman asked.

"Well," I said. "He meets this girl through a sort of accident. Her brother gets jumped by a gang of toughs, see, and Martin just happens to be passing by, and he jumps in and saves the guy. So the guy he saves invites him home for dinner—to show his gratitude, you know, and here he meets this guy's younger sister."

"We're sailing cross the river from Liverpool," sang the guitar player. "Heave away, Santy Anno. Around Cape Horn to Frisco Bay, way out in Californio."

"All right," the girl next to me said. "He meets the girl. Go on. Sounds like a good love story."

"Sounds like an American version of Pygmalion to me." This from the fellow who had said London was always beating the drum for Karl Marx. "Sounds like *My Fair Lady* in reverse."

"Sort of," I said. "But not really. But it starts out as if that's where it's going. See, these people who invite Martin home for dinner are really upper class types. At least, that's what he thinks. He's never been in a home like this, you know, with crystal and china, and oil paintings hanging on walls. And he's never met a girl like this Ruth Morse—that's the sister's name. And he falls head over heels in love with her. But the problem is that he knows he's not in her class. She's never gonna love a sailor."

"Don't tell me," said the Earthquake, in a rare flash of insightfulness. "She loves him in spite of himself."

"Not exactly," I said. "She won't admit it to herself, but she loves him for the very reason he loves her. He's from another world, one that she has never dreamed existed. His face is tanned, and he's muscular, and—well—dangerous." I turned to the girl who was leaning closer toward me. The fire light shone in her eyes. "Are you attracted to dangerous men?" I asked.

"Not me," she said.

"Do you mean to tell me that you wouldn't go out with Jesse James if he asked you?"

"No."

"I would," another girl said.

"So would I," said one of the guys, and made a limp-wristed gesture.

"What about the story?" asked Bowman.

"Well," I said, "Martin decides he has to go to school and get educated. He has to be somebody so that he can marry Ruth Morse. And Ruth, why she takes him under her wing and begins giving him advice, about what to read, what is art and what isn't."

"Pygmalion," said the wise guy.

"Yep, except things begin to get out of hand."

"They always do," the wise guy responded. "Didn't Eliza Doolittle become a bit too much for Professor Higgins to deal with?"

"But Eliza really is the Professor's creation. Ruth Morse doesn't create Martin. She only thinks she does, and she finds out pretty soon that her supposed creation is completely out of her class. Martin Eden is a genius, see, but he doesn't know it. He's never been exposed to the world of learning. But once he starts to read, why his whole world begins to change. One book makes reference to two more, and those two bring up five others, and pretty soon he's reading everything he can get his hands on."

"I'm sort of curious about the girl's family," the girl sitting next to Bowman said. "Do they like their daughter hanging around with a sailor?"

"I'm a sailor," Bowman told her. "Does your mother like you hanging around me?"

"You're not a sailor," she said. "He might be," nodding toward the Earthquake.

"All three of us are," the Earthquake said. "Don't let these guys fool you with a bunch of fancy talk. They're just a couple of sailors with inflated opinions of themselves."

"Not all sailors drool and speak in monosyllables," I said. "Ain't that right, Bowman?"

"Speaking for myself," Bowman replied, "I try to confine my drooling to weekends. As to the other, I'll admit that I frequently find myself deviating into polysyllabic expression without giving it a thought. But then I catch myself and go back to the standard grunts which make up the bulk of maritime vocabulary."

"You guys are a scream," Bowman's girl said.

"Yeah," said the Earthquake. "A regular riot. But back to the story. What about Ruth's parents. Surely they don't let Martin Eden hang around."

"Actually," I said, "they do. They realize that their daughter is, shall we say, unsophisticated in the grosser elements of love, and they think she is involved in a fascination that will be short lived. What they don't figure on—what none of them figure on—is that Martin Eden is smarter than any of them. They were born to wealth and education, and they can feed back college lectures by rote. But they really can't think for themselves. And pretty soon Martin discovers this. They're purely superficial. And it surprises him."

I paused, and I found myself looking deep into the fire, thinking about the story and its implications for me. I must have been silent longer than I thought. One of the girls brought me back from my introspective journey by saying:

"Okay, then what?"

"Oh," I said. "Well, then he decides to become a writer, and…well, that's as far as I got."

"Does he get the girl?"

"I don't know."

"Does he succeed as a writer?"

"I don't know. Get the book and read it."

"This pisses me off, Mill," the Earthquake said. "You really had me going there. Now you tell me you don't know what happened."

"You bought a copy of the book today, Earthquake. Read it and find out how it ends."

Apparently reading the book for himself hadn't occurred to him.

"You can tell me the rest at the pool," he said.

The guitar player sang, "Once there were green fields kissed by the sun. Once there were valleys where rivers used to run…" Couples began drifting away from the fire together. One of the girls said something about coming back tomorrow, but Bowman told her we had to be on duty at the swimming pool.

"I thought you said you were sailors," the wise guy put in.

"We are," said Bowman. "We're assigned to the swimming pool at Miramar as lifeguards."

"Hey, that's a great pool," one of the guys said. "I was out there with a friend once. He's an ensign."

"Maybe we could come out and visit you," Bowman's girl said. "And hear the rest of Mill's story."

"Not mine," I said. "Jack London's. What's your name?"

"Marge Taylor."

"Read the book, Marge."

"Too busy. Going to summer school."

I could hear laughter and muttered words off in the darkness. Bowman and Marge Taylor left the fire and went off in the darkness together, and I was left at the fire with a girl I had never seen, and with Earthquake O'Toole, who I had seen more often than I wanted. But the Earthquake, who had been consuming beer all day, had the good grace to fall backward in the sand and lose whatever measure of consciousness he possessed, which left me alone with the girl, and with a ripe opportunity that turned out not to be ripe.

Her name was Betsy Taylor, and she was fifteen years old.

"Fifteen!" I said. "Good grief, girl. Do your parents know you're out here at night with a bunch of sailors?"

"Sort of like Ruth Morse, aren't I."

"Ruth Morse was of age," I said.

"Oh, how old are you?"

"Nineteen," I said.

"Do your parents know where you are?" she asked.

I laughed. "I guess Marge is your big sister."

"Yes, and a real pain," she said.

"How old is she?"

"Seventeen."

"Oh, hell!" I said. I jumped up, ran about twenty yards in the direction I'd seen Bowman and Marge Taylor take, and yelled into the darkness, "Be careful, Bowman. You're dealing with jailbait there. San Quentin quail, boy."

It took Bowman all of about fifteen seconds to come plowing out of the darkness, across the sand of the beach, looking over his shoulder as if he were the object of an intensive manhunt, dragging his bewildered and disheveled partner behind him.

"What the hell are you talking about?" he demanded.

I pointed at Marge. "Seventeen," I said.

"Whaaaat," Marge shouted. "I'm nineteen years old."

"That ain't what your little sister says." I pointed over to where Betsy sat beside the fire, grinning like...well, sailors have an obscene expression for it. Grinning like a possum, with a few added touches.

"You little creep," Marge shrieked.

"Mom and Dad told us to stay out of trouble," Betsy said.

"I'm nineteen years old," Marge shouted, and stamped her foot on the wet sand.

"You are not," said Betsy. "You're only eighteen."

"I'll be nineteen in a month."

"Brother," Bowman said. "It's getting where you have to check IDs before you pick up a girl."

Marge whirled on him. "I'm not a pickup," she screamed.

"Don't worry, honey," I said. "I'm sure he'll still respect you in the morning."

"Ooooh," said Marge. "Let's go, Betsy."

Betsy jumped merrily up, laughed, waved, said, "I had a great time, guys," and off she went behind her enraged sister.

"I was just about to fall in love with you, Marge," Bowman called after them. "At least I was just about to tell you I was. But don't do anything foolish. You still have lots to live for."

He turned to me. "She'll probably name her first son after me," he said.

We collapsed on the beach, rolling and laughing.

"Everyone wound up with someone," I finally said, as we lay still, looking up at the stars. "We wound up with the Earthquake."

"Yeah," Bowman said. "And I'm not sure he's still alive."

Alive he was; but he was drunk, utterly dead to the world, and he had emptied the contents of his stomach—probably two six-packs of beer—in a great variegated mess beside him. If he had rolled the wrong direction he would have drowned in his own vomit. I looked at Bowman. He looked at me. Great minds run in the same grooves, and close friends frequently know the right thing to do without ever saying a word to one another. We took off O'Toole's pants, turned his underwear backward, filled them with vomit, and put his pants back on him. I don't know what the Earthquake thought when he awoke the next morning with an aching head and found himself in this wretched and puzzling condition, but I do know that when we were back on duty at the pool, we were one lifeguard short for the whole morning because the Earthquake checked in at sick bay. A corpsman told me later (in the strictest confidence, you understand, which confidence I now violated by announcing it to the world) that the Earthquake complained of a serious digestive disorder. He was putting hot dogs in at one end and they were coming out the other in almost pristine condition.

Chapter 6

Up Jumped the Pantheon

"You know," Bowman said, as we were reliving the backward shorts caper, "folks just don't have good, clean fun like that anymore."

We sat on the rocks overlooking La Jolla Cove. The afternoon sun was slanting over us, bathing the world in dusty gold. Far out at sea, in the blue-gray distance, a merchantman was plowing south, bound probably from San Pedro to some distant port.

"Hand me a brew, son," I said. "Let me pour another libation on the altar. Sing to me, Erato, of young gods and forgotten times. Crown my erstwhile golden locks with leaves of myrtle while I strike the lyre and descend bodily into the hallowed halls of the departed. Earthquake, if you are indeed conscious—which you never were during your earthly sojourn—you now realize what a rotten trick we played on you. Do you still consider us your best friends? Are you able to forgive and to join us in belated laughter?"

"That," Bowman said, "is the great mystery yet to be solved. The riddle of the sphinx begs for an Oedipus."

"Ah," I responded, "the answer to the riddle was man, going on four legs in the morning, two legs at noon, and three legs in the evening. Our riddle involves a creature who crept along his entire life on all fours—when he wasn't wriggling on his belly."

"You have a real mean streak in you, Miller."

"Yes. But listen to yourself. You accuse me of meanness, but when did you, or either of us, for that matter, ever show any real kindness to this guy? Now here we sit with his ashes, heirs to his dubious treasure…"

"Hold on now, whatever we did to him must have been all right with him. No, my boy, you can quit inviting me to join you in self-flagellation. The fact of the matter is we took him into the inner circle. He was a member of the Symposium with all the rights and privileges attendant thereunto. And we never invited anyone else. Others, if they came at all, came as party-crashers."

"True," I said. "Very true. I guess he got out of it what he wanted to get out of it."

We were quiet for awhile, enjoying the sounds of pounding surf on the rocks far below, and the smell of the great Pacific Ocean.

"Boy, what a bunch of snobs we were," I finally said.

"Snobs?" Bowman said. "How were we snobs? Elitists maybe. Maybe a bit pretentious. Certainly not snobs. The fact is, if you'll recall, the other guys weren't all that interested in what we were doing. They thought we were a little crazy. We didn't tell any of them they couldn't sit in with us."

"We didn't tell them they could either."

"We didn't tell them anything. We just did our thing and let everyone else do theirs. Ours happened to have been the Symposium."

"How did we get going on that? Do you remember?"

"As I recall, after the evening of backward skivvies, I wanted to hear more about *Martin Eden*. So did Earthquake, for some reason. You finished it in two days of marathon reading, and you spent the rest of the week telling us about it."

"The Symposium…" I said, looking away into the distance. "Wednesday evenings."

"It was Thursday."

"No, Bowman, it was Wednesday. I remember because that's the night *Maverick* was on, and we had to wait till that was over to meet. You were a *Maverick* nut."

"Wrong, Miller. It was Thursday, and we had to work around the *Alaskans*. You were a nut for the *Alaskans*. Besides, I never gave a damn for *Maverick*. I was a *Mister Lucky* fan. Oh, Mister Lucky, la-di-da, scooby doo, doo wah…And, anyway, Maverick was on Saturday night."

In my heart I knew the Symposium met on Wednesday night, and I'm still convinced it did, but I am just as convinced that it doesn't make a great deal of difference. It was nothing formal, and generally we didn't meet at all. When we did, it was usually at the pool after it closed and sometimes at the park across the street, and we discussed philosophy and literature, and tried out harebrained, adolescent ideas on one another. This was one of those unplanned, seemingly spontaneous, events that made a major difference in Bowman's life, and in mine, and, as it turned out, in Earthquake O'Toole's.

"Does the Earthquake mention anything about the Symposium in his diary?" I asked.

"Let's see," Bowman said. "It's getting kind of hard to read out here. Now that would have been in early June. Right." He was leafing through Earthquake's diary.

"Late May or early June," I said.

"Listen to this entry," Bowman said. "Quote: I am one sick son-of-a-bitch. I think Miller and Bowman tried to poison me last night down at the Shores. Those two are not only crazy, they're dangerous. If I ever drink with them again, I'll keep a close eye on the bottle. Woke up this morning with the worse case of diarrhea I ever had in my life, and the worst hangover. And over and over in my head Mill's voice—Jack London, Jack London, Jack London."

"What's the date on that entry?" I asked.

"May 31."

"Well, then the Symposium couldn't have started before June first. A simple matter of logic, my boy."

"Wasn't it about the time of the card game?"

"The card game?"

"The card game," Bowman repeated. "Surely you haven't forgotten that. A Parthenon beats three Apollos."

"Oh, hell," I muttered. "My brain has started to calcify on me. How could I forget the card game? It was two or three mornings after the backward shorts caper. We woke up to heavy rain."

I remembered the rainstorm because it was accompanied by something we seldom experienced in San Diego—thunder and lightning. I don't know why this is such a rare occurrence in Southern California, though I'm sure a good meteorologist could tell me if I were curious enough to pursue the matter, but in all the time I spent in the San Diego area, I saw electrical activity with a rain storm only once or twice.

We left the barracks in what promised to be a veritable deluge. By the time we were out of the chow hall, the gutters were running full of water and thunder was rattling above us. Normally, we walked to the pool, but this morning we managed to catch a ride in a pickup truck with one of our buddies who was delivering some boxes of popcorn to the movie theater. So far, so good. He had the boxes covered with a canvas tarp, and Bowman and I got under it and managed to stay dry. The Earthquake and Hopewell rode in the cab with the driver. But once we got out of the truck at the theater, we had about a seventy-five yard run, across the street, and around the outside of the pool, to get to the entrance. We arrived soaked. Chief Crouch met us at the front door, soaked in more ways than one.

"Get out of them wet clothes," he said. "Look at the mess you're making. Earthquake, get a swab and get this deck mopped up."

"Get a swab, Mill," the Earthquake said.

"The Chief told you to get it."

"Yeah, but I outrank you, Seaman Miller. Get this deck swabbed."

"I hate to admit it, Mill," Bowman said, "but for once the Earthquake is right."

"What are you gonna do?" I asked Bowman.

"I'm gonna stand here like the third-class petty officer I am and watch you swab the deck, Seaman Miller."

"Well, what a couple of horse's asses," I said.

"Get the deck swabbed, Miller," said Chief Crouch. "Even I agree with O'Toole."

"Boy, what a day," I said. "When the world lines up with Earthquake O'Toole against Miller, evil and destruction must be just around the corner. Gather the animals two by two into the ark, for I will destroy mankind from off the face of the earth."

"All right, Reverend," the Chief growled, "get busy on that deck."

We cleaned up, changed into swimming trunks and sweat shirts, and gathered in the Chief's office, where there was hot coffee and absolutely nothing to do: electrical activity equals no swimming. But relieving boredom is a way of life in the Navy, as anyone who has ever spent long amounts of time at sea can testify; and the relief of boredom usually takes one of several forms. The telling of sea stories (So we rolled into Hong Kong, and then...) is a typical sailor way of killing time. Drinking is another. And then, there is always the playing of games.

"Too bad we ain't got an acey-deucy board," the Chief said.

Acey-deucy is a Navy version of backgammon, played for so many years aboard so many ships by so many sailors that it has become a tradition—sort of like chess at Oxford. But, as the Chief's comment indicates, we didn't have an acey-deucy board.

"Got any cards?" Hopewell asked.

"Yeah," said the Chief, and produced a battered deck from a desk drawer. "But I ain't got a cribbage board."

Cribbage is another shipboard favorite.

"How about a little poker," said Hopewell.

"Why not," said the Chief.

We pulled the desk to the middle of the room, circled the chairs around it, and got into the card game that became a part of the legend which is the Greek Summer and indirectly led to the Chief's vain attempt at total sobriety.

"All right," said the Chief, "here's how we'll do it. Get a box of book matches from the snack bar. Each match is worth twenty-five cents. At the end of the game, we'll figure out who owes what to who, and we'll pay up on payday."

"There's only one way to do it," Bowman said. "We have to start even, with the same amount of matches. That way we can tell who the winners are and who the losers are."

We finally came up with a box of book matches, worth ten cents a match in our makeshift bank, and a box of wooden ones, worth twenty-five cents each, and split them up so that each of us started with twenty dollars.

The Chief brought the radio around from the reception counter. "Well, all you cats and kittens," the disk jockey merrily declared, "we have a wet day, so stay in and keep your fur dry, and we'll keep you up to date. Here's Sam Cooke and Chain Gang."

"That's the sound of the men, working on the chain gang," Sam Cooke informed us.

Above us, the thunder rumbled, and the rain came down, and one of history's most notable games of chance was underway. The stakes, as it turned out, were staggering beyond belief, for on the table were the heroes of Greek antiquity, and one of the heroines, as well. I don't know, for neither Bowman nor I could remember, who took the game in its classical direction, but I will give my own version of how it occurred. I remember for sure that the Earthquake was dealing, and that he had called five card stud.

"Ante one dime," he said.

We all kicked in, and around came the hole card and then the first card face up. The Earthquake called them as he dealt them, like he had seen it done in the movies no doubt, or like he thought gambling etiquette demanded, considering himself something of an authority in this area.

"Six. Six. A king. Jack. A Deuce. Your king bets, Bowman."

"Well, boys," peeking at his hole card, "that'll cost you a dime."

"Oh, big spender," said the Chief. "And a quarter."

"You don't suppose he has a pair of sixes," the Earthquake said.

"You guys are nuts," Hopewell said.

"Are you in, or ain't you?"

"Yeah, I'm in."

"Here we go round again," said the Earthquake. "Eight. No help. Five. Nothing. Wow! Two kings. Nine. No help there."

"You say nothing," said the Chief.

"The Chief's sitting on a possible straight," Bowman said. "So's Hopewell."

The Earthquake shrugged. "But lookey here now. Mill draws two jacks."

"London, two times," I said.

"Martin Eden twice," said Bowman.

"You two are driving me up a wall with that Jack London stuff," said the Earthquake.

"Amen to that," Hopewell said.

"Two Apollos bet, Bowman," said O'Toole.

"Check to the Chief."

"One dollar."

"If you think you're fooling me, Chief, you've got another think coming." Bowman looked again at his hole card. "There you sit with a handful of crap, and me with two Apollos showing. You're not bluffing me out."

"Well," I said, looking at my hole card. "I don't know..."

"Whaddaya mean, you don't know?" said the Earthquake. "You've got three Jack Londons possible. Are you gonna let the Chief run you off with a bunch of doo-doo?"

"Doo-doo," said Bowman. "What a quaint expression. Did you pick that up in parochial school?"

"How about a bet, boys," said Hopewell.

"All right. Everyone in. Here we go round the mulberry bush. A jack to Hopewell. Eight. Ten. Another ten. And the dealer draws an ace. My, my, my. The big boy."

"The ring," I said.

"The ring of Guy-jeez," said the Earthquake.

"I don't know what the hell you guys are talking about," said the Chief.

"Students of philosophy," said Bowman. "Disciples of Socrates."

"Well, your two Apollos still bet," I said.

"This time it's two bucks," said Bowman.

Hopewell folded. I folded. The Chief raised a dollar. The Earthquake saw that and raised another dollar. Bowman, the Chief, Earthquake O'Toole were in for the final card, the suspense lay in heaps and piles, and the rain came down.

"Nine," said the Earthquake. "A very possible straight. Another nine. Who knows. Depends on what you've got in the hole. Maybe two pair. Those Apollos are wicked looking. And the dealer draws a four."

We whooped and hollered, and Bowman said, "My two Apollos are still high." He looked at his hole card, drummed his fingers on the table, and said, "One dollar to you."

"Maybe he's got two pair," the Earthquake said. "Maybe not."

"We need something to drink other than this coffee," said Hopewell. "You make rotten coffee, Chief."

"You don't like it, make it yourself next time," the Chief said. "Now don't bother me, son. I'm trying to think. Here's your dollar, Bowman. And it'll cost you another five to stay in."

"Six dollars to you, Earthquake," I said.

"Shut up, Miller," said the Earthquake. "You may be some sort of philosopher, but you're on my turf now. I cut my teeth on a deck of cards."

"Who is the short, fat stranger there?" I sang. "Maverick is the name."

The boys guffawed. The Earthquake thrust his middle finger into my face, then said, "All right, Chief, here's your six dollars, and an extra one just to sweeten the pot."

The Chief looked at the Earthquake with what has to have been the blankest expression I have ever seen, and with no more concern than a man yawning, he pushed four wooden matches into the center of the table.

"Seven dollars, Bowman," Hopewell said.

"Man, there's a lot of match wood in there," I said.

"This is nothing," said the Chief. "I've seen pots of over a thousand. But that was back in the days when men were men."

"Oh, kindly spare me that shit, Chief," Bowman said. "Okay, here's your seven dollars. Let's see your cards."

The Chief hesitated, reached out slowly, and turned over a deuce.

The Earthquake smirked. "Just as I thought," he said. "A handful of doo-doo. What about you, Bowman?"

"I called you," Bowman said.

"Okay," said the Earthquake. He flipped his hole card over. It was an ace.

"The ring of Guy-jeez twice," I said.

Bowman's face grew red and his jaws tightened. "You're looking at what I've got," he said. "Go ahead and drag it in, you no good shanty mick."

"Ah," said Earthquake O'Toole, rubbing his hands rapidly together. "Saint Bridget is still smiling on the Irish. I knew you didn't have another Apollo in the hole, Bowman. I knew it by the way you were betting. The Chief was the one I was worried about."

"Shut up and deal," said Bowman.

"It'll be five card stud again, gentlemen," said the Chief, "and this time the ante will be one buck. Everyone in."

"I wish we had something to drink other than your coffee, Chief," Hopewell said, a wish he had already voiced.

But this time he got his wish. Like Houdini pulling a rabbit out of a hat, the Chief fetched up a bottle from somewhere under the desk and slammed it down on the table. It was about three-quarters of a fifth of Old Grand Dad. I, for one, was surprised that the Chief had a bottle of anything that was that full, and it is my guess, forty years after the fact, that we were looking at his daily ration, and that he had already consumed a quarter of the bottle.

"You boys'll replace this on payday," said the Chief. "Now won't you?"

"Sure, Chief," the Earthquake said, his eyes twinkling like a kid's at Christmas.

Old Grand Dad. It tasted awful.

"Wish we had something to mix it with," Hopewell said.

"Well, we ain't got nothing, sister woman," the Chief said. "Mix it with coffee."

We did. That tasted even worse. But after a few swallows it seemed to be the finest drink ever devised for consumption by the United States Navy, and it went down easier and easier, and the cards fell on the table, and money, in the form of match sticks, changed hands.

We rocked along like this for the better part of the morning, losing money to the Earthquake, and slopping down Old Grand Dad like there was no tomorrow. We were creating a whole new language for poker playing, one which became standard for all our games that summer. The king was Apollo. The jack began as Martin Eden but gradually metamorphosed to Dionysus. The queen was the Amazon. O'Toole balked at this one because he felt that our section leader was a pushy slut who had failed to show him the proper respect, and he said that he intended to either seduce her or whip her butt.

"O'Toole," said the Chief, "you couldn't seduce your own fist."

"Wanna bet?" the Earthquake demanded. "I seduced it twice only last night."

"Well, I know damn well you can't whip her," Bowman said.

"Hell, if she dropped one of her boobs on you it'd break your neck," said Hopewell.

"All right," the Earthquake said. "All right. You've got two Amazons, Mill. What are you gonna do?"

A full house became a Parthenon in our jargon. A straight was a Socrates. A flush—Plato. A straight flush, which we never saw that summer, was an Athens.

Who knows where we might have gone with this business, probably to the Elysian Fields. O'Toole was sitting there with three aces showing (excuse me, three rings of Guy-jeez) when the door to the office swung back and there, in a long, black raincoat, stood Commander Stanford, the commanding officer of Special Services. Things got quiet very quickly. The Chief, in a silly attempt to hide the bottle by putting his hat over it, knocked it over and it spilled in a beautiful amber puddle in the middle of the desk. I thought the Chief was going to cry—not at getting caught drinking on duty, but at the loss of the whiskey. The rest of us simply froze, as if caught in mortal sin by an angry deity.

"Ten-hut!" the Chief called, and rose, swaying like a tree in a high wind.

I started up, but had to grip the desk to keep from falling, and a wobbly crouch was the closest thing to an attention I could manage. Hopewell just sat there. Bowman fell sideways off the chair, crawled for what seemed several minutes on the floor until he found the chair in which Hopewell sat, and manhandled himself up to a position not much better than the one I had achieved.

The Earthquake gave out his goofy giggle.

"All present and accounted for, sir," the Chief said.

"Yes, and in top condition, too," Commander Stanford said. "This place smells like Yokosuka on a Saturday night. Sit down. Hell, sit down before you all fall down."

"Yes, sir, Commander," said the Chief, motioning us down like a choir director after the last note of an oratorio. "I was just explaining to the boys…"

"Shut up, Chief. Who brought in the whiskey?"

"What whiskey would that be, sir?" the Chief asked.

Commander Stanford dipped an index finger into the puddle on the desk, raised it to his lips, and said, "This whiskey, Chief Crouch."

"Oh, that," said the Chief. "That's just a little bottle we keep around for medicinal purposes. Snake bites and stuff, you know. You never can tell when a snake might bite someone."

"I'll see you in my office right now, Chief," said the Commander. The rest of you, get this dump cleaned up. There is about to be weeping and gnashing of teeth." And he whirled on his heel and walked out into the rain.

"Keep them cards exactly where they are," the Chief said, pulling on his raincoat and fumbling for his whiskey spattered hat. "We'll go on with the game as soon as I get back."

After the Chief had left, we sat silently, looking down at the cards and the now empty whiskey bottle.

"When he gets back," I finally said. "What makes him think he's coming back. He'll be lucky if they don't have him keel hauled."

"Him," said Bowman. "What about us? We're done for. Insignia cut away. Rolling drums. Ten years and transportation to Madagascar."

"You guys are so stupid," Earthquake O'Toole said. "You've spent too much time in the books, but you ain't got no street smarts."

"Okay, mister street smarts," I said. "How do you suggest we get out of this one? Drinking on duty. Uniform Code of Military Justice, section so-and-so, paragraph so-and-so. We'll be busting rocks in Portsmouth by this time next week."

"For what?" the Earthquake demanded.

"I told you," I said. "Drinking on duty."

"*Mea culpa. Mea culpa. Mea maxima culpa.*" Bowman thumped himself on the chest.

"This ain't no joke, Bowman," said Hopewell.

"You think I think it's a joke?" Bowman said.

"Then why are you sitting there talking crazy?" Hopewell asked.

"All right, you poor idiot children," the Earthquake said. "I guess I have to spell it out to you. Who said any of us were drinking on duty? Did the Commander say we were?"

"Well, he saw us..." I began.

"What did he see?" the Earthquake wanted to know. "What's in your cups? Looks like coffee to me. Dump it down the sink. Jump in the pool clothes and all. Then get in the shower. Stick your fingers down your throats and puke your stomachs dry."

"But what if they try to make us walk a straight line?" Bowman said.

"Or draw a blood sample?" I said.

"They ain't gonna do that," said the Earthquake. "I'll tell you what the Commander saw. He saw the Chief, a known lush, with a bottle of whiskey that got knocked over. Sure the place smelled like a distillery. Why not, with whiskey spilled all over the desk. Not one of us touched a drop. Everybody got it."

"But what if the Chief rats us out?" Hopewell said.

"He won't," the Earthquake said. "If he does—why, it's his word against ours. Now, boys, we have to stick together on this one. None of us drank a thing. Got it."

"That means we have to saw the limb off behind the Chief," Bowman said.

"Yeah," the Earthquake said. "War is hell, ain't it. Well, his goose is cooked anyway. You wanna go down the tubes with him?"

"All right," I said. "I'm in. We go in there and lie like cheap watches."

"Anyway," said the Earthquake, "I'm in the clear."

"How do you figure that?" I asked.

"Don't you see, Mill? I was holding three rings of Guy-jeez. I was invisible."

Difficult as it may be to believe, Earthquake O'Toole called it perfectly. I mean as to his invisibility. For reasons that none of us understood—with the possible exception of the Earthquake—he wasn't even called in with us. Puked, washed, scared out of our wits, Bowman, Hopewell and I wound up standing at attention before the desk of Commander Stanford. But it wasn't just his own invisibility that he was right about. The Earthquake called the entire action to the letter. We all three denied touching a drop. The Commander was stunned. How could we stand there and tell him such an obvious lie.

"I know it looks bad, Commander," Bowman said. "But the truth is that we were drinking coffee. We know better than to drink on duty, sir. Sure we were playing cards, but the pool was closed, and we had to kill the time somehow."

"Is that your story too, Miller?"

"Yessir."

"Hopewell."

"Absolutely, Commander."

"You horses asses get out of here," said the Commander. "Get back to the pool. And keep this quiet. I sent the Chief over to sick bay."

Chapter 7

▼

Dionysian Frenzy

Well, the boys talked their way right out of the mess they were in. Good thing for them I was there. They were going to go over there and admit to the whole thing and throw themselves on the mercy of the court. Good grief! How stupid can you get. Anyway, all's well that ends well. I still intend to find out more about the Ring of Guy-jeez.

—The Diary of Earthquake O'Toole

"You know," I said to Bowman. "I'm getting the uncomfortable feeling that O'Toole, in his fumbling way, got closer to the truth of the Greek Summer than either of us ever did with all our myth-making."

"Not likely."

"Well, to us the whole Summer was spent in the rarified oxygen of philosophical speculation. To O'Toole, it was just a big party from dawn to dusk. Sure we read Plato and Jack London. But it seems I was always nursing a hangover."

"Yeah. Well, I don't give a damn about the hangovers. But I was just thinking about Chief Crouch and his permanent hangover. That business about him being a war hero bothers me to this day. I've never been able to shake the feeling that we got played for suckers right down the line. I'm not sure Stanford didn't lie to us about the whole thing."

"But why would he?"

"Some ulterior motive. Maybe he owed the Chief money. Maybe the Chief had something on him and was blackmailing him."

"Bowman," I said, "everything we were able to learn convinces me that Stanford told the plain, unadorned truth. But suppose he didn't. What difference does it make? Everyone gets hustled at one time or another, and it all turned out okay in the end."

"I guess it did," Bowman answered. "Stanford stroked out, the Chief got retired out and drank himself to death. We ran the Amazon off by being stupid...Brother, that really hurt. I was in love with her, Mill."

"Bowman, this is me, Miller. Remember? If you were in love with the Amazon I'm a three-legged police dog. We've been around too long to start deluding ourselves over that."

"Do you mean to sit there and tell me you doubt my love for Betty Ann Greybow?"

"Do you mean to sit there and tell me," I replied, "that you expect me to take you seriously?" I paused. "How did we get going on this line?"

"The Chief being a war hero. Some hero! Remember how he came back after the card game and called general quarters. You haven't forgotten that one have you?"

"Until senility sets in, I will never forget that one."

It was the day after the card game, and the sun rose in a blue, rain-washed sky. Ten o'clock, the front doors opened, the crowd rushed in, and Chief Crouch, drunk as a lord, got on the public address system.

"Now general quarters, general quarters, all hands man your battle stations. This is not a drill. Repeat. This is not a drill."

I was sitting on the mid-pool tower. Bowman was standing across the pool from me, but farther down toward the deep end. Hopewell was on the tower at the shallow end. The Earthquake was out front at the check-in counter, where the microphone for making public announcements was located. When the chief sounded general quarters,[1] the Amazon came out of the office with her hands on her hips, looked around the pool, across at me, and shrugged. Then the Chief came marching out the door from the entrance area, directly into the pool in about eight feet of water, and sank like a rock. His hat was left floating on the

---

1. In the Navy, general quarters is serious business. It means an attack is imminent. But I never heard general quarters sounded, even in a drill, while I was ashore. This is shipboard business.

surface. I dived into the pool immediately, as did Bowman, and the two of us wrestled him up from the bottom, and over to the side, where the Amazon grabbed him by both shoulders and dragged him out. He fought us, in a feeble fashion, cursed a great deal, and finally gave in when the Amazon sat on him and Bowman threatened to break his arm.

"This is the last damn straw," the Amazon said. "We've got to watch two-hundred screaming kids and one drunk CPO. I've had it. Either he goes or I go."

"Cool down, Amazon," I said. "He's okay."

"Figure it out, Miller," she said. "If something happens to one of these kids in here, who do you think is responsible?"

She waited for me to answer, then said, as I only stood shaking my head, "I'm going over to see Commander Stanford. Keep things running till I get back."

She was gone about an hour. When she came back, she had two corpsmen with her, and back the Chief went to sick bay again, this time in restraints. I had just climbed up on the tower at the shallow end of the pool, and I noticed Bowman, on the mid-pool tower, talking to the Amazon, leaning down to hear what she was saying, nodding. Then she walked down to me.

"The Commander's going to come over and talk to us after the pool closes tonight. Chief Crouch is on his way to Balboa to the psycho ward to dry out."

"Is he coming back?"

"I don't know. I feel like a regular Benedict Arnold. I really like the old lush, but I'm afraid someone is going to get hurt with him around here. Of all places to send him."

"Yeah," I said. "Looks like they'd find a nice desk job for him somewhere in Nome, Alaska."

That evening after the pool closed and we were cleaning up, Commander Stanford came in and got us all together in the office. He didn't seem to know how to proceed with whatever it was he was trying to proceed with. He began to speak. Stopped. Took off his hat and threw it on the desk, sat down and ran his hand through his thinning hair, started to speak again, got as far as, "Chief Crouch..." Then he stopped and seemed to have forgotten why he was there at all.

"Is the Chief all right, sir?" Bowman asked.

"They've got him on a locked ward at Balboa," said the Commander. "Feeding him reduced amounts of booze to keep him from going into d.t.'s. Well, I can do one of two things. I can transfer him...But, hell, no one wants him. I'd have to beg on my hands and knees to get him a job cleaning the head. Or, the other thing I can do is cover for him." He folded his arms across his chest, rather defiantly, I thought.

"I'm gonna cover for him, which means he's on sick leave. Officially he has a bad case of bronchitis. I need you to help me out," he said.

Commander Stanford was not what I would have called a humble man, though I always thought he was a fair one, in his own way. He was tall, and stiff, and very military, with blue eyes that looked right through you, and he had the sort of arrogant bearing that comes with authority. But just now he was neither arrogant nor authoritative, which is probably why he was finding it so difficult to talk to us. He looked from one of us to the other in a sort of hopeless way that was not at all characteristic of him. It was obvious that there was something he wasn't telling us, and that he didn't quite know how to tell us.

The Amazon lubricated the process like a skilled public relations executive (which she may have become, for all I know) by saying, "How can we help you, Commander?"

"Look," he said. "Chief Crouch is only a few months away from retirement. In September he goes out with twenty. I want to see him get there with a clean record and all his chief stripes on him. But at his present clip, he'll never make it."

He paused, swallowed, looked again from one of us to the other. There was still something he wasn't telling us.

"How can we help you, Commander?" the Amazon asked again.

"What can we do, sir?" Bowman asked. "We'll do it...If we can."

"Sure," I said.

The Commander took a deep breath. He was looking at me, or perhaps over my shoulder, out the door and off into eternity.

"I've known the Chief since he was about your age, Miller," he said. "In fact, you sort of remind me of what he was like when I first met him."

"Me?" I said, pointing to myself.

"Oh," he said, "I know he's a wreck now. But that's what booze and whores will do for you. Pardon my French, Miss Greybow."

"I'm not that delicate," said the Amazon.

"We were at the Coral Sea together," he said, as if he hadn't heard her. "Deck seamen in the black shoe Navy aboard the Yorktown." He had this faraway look. I don't know about the others, but I was getting uncomfortable with all this *de profundis* stuff. As Scott Fitzgerald once said, I wanted no riotous excursions with privileged glimpses into the human heart. I wanted the old, arrogant Commander to come back and drill us through with those cold, blue eyes. But the

Amazon was with him heart and soul, shaking her head and biting her lip, as if she were a sympathetic bartender at three o'clock in the morning. And on he went, raking up the past.

"It was a bloody mess. Not too many know this, but more sailors were killed at the Coral Sea than Marines were on Guadalcanal. We were right in the middle of it. Took a direct hit that blew off the forecastle. Jim Crouch had half his clothes torn off and was bleeding so badly from his nose and ears that I don't know how he stayed on his feet. But he did. He ran the length of the deck, dove over the fantail, swam through burning oil and pulled back one of our men who'd gone overboard. Then he went back and got another one. A Zero strafed us. He took a shot through his forearm, but he went back and got a third man out. Jim got the Navy Cross for that. I would have given him the Medal of Honor if it had been up to me."

"Chief Crouch has the Navy Cross?" mumbled a bewildered Hopewell.

We were all uncomfortable and squirming by this time, except for the Amazon, an obvious sucker for a hard luck story in spite of her feigned toughness. She took off her sunglasses. It was the first time I had seen her without them. Her eyes were dark and misty with tears.

"I told you I felt like Benedict Arnold," she said to me.

"Come on, Amazon," I said.

"You did the right thing, Miss Greybow," said the Commander. "No need to apologize. But..." He was struggling, and pretty soon he was crying along with the Amazon. "Oh, hell," he said, "I love that old drunk, and I intend to see him retired with honors. So I'll say it again. I need your help. We're going to cover for him until we can pipe him ashore. O'Toole, you're the ranking petty officer in this section now. You made grade six months before Bowman. You're in charge."

The Earthquake had been acting up to this time as if nothing that had been said had anything to do with him, or maybe that the entire conversation were being carried on in a language he didn't speak. But the statement, "You're in charge," registered with him all too clearly. He looked as if he had been hit with a large club.

"What about the Amazon?" he said. "The Chief said she was in charge."

"However you've been doing things, just keep on doing them that way. You never really needed the Chief. Have you been running things, Miss Greybow?"

"Yes, I have."

"Go on. But for my part, O'Toole, I'm holding you responsible."

Responsibility was the very thing Earthquake O'Toole spent his life trying to avoid.

"The Chief said the Amazon's in charge," he said again.

"Come with me," Commander Stanford told him. "We'll talk about it. I want you to understand exactly what I expect of you, O'Toole."

Just then, I wouldn't have been surprised if the Earthquake had run out the front doors and headed for Mexico: he had a bewildered, cornered look like a man ordered into combat with an unloaded weapon. But he went along with the Commander, shaking his head and muttering to himself.

"I'm not taking orders from that goofy Irishman," Bowman said after Commander Stanford and the Earthquake had left. "You hear me, Amazon?"

Hopewell threw back his head and laughed. "I think it's funny as hell," he said. "That's the Navy for you. How did we ever win the war? You've got a imbecile covering for a drunk. It's just like the Marines say: the unwilling led by the unqualified to do the unnecessary."

The Amazon said, "We won the war, you creep, because of people like Chief Crouch.

"The first thing O'Toole will do," I said, "is schedule himself to occupy the cot in there and leave us to watch the pool. Just wait and see if he doesn't."

"No he won't," the Amazon said. "I promise you that."

"So will I," Bowman said. "I'll drown his pear-shaped ass if he tries it."

Hopewell was still laughing. "It's funny as hell," he repeated.

The Amazon took Bowman aside, and Hopewell and I went into the locker room, stripped out of our swim trunks, and got into the shower.

"There's a man in the funny papers we all know," Hopewell began singing. "Alley oop, boop, boop, boop. .a boop, boop ."

"There's a guy named O'Toole who looks a lot like him," I sang.

Hopewell laughed.

"I hope this turns out to be as funny as you think it is," I said.

Bowman came in, stark naked, and grinning from ear to ear.

"Idiots," I said. "I'm surrounded by them. You're singing and you're grinning. Boy, if I ever get out of this chicken outfit, I'll never leave mother's home for the rest of my life."

Later, as Bowman and I stood on the front steps in gathering shadows, he said, "I couldn't talk in there with Hopewell listening, but you and I have been invited out for the evening."

"By the Amazon?"

"The Amazon. She's got the blues. Wants a little sophisticated male companionship."

"What are we gonna do?"

"What do you care? It's a night out."

"Two of us and one Amazon."

"Oh, that's the good news. She's got a younger sister."

"Oh, no you don't, Bowman," I said. "No you don't, old buddy. No blind dates. The last one I was on, this guy tells me he's got me lined up with a girl. 'She ain't bad,' he says when I ask him what she looks like. Man, I never saw such a woman in my life. She looked like her face caught fire and someone put it out with a pick ax."

"Look, if you don't like her, I'll take her and you take the Amazon."

"The Amazon won't go for that. I think she's got the hots for you, Bowman. I'm just a pimple-faced kid. Besides, I can't get in any place where they serve anything stronger than iced tea."

"Come on, Mill…"

"All right. But if she's a dog, you and I are through."

She was gorgeous, a smaller version of the Amazon, and it turned out she had been just as reluctant to go on a blind date as I was.

"I almost didn't come," she told me. "Betty Ann said you are real cute."

"Well, I am, ain't I."

She smiled. "Not too shabby," she said.

"I'm a philosopher too," I said. "And poet and a lover."

"She told me that too. Well, the philosopher part."

The women had picked us up at the front gate. The Amazon let Bowman drive, and I was in the back seat with little sister, Mary Alice Greybow, or Maggie as she came to be known.

"Where are we going?" I asked.

"Oh," she said, "just, you know, around." She drew a circle in the air with her index finger.

Maggie and the Amazon both had on shorts, sandals, and blouses that displayed their physical endowments to a very good advantage.

"What in the world went on at the pool today?" Maggie asked. "Betty Ann came home in tears."

"I heard that," the Amazon said from the front seat.

"Well, it's true," Maggie said.

"The Amazon…"

"What a terrible name," Maggie said. "She told me about that too. Why do you call her that?"

"It's a term of respect," Bowman said. "By the way, where are we going?"

"Just around," said the Amazon.

"Drive to the beach," I said. "Torrey Pines. Shall I comb my hair behind? Do I dare to eat a peach? I shall wear white flannel trousers and walk upon the beach."

"Ezra Pound," Maggie said.

"T.S. Eliot," said the Amazon.

"Don't ask me," said Bowman. "But it ain't Shakespeare, that's for sure."

"It's Eliot," I said.

"Okay," Bowman said. "Here we go to the beach."

"They that go down to the sea in ships," I said, "that do business in great waters, these see the works of the Lord and his wonders in the deep."

"Eliot," said Bowman.

"Bible," I said. "Psalms."

I kept throwing out poetry because that's what I have always done when I get into a situation I don't know how to handle, and the present situation was one I certainly didn't know how to handle. Everyone has heard the old saw about a sailor having a girl in every port, but in my experience, the only sorts of girls that sailors have in every port, in fact the only ones that consistently hang around sailors, are those who will take up with anybody if the price is right. Maggie was not that type, and neither was her older sister, and while Bowman may have been in his element, I was not. If I held Maggie's hand, she might box my ears. So I did nothing. We drove in silence for several miles, both of us looking straight ahead, while in the front seat Bowman and the Amazon kept up a lively banter. Actually, it was more like a psychiatric session, with Bowman acting the part of the therapist and the Amazon leaning back on the front seat, and telling out her grief to the naked stars.

"I feel awful about what happened to Chief Crouch," she said. "I think maybe I should have just let the whole thing go."

"He's got to get off the sauce," Bowman said. "He's his own worst enemy."

"And Richard Cory, one calm summer night..." I began.

"I know that one," said Maggie.

We got to the beach. It was dark and windy, and the surf was breaking in long, phosphorescent ribbons. Orion stood over us to the south and the Great Bear was high up in the north. We parked the car, locked it, and made our way down the cliffs to the long stretch of sand. We could see winking lights off in the distance, the lights of cities, and directly ahead, far out at sea, a red running light.

I pointed it out to Maggie. "She's bound south," I said.

"How do you know?"

"The red light. Port side."

"We're walking up there," Bowman said. The Amazon had her arm hooked through his and was leaning against him.

I was stuck for an answer, though no answer was required. The unspoken message was that he didn't care what Maggie and I did, just so long as we left him and the Amazon alone.

"Come on, Miller," Maggie said. "Let's go down there and look for shells."

"Okay," I said.

She hooked her arm in mine, then, without so much as a word, she put her free hand behind my head, drew me down to her, and kissed me in a way to suggest that she knew what she was doing. Her lips were soft and wet, and she smelled of fragrant flowers, or perhaps of a dewy meadow on a cool spring morning. To tell the truth, I was never able to decide what Maggie smelled like, but it was good, whatever it was. I wrote several poems about her, but none has survived, which is probably just as well, for very little of a young man's poetry is worth reading the day after it is written.

The evening promised great things, but it remained only a promise, just a lot of kissing and heavy breathing. Still, it was better than sitting in the barracks and watching TV or reading. Maggie, at least two jumps ahead of me at all times, and probably figuring we would wind up on the beach, had brought some book matches. I built a fire. Building fires on the beach became one of my specialties that summer.

"It's sort of cold," she said.

"That's what I'm here for," I said.

"Oh, to warm me up."

"Unless you have a better plan."

"No," she said. "Go ahead. Within reason, if you know what I mean."

"I think I get the drift," I said.

Between kisses and clutches we started finding out about each other. I learned that she was a freshman at San Diego J.C., the same school at which Bowman had taken the night philosophy course. When I asked why she wasn't in the school with the Amazon, up in Washington, she said that she didn't want to go up there. It was too rainy to suit her. She was thinking about USC or maybe Berkeley.

"What about you?" she asked.

"I don't know," I said. "I really don't."

"Betty Ann says you're really smart. At least she says that's what your buddy Bowman says."

"Maybe I am. I don't know. I almost flunked out of college. That doesn't sound too smart to me."

"So what do you want to do?" she asked.

"I don't know about that either. I guess I don't know much about anything. I feel sort of like Holden Caulfield."

"*The Catcher in the Rye*," she said. "Didn't you love that book?"

"It made me uncomfortable," I said. "I read it while I was working real hard at flunking out of school. The night I decided to leave college, I swear, I felt just like Holden Caulfield."

We had separated and were sitting on opposite sides of the fire. She was hugging herself, staring into the flames, and I was watching her.

"Do you guys get together and discuss philosophy?" she asked.

"We keep saying we're going to," I said. "But we haven't actually done it yet. Mostly Bowman and I read stuff, then we talk about it at the pool when we're on breaks. I think we're supposed to meet at the park across from the pool. Maybe tomorrow night."

"What do you talk about?"

"Well. We've been talking some about Plato's *Republic*. And we talk about Jack London."

"About Buck the sled dog?"

"There was more to London than that."

"I've never actually read him. But I saw the Clark Gable movie."

"If I asked you to do me a favor, would you do it?" I looked at her. She looked back.

"I guess it would depend on what the favor was."

"It's nothing crazy. Would you get London's book *Martin Eden* and read it?"

"*Martin Eden*?"

"Would you? And then tell me what you think of it. Maybe your sister would read it too."

"Why do you want us to read it?" she asked.

"Well, you want to know what we discuss. That's what we've been talking about for days now. I'd just like to know what you think of it."

"Okay."

"Are you gonna be home tomorrow?"

"Probably."

"Would it be all right if I call you?"

"Sure. I think I'd like that."

We sat silently for awhile.

"Come on," I said. "Let's go look for shells."

"Okay"

She jumped up and brushed the sand off her pants, and we started off together, hand in hand, in the opposite direction of the one Bowman and the Amazon had taken. I had no idea what they were doing, but whatever it was, I didn't want to surprise them.

"The Symposium," she whispered in my ear.

"What's that?"

"That's what Betty Ann calls your get togethers."

"Our non-existent get togethers, you mean. The Symposium, huh?"

"Yes. I think it's just neat. I don't know anyone who does something like that. It's sort of like going to church, but there's no church. It's sort of like being back in Athens or somewhere, with togas and sandals and wineskins."

"*The Symposium* was one of Plato's dialogues. I started to read it once, but I got sick of it. It's all about homosexual love."

"And you and Bowman aren't homosexuals, are you?"

"Are you kidding?"

"Well," she said, "I don't know why she called it the Symposium. But she seemed to know what she was talking about. And I still think it's neat that you're getting together."

"I guess it is," I said. "Maybe we'd better start doing it and quit talking about it."

"Can I come?"

"Sure," I said. "I guess so. If we ever start doing it."

"Miller," I heard Bowman calling from behind us. "Where the hell are you?"

"Down here," I called back.

"Let's go. The Amazon says she has to get home."

"Okay."

Back in the car, things got very quiet, as Maggie and I dived back into the joys of exploring our new, erotic relationship and Bowman drove with one hand and did with the other whatever he was able.

"She's a tease," he said when we were walking back to the barracks after the girls had let us out. "I might have known it. What about Maggie?"

"She's all right," I said. "I like her."

"All the Amazon wanted to do was talk about poor old Chief Crouch. I guess I helped her work through some goofy problem she's having with guilt."

"Well," I said, "wasn't that why she wanted to go out?"

"Yeah, but I was expecting more positive developments once I got her alone and turned on the old Bowman charm."

We walked along, our heels clicking on the pavement, out of darkness into an island of orange light created by a street lamp, then into darkness and toward another island. The barracks we passed looked sterile, blank, like temporary dwellings for temporary dwellers—which is, of course, what they were. I hated them. Barracks life was as good a reason as any I ever knew not to reenlist in the military; barracks life, and the food, and the absence of women, and the stupid orders you had to obey just because some guy with stripes on his sleeve told you to do them. I guess there were lots of reasons. I told Bowman all this, but he wasn't listening. He was somewhere else, mentally.

"You know, Miller, there's something strange about this business with Chief Crouch."

We had come to our barracks and were about to go inside, but Bowman stopped, sat down on the grass, lay back and looked up at the stars. I sat down beside him.

"What's a Symposium?" I asked.

"One of Plato's dialogues," he said.

"Have you ever read it?"

"No."

"I think the Amazon thinks we're fags," I said.

"What the hell gives you that idea?" he said. "Why I'll slap the shit outta her. To tell you the truth, I'm not sure she's not."

"I'm sure Maggie ain't."

"Ah, you're talking crazy."

"Yeah. Well, what's so strange about the business with Chief Crouch. If you ask me, anything to do with Chief Crouch is a little bit strange."

"Maybe the Earthquake can give us some insight," Bowman said. "He must come from a long line of drunks. But that's not what I mean when I say there's something strange about it. It's what Commander Stanford said today at the pool, about the Chief getting the Navy Cross and all."

"I guess lots of war heroes take to the bottle. I've heard that anyway."

"But remember how the Commander said that he and Crouch were in the black shoe Navy at the Coral Sea. He said they were aboard the Yorktown, and that it took a direct hit and had its bow blown off."

"Yeah."

"The Yorktown wasn't sunk at the Coral Sea. My uncle was aboard the Yorktown. She went down at Midway."

"Well…surely Commander Stanford wouldn't lie to us. Would he?"

"An officer and a gentleman," said Bowman.

"Brother," I said. "I don't get it."

"I hate being used," Bowman said. "I wonder how we could find out about Chief Crouch. Did you ever notice any scars on his arms?"

"You mean from a Jap machine gun? I don't guess so. But then I haven't been looking."

Bowman and I were getting madder the more we talked.

"The Amazon kept talking tonight about the Chief's heroic deeds at the Coral Sea aboard the Yorktown," he said. "And something about it just didn't sound right. Then I remembered my Uncle Dan. I was only about four years old, but I remember the telegram to this day. Midway."

"Hell," I said. "The Amazon wouldn't know about that. Not unless she's some sort of history buff."

"Well Commander Stanford sure as hell would. Look, don't say anything to the Amazon about this. She's a direct line to the Commander."

"Okay. But what are you gonna do?"

"I'm gonna find out the truth. I don't like being used."

"You said that already."

"I've got a yeoman buddy. I think I'll ask him to look at the Chief's personnel file."

"I think that's illegal," I said.

"I didn't say I'm gonna run an ad in the paper about it. I'm just gonna ask him to check it out."

"Bruce Bowman," I said. "The Sam Spade of the aquatics world. I was paddling around my pool and in she walked. She was beautiful, gorgeous, luscious."

"I don't like being used," Bowman said.

Chapter 8

The Symposium

I don't like the way things have come out. None of the guys have any use for me now that I'm in charge. But I'm not really in charge. The Amazon keeps running things. I hate that bitch. Mill is on me about reading Martin Eden. *I don't like to read. I'm not sure I like Mill. He and Bowman are going to get together and discuss philosophy, or something like that. These guys are amazing. The real world has yet to greet them.*

—The Diary of Earthquake O'Toole

I made an interesting discovery after Bowman and I spent the evening at the Cove pawing through Earthquake's diary and trying to understand the man's final actions. For years, every time Bowman and I got together, we relived the Greek Summer. It became, for us, an epic adventure, the ultimate life-changing event, the baptism by total immersion into the golden fire of philosophical speculation, the transporting event that carried us up on eagle's wings to the hallowed halls of the gods. And so on, and so forth. What I discovered was that the Greek Summer was a disorganized and disjointed series of events that make little sense, and that the thread of philosophical inquiry that Bowman and I wove through these events was our own attempt to convince ourselves that they had some larger, underlying meaning.

I don't mean to suggest that the Greek Summer wasn't life-changing for both of us. But it was nothing organized. Nothing planned. We couldn't go back and do it over if we wanted to.

It just happened.

Take the Symposium as an example. When the Amazon referred to our get-togethers using this word, we thought she was suggesting we were homosexuals in love with one another. Actually, she knew more than we did. I looked the word up, found out it came from two Greek words *sym* and *pinein*, and that it meant to drink together and to exchange ideas. I shared this with Bowman, and we both felt better immediately. The word described our sessions perfectly. But for all that, and for all the glamour we tried to cloth ourselves in after the fact, the Symposium was really nothing more than a bull session that started off with a collection of semi-conscious minds and usually wound up with a group of drunk ones.

We actually had to be prodded into meeting at all. So far, all we had done was talk about it; but after the evening on the beach with the Amazon and Maggie, and because I really wanted to live up to her stated opinion of me as some sort of genius, I got the thing off dead center by inviting Bowman to a philosophical discussion in the park across from the pool. I still think it was on a Wednesday, and that Bowman has got the day confused because of his more basic confusion about the television schedule.

I called Maggie that afternoon from the pool when I was on break. She seemed genuinely glad to hear from me, which was a relief, because her older sister seemed distant all that day. I was still wondering what had gone on between her and Bowman, but beyond his saying that she was a tease, and his insistence that she was somehow conniving with Commander Stanford to use us, I couldn't get much out of him.

"I had a great time last night," Maggie said.

"So did I," I said. "I dreamed about you."

"You did not."

"Yes. I did."

This was an absolute lie, but it really rang her bell.

"And what did you dream?"

"That's a secret," I said.

"Oh, well. I can imagine."

"Listen. We're going to get together after the pool closes. The Symposium, you know. You said you wanted to come."

"I do. I really do. But I can't tonight. Other plans. Besides, I can't get on the base—can I?"

"I guess not. We'll hold the next one down on the beach."

"Great."

"Write me down on your appointment book."

"Okay. And if you dream about me tonight, make it a sweet dream."

She kissed the receiver and sent waves of passion rushing around my loins like charges of electricity. I had to get up and walk around the pool to keep the top of my skull from blowing off. The Amazon approached me down by the high diving board.

"You look like you discovered mama's cookie jar," she said.

"I was just talking to your sister," I said.

"Oh," she said, and smirked slightly. "Yeah, she likes you too. But I never saw a boy she didn't like."

"Boy, Amazon," I said. "You really know how to bust a guy's balloon."

She threw back her head and laughed. "Don't worry about it," she said. "She's good for the summer anyway. After that—who knows?"

"Who knows?" I repeated.

She walked over to the board and called to a kid who was bouncing up and down on it, "Hey, buddy, that's a diving board, not a trampoline. Either dive or get off it." She stuck one foot into the pool, took it out, and walked back to me. "I talked to Commander Stanford awhile ago," she said. "The Chief's coming back next Monday. All dried out and ready for duty."

"I'll bet," I said. "You're gonna make someone a nice nanny. I'll write you a letter of recommendation. After the Chief and Earthquake O'Toole, a house full of brawling kids will be like a Sunday school picnic."

She shook her head. "Yeah," she said, and she looked at me as if to say that I wasn't much better.

"You want to go down to the beach again?" I said.

Her face was expressionless. I wished she hadn't had dark glasses on, for her eyes would have been very revealing.

Brook Benton was singing on the radio, "That's how I will love you, oh darling, endlessly."

What in hell and damnation, I wondered, had she and Bowman been up to?

"The Symposium will meet after the pool closes," I said. "Ultimate truth and beauty will be revealed. The secrets of the universe will yield to the sharp logic of…"

She had already turned back to the diving board. "I mean it, buddy. Get off that board now!"

"Oh, my love, you are my heaven," Brook Benton sang. "You are my kingdom. You are my crown…"

I walked the length of the pool to where Bowman sat on the shallow end's tower.

"What's with the Amazon?" I asked. "I mentioned last night and it was like I was blasted with an arctic wind."

"She's in love with me, son," he said.

"That's love?"

"Yeah, and you know what Elmer Gantry said. 'Love is the morning and the evening star. Love is the inspiration of poets and philosophers.'"

"Love is an arctic blast from the Amazon," I said.

"I can warm her up with a wave of my hand, this very hand."

"She says Chief Crouch is coming back next week."

"Yeah," he said. "Well, I talked to my yeoman buddy this morning at breakfast. Mum's the word. He's gonna see what he can find out."

"Oh, boy," I said. "I intend to plead ignorance on this one if we're ever caught."

"Caught at what? Plausible deniability, or something like that. I heard someone say it once. Plausible deniability. I don't know nothing. I ain't seen nothing."

"You just don't want to be used."

"That, by damn, is correct. The Yorktown, my ass."

"In the meantime, Sam Spade, what are we gonna talk about tonight at the Symposium?"

"We'll think of something."

And, of course, we did, but it would be ridiculous of me to pretend, forty years after the fact, that I remember what it was. There was not, as I have already suggested, a set meeting place. Sometimes it was the park. Sometimes a local bar that I could get served at because they never checked IDs until, as I later learned, the cops caught them serving minors, fined them, and threatened the owners with jail. Sometimes we congregated on one of the beaches with the girls. And many times we met at the pool on our days off and laid around on the grass on the west side of the enclosed area. It was sort of—if I can get away with ripping off Hemingway—a moveable feast in which we nibbled on whatever dainties were placed before us. The only three people who showed up without fail were Bowman, Earthquake O'Toole, and me. Hopewell hung around sometimes, if we met at the pool, never said much, seemed bored to distraction. The Amazon and

Maggie showed up once. Bowman never understood, and I never understood, why the Earthquake came. And, of course, the mystery only deepened when he died and left us his diary and the letter telling us how we were the only friends he'd ever had.

As to what we discussed…Well, I was getting to that. I can only give a general idea of what these sessions were like, at least as I remember them. They went something like this.

Miller: I was looking at this Cave business last night, *Republic*, Book VII. Hell, I can't figure out what he's talking about. It's supposed to be about enlightenment, but it sure didn't enlighten me any. Did you talk about this in college, Bowman?

Bowman: Yeah. We got into it. This is a very famous passage. The professor said it's one of the most famous pieces of writing in world literature.

Earthquake: (Belches and scratches himself).

Miller: There's this cave, and all these characters are chained to chairs looking at a wall. And there's this shadow play going on. And they think this is how the real world is.

Bowman: But reality is the figures behind the shadows. Plato was after the truth instead of just shadows of the truth?

Miller: So what is the truth.

Earthquake: (Picks his nose). The truth is that I don't like the friggin' Navy. Every time I think life is rolling along the way it ought to, someone with stripes on his sleeves or gold on his collar throws a monkey wrench into the works.

Miller: The truth is that if there is no such thing as the truth, then we can't really know anything, and the whole business grinds to a halt. Hey, maybe the Earthquake's onto something. Maybe God threw a monkey into the works.

Bowman: But Plato thought there was truth. But he thought you have to get behind the curtain of mere appearance to get at it. It's all about the forms and ideals, all that kind of stuff.

Miller: But what's that mean?

Earthquake: I was gonna ask that myself, but I didn't want to seem as stupid as you just did, Mill.

Bowman: This is going nowhere fast.

Miller: Okay. What is truth? If I believe I can fly, is that the truth.

Hopewell: Not if you're in a plane O'Toole just worked on.

Earthquake: Kiss my ass.

Miller: No. Listen. Everyone out here has his own version of the truth. We've got Muslims, Christians, Hindus. And they all have a different version of the truth. Now which one of them is right?

Bowman: Yeah, but Plato would say this is just the problem. Everyone is just looking at shadows. There is a real, honest-to-God truth behind it all. We just have to find it.

Earthquake: I knew a guy once who believed when you died, if you went to hell, you'd have to do the worst thing you could think of for all eternity. He said if you hate cleaning out chicken houses, then you'd find yourself in a giant chicken house full of chicken shit, and no matter how much you worked, it would never get clean.

Hopewell: Just think, O'Toole. If you go to hell, you'll be enlisted in the United States Navy for eternity, cleaning out heads...

Earthquake: All right! All right! I'm trying to make a serious point here.

Miller: Then heaven would be whatever you like most, forever and ever. Man, I see myself as a lifeguard in a swimming pool, with women that look like Maggie running around in bikinis and rubbing suntan lotion on me.

Bowman: Heaven is a woman with gigantic jugs.

Miller: Yes. Amen. Preach it, brother.

Earthquake: And you guys call yourselves philosophers. Hell, you've set the whole field back a thousand years.

Hopewell: What's your heaven, O'Toole? A pound of pork ribs and a bottle of beer?

Earthquake: (giggles and belches again). It sure ain't the Amazon. If I died and went to hell, I'd wake up in a hospital ward with an army of nurses looking like her. And they'd all have big hypodermic needles. And they'd say, "Bend over and grab your ankles."

Miller: Is this metaphysics, or what?

Bowman: I wonder if Plato ever belched and scratched himself.

As the most tolerant of observers can easily discern, our discussions didn't always achieve a very lofty level. But some were better than others. We didn't do well on Plato because we didn't have anyone to guide us, and aside from Bowman, with his one semester of philosophy, and myself, with my one semester, which I slept through, we had no philosophical foundation to build on. But anemic as it all sounds, and difficult as it may be to believe, I, for one, was fascinated by the world of ideas.

We were saved from utter confusion and aimlessness when Bowman came up with Will Durant's *Story of Philosophy*, which he picked up in Mr. Stuart's used bookstore one fine day. In fact, we mentioned to Mr. Stuart that we were trying to understand philosophy, but that we just couldn't seem to get to first base with it.

"Oh, it's tough," he said, smiling. "Let me see if I can get something to help you."

He went straight to it, tucked away, as it was, on a lower shelf of his philosophy section, where it had been gathering dust for, according to him, five years.

He blew the dust off it.

"I picked this up in an estate sale five years ago," he said. "Bought the entire library of one of the city's matrons. I still have most of it. You can have it for a quarter."

Bowman bought it.

"Do you have another one?" I asked.

"No. That's my only one."

"You are an amazing man," I said. "Do you actually know what you have in here, and where everything is?"

"This," he said, spreading out his arms, "is my life. Don't you know about your own life?"

"I'm not so sure," said Bowman. "That's why we're into philosophy. It's supposed to clear up the cobwebs. So far, it's only added a few."

"He published this back in the twenties," Mr. Stuart said as he took Bowman's quarter and handed him the book. "It made a rich and famous man of him. It may not make either of you famous, but I predict it will make both of you rich—if you get my drift."

It was a paperback, Pocket Library edition, somewhat worn, very dusty, but in otherwise good condition. Bowman took it and entered into a self-imposed state of mental solitary confinement from which he emerged now and then like a man looking at the world for the first time. He was like I had been with *Martin Eden*, except he didn't talk about what he was reading. He just read, and read, and went about his daily activities as if he were somewhere else—which I suppose he was.

About a week later, he handed me the book. "Boy, Mill," he said, "this is the greatest thing that ever happened to me. I actually understand something about Western philosophy. We've been complete fools. Fools, son."

I couldn't resist saying, "Well, while you've been buried in that book, Commander Stanford and the Amazon have been getting away with using us. Did you forget your mission? Chief Crouch is back, quiet as a mouse."

"Let 'em alone," he said. "Let 'em do what they wanna do. We've got bigger fish to fry."

So I dived into *The Story of Philosophy*, and in short order I was walking around like a man in a trance. I have always been a fast reader. It took me three days to read through this book, then I went back for seconds. I would wake up in the morning thinking about the Platonic forms, wander down to the chow hall for breakfast with Aristotelian logic knocking around my brain, climb up on the lifeguard tower and sit there struggling with Nietzsche's nihlism and his God-is-dead ethics. I would be walking along, I'd hear my name called, and I'd become aware that I had been engaged for some time in a conversation with one of the boys and that I had no ideaa what had been said.

Maggie called me one evening at about eight o'clock. I was in the upstairs reading room working my way through Durant's chapter on Schopenhauer when the master-at-arms came in and said I had a phone call.

"Unless it's my mother or God, I ain't here," I said.

"It's a girl named Maggie," he said.

I looked up. "All right," I said, and closed the book.

"Thought that might stir you to action," he said, with a knowing leer.

"Where have you been?" she said, when I got to the phone. "I thought you were going to call me. Are you all right?"

"I'm fine, Maggie. I've been reading this book."

"You have got to be kidding me. Dead silence on your end, and you've been reading a book? Can't you put it down once in a while?"

"Sure. How are you?"

"Are you sure you're all right. Because you sound sick or something."

"No. I'm just coming back from a long way off. I was in Nineteenth Century Europe with the German Idealists."

"You're off tomorrow," she said. "Betty Ann told me. If you and Bowman can tear yourself away from the German Idealists, we'd like to invite you for a day at La Jolla."

"Well, sure," I said. "I think we can work that in. What time?"

"We'll be down there around one o'clock. Bring beer. We'll bring food. Bring bathing suits. And bring the German Idealists with you. You promised I could go to the Symposium."

"Maggie," I said, "I'm glad you called. I've been up in the rarefied oxygen with the philosophers long enough. I'm coming down to earth, girl, raring for action."

"Don't get too rambunctious, mister."

After I hung up, I looked for Bowman. I found him in Earthquake's cubicle, involved in an argument with our erstwhile leader (dethroned, much to his satisfaction, upon the return of Chief Crouch) over *Martin Eden*. I couldn't believe it.

By all appearances, O'Toole had actually been reading the book. The disagreement centered in on whether or not the sailor, Martin Eden, was a believable character.

"No one can come out of a ship's forecastle that ignorant," the Earthquake said, "and be discussing poetry and philosophy with college educated people in a matter of months."

"The book is autobiographical, Earthquake," Bowman said. "London is writing about himself. He is Martin Eden, and he did just what Martin Eden did.'

"You actually believe that?"

"Why not? There are a few people out there with functioning brains, you know."

"Fellows," I said, "let me break in on this delightful exchange. We're invited to the beach tomorrow, Bowman."

"I know," he said. "The Amazon told me. O'Toole's coming along. They got some girl who's willing to be seen in public with him."

I said nothing, only looked at the Earthquake and tried to figure out what his girl would look like. Wouldn't it be something, I reflected, if she turned out to be some kind of knockout, and Bowman and I were left drooling with suppressed desire.

"Nah," I said out loud.

"Nah, what?" the Earthquake asked.

"Nothing. Just thinking about something."

The Earthquake lay on his bunk, folded his hands over his belly, and looked up at the ceiling. He had obviously lapsed into deep thought, and given the argument he and Bowman had been having when I entered the cubicle, I thought perhaps he was about to come out with an observation of great value.

"Whatsamatter, Earthquake?" Bowman finally said.

"I was just wondering," he said. "I hope those girls bring something to eat other than hot dogs and potato chips."

"We're not going to a banquet," I said.

"Yeah," he said. "But I get tired of hot dogs and potato chips. I'd like some steak. Some baked potatoes. Maybe even some good potato salad. I haven't had decent potato salad since I joined the Navy. Boy! And how about some homemade ice cream. I could sure go for that. And chocolate chip cookies! And pie! Apple pie! I love good, hot apple pie, with a slab of cheddar cheese on it."

"Girls, Earthquake," Bowman said. "There'll be girls there. They can bring jellybeans and root beer for all I care. How about if you take the Amazon, Mill, and I take Maggie?"

"Not on your life. The Amazon has yet to acknowledge she lives on the same planet with me. That's your girl, Bowman. She's in love with you. You said so yourself."

"Yeah, but irresistible as I am, Maggie probably is, too."

"Now that Chief Crouch is back The Amazon seems downright civil," the Earthquake said. "For awhile there, every time I said good morning, she was stuck for an answer."

"Speaking of Chief Crouch," I said, "how's your detective work coming along, Bowman?"

"Thanks, Miller," Bowman responded. "You were supposed to keep a lid on it." He pointed to the Earthquake, still stretched out on the bed and gazing up at the ceiling.

"What?" said Earthquake.

"He's still thinking of apple pie with cheese," I said. "He didn't even hear what I said."

"Detective work," Earthquake said. "You think I'm stupid. I know what you're doing anyway. Prebble told me."

Prebble was Bowman's yeoman buddy.

"Plausible deniability," I said. "I ain't seen nothing. I heard nothing."

"This is just great," Bowman said. "I told him not to tell anybody. I made him swear he'd keep it quiet. So who does he tell? The Walter Winchell of the First Fleet—P.G. Earthquake O'Toole."

"I'll keep your secret better than Prebble ever did," said the Earthquake. "And anyway, you're on a wild goose chase. The Yorktown was, in fact, at the Coral Sea."

"The Yorktown was sunk at Midway, old buddy."

"That's right, Bowman," the Earthquake said. "But it was at the Coral Sea. It was damaged there. Dive bombed. Then it was repaired and put back into action in time to get sunk at Midway."

"You are full of…"

"Wanna bet?" Earthquake said, sitting up and swinging his feet around to the floor. He thrust out his right hand. "Come on. I'll bet you ten right now."

"How do you know so much?" Bowman asked.

"Because I had an uncle on the Yorktown," Earthquake said.

"Well, it's a small world," I said. "Bowman's uncle was on the Yorktown."

"This is just too damn scary," Bowman said.

"It's all kind of cosmic," I said.

"Your uncle and my uncle were aboard ship together."

"And Chief Crouch," I said. "Don't forget Chief Crouch."

"Tell me something, O'Toole," Bowman said. "Is your uncle still alive?"

"Hell no, dummy. He went down with the ship."

"So did mine. So how the hell come Chief Crouch survived?"

"He was wounded at the Coral Sea," I said. "He was probably in a hospital in Pearl when the Japs hit Midway."

Bowman had a stunned, rather hurt expression, and he suddenly turned and left, thinking, no doubt, that fate had played some great joke on him. In fact, he told me later that he was paying off a debt for bad karma, that in a previous existence he had probably burned down a church, or raped a nun, and now it was his fate to be tied eternally to the O'Toole family.

I knew better.

After Bowman stomped out of the cubicle, O'Toole started to laugh. "Bullshit, Mill. Pure, undiluted bullshit," he said. "None of my uncles were even in the Navy. But did you get a look at Bowman's face? Wow, I wouldn't trade that look for all the apple pie in the Amazon's refrigerator."

"Then how did you know Bowman's uncle was?"

"He mentioned it to Prebble. Boy, did you see his face? Are you gonna tell him? Hell, don't tell him. Let him lay awake all night worrying about it."

I chuckled. "You son-of-a-bitch," I said.

"Hell," he said, "Prebble didn't tell me much of anything else, except that we have a genuine war hero working with us, and to tell Bowman that the Yorktown was definitely at the Coral Sea. I put the rest together."

O'Toole was no philosopher, but he did demonstrate, at least on this occasion, a street-level logic that Sherlock Holmes could have envied. And, no, I didn't tell Bowman for about a week. It was too much fun to watch him stewing about it. At one point he told me he was going to have to check his facts out, that he believed his uncle may have been on the Enterprise, or maybe the Lexington. In fact, maybe it wasn't even a carrier. It might have been the North Carolina or the Indianapolis. When I finally told him the truth, he didn't take it kindly; but he got over it.

Chapter 9

Living the Good Life

"I thank God that I was born Greek and not barbarian, freeman and not slave, man and not woman; but above all, that I was born in the age of Socrates."

—Plato.

What this country needs is more white meat on the chicken.
—The Diary of Earthquake O'Toole

I read the first of the statements quoted above as we lay on the beach with the girls on a golden afternoon in the summer of 1960, the long gone Greek Summer, when we were young and beautiful. Well, when we were all young, and some of us were beautiful.

Bowman read the second statement from Earthquake's diary on a waning evening in our autumn years, as we sat on the rocks above La Jolla Cove drinking beer and trying to find some ultimate meaning to our lives, and to the life of our erstwhile departed associate. Humans seem to have a need to do that, and thus there will probably always be philosophers, poets, prophets, religious hucksters, divine interventionists.

"This chicken business is something I remember," Bowman said. "It was when we went to the beach with the Amazon and her sister, and we brought O'Toole with us."

"Yeah. And that goofy looking girl came along."

"Goofy or not, she was a jewel compared to O'Toole."

"She sort of reminds me of that girl who played Robin Williams' girlfriend in *The Fisher King*. But she sure didn't go for the Earthquake. I didn't expect her to. What was her name?"

"Act like you've got good sense, Miller. After forty years, you think I can remember a girl I saw one time. Wait! Wait a minute. Here it is. O'Toole actually put it down. Wilma Strupp."

"Wilma Strupp," I said.

"And listen to this. 'Miller and Bowman have done it to me again. They fixed me up with a regular iceberg. There's something wrong with the girl. I think she must have been raped when she was a kid. Touch her and she jumps away like she's been burnt.'"

"You know," I said, "I actually remember him saying that as we were driving home that night. We were comparing notes, how did you make out and all that. Then the Earthquake throws his rape theory at us, to cover for the fact that old Wilma wouldn't let him near her."

"The main thing I remember is the Amazon getting pissed off at that Plato passage."

"Boy, did she ever." I laughed. "And that was in the days before the Swarthmore crowd started burning their bras."

"Yeah, the Amazon was a pre-Friedan bra-burner all right. How did that go? I thank God that I was not born a woman?"

"That I was born Greek and not barbarian, freeman and not slave, man and not woman."

"And do you remember what the Amazon said?"

In fact, I remember it all too well.

"Oh, barf," she said. "Plato was as queer as a three dollar bill. He probably wished he had been born a woman so that he could spread his legs for Crito."

"I don't think he swung from that side of the plate," I said. "I think these guys were pedaphiles."

"Well Achilles and Patroclus sure weren't pedaphiles," the Amazon said. "They were swinging from whichever side of the plate they wanted to. Lucky for us the Trojans did them in."

"Frankly, I don't care one way or the other," I said.

Wilma, a quiet, mousy girl who looked like she'd styled her hair with an egg-beater, said, "I hope that I haven't fallen in with a group of sodomites."

"I'm a chicken and potato salad man myself," said the Earthquake.

Bowman was lying with his head in the Amazon's lap. He turned slightly toward the Earthquake and said, "But after all, a little baked Sodom never hurt anyone did it?"

"I think that's a southern dish," said the Earthquake. "Mill can tell you about it. It's responsible for all those drooling morons down there. Sodom on the half-shell."

I was trying to get close to Maggie, but Wilma had insinuated herself between the two of us, evidently because she thought I would protect her from the clutches of the Earthquake. The Earthquake, however, was intent on getting into the food basket the girls had brought along, and in this state of mind, he would have been dangerous to Wilma only if she could have been toasted on a bun and eaten.

"Plato," I began…"Oh, by the way, open me a can of that golden brew there, boy."

"Open it yourself."

"I'll get it," said Maggie.

Maggie was absolutely stunning that day, long-legged and tan, with golden brown hair pulled back in a ponytail that fell below her shoulders. I always thought of ripe peaches when I saw her, mature plump ones just off the tree, full of juice, please-bite-me-or-I'll-never-speak-to-you-again peaches. She had a way of wrinkling her nose when she laughed, and of throwing back her head and displaying a full set of white, even teeth. I thought then, and still think, that she ought to have been in movies; but she was probably lacking that one quality that looks can't make up for—dramatic talent.

Oh, well. A full house isn't too bad unless you insist on an ace-high straight flush.

"The Greeks," said Bowman, "were the first people we know of—certainly the first people in the West—who believed, really believed, that they could explain the universe without resorting to gods and myths. That's what Mr. Stuart said."

"They had plenty of gods and myths," said Wilma Strupp.

"Ah, but the philosophers could see through that. They knew these were only symbolic explanations."

"Was Plato an atheist?" Maggie asked.

"No." I said.

"Are you?"

"I don't know."

"I think he is," Bowman said.

"I don't know what I am," I said. "I think I'm a philosopher. This summer has changed my mind about a lot of things. I think I'm going back to school and major in philosophy."

"The Greeks didn't eat chicken and they didn't drink beer," said the Earthquake. "They lived on roast lamb and wine."

"They were looking for the truths that underlie the universe," I said. "Mr. Stuart said they were convinced that the universe as it appears is undergirded by eternal, unchanging ideals, and they thought they could discover them by correct thinking. There's something very exciting about people like that."

"There's something very weird about people like that," Wilma Strupp said. "By the way, why do they call you Earthquake?" This was the first time, so far as I remember, that she had actually addressed O'Toole.

"Those two smart bastards tagged me with it," the Earthquake said, motioning in the general direction of Bowman and myself.

"We did not," I said. "I don't know where he got it."

"What's your real name?" Wilma asked.

"Call me Earthquake," he said.

"I know his real name," said the Amazon, she was running her fingers through Bowman's sun-bleached hair. He had his eyes closed, obviously enjoying the affection of a woman whom I could never understand. One day she wanted to punch you out, the next she wanted flowers and violin music, and to be told the standard things: your eyes are like stars, etc. etc.

"You only think you know my real name," the Earthquake said. "I enlisted under a false name."

"Percival Gregory O'Toole," the Amazon said.

"Percival," Wilma said, and giggled. "No wonder you want to be called Earthquake."

"I'm telling you," he said, "that's not my real name. I had to get out of town quick, and cover my tracks, and I enlisted under a false name."

I have never seen the Earthquake more serious. Maggie looked at me, frowned, and I looked back and shrugged.

"Why did you have to get out of town so quick?" Bowman asked. He still had his head in the Amazon's lap, and she was still twining her fingers in his hair. He did not so much as open his eyes or look around. He sounded bored.

"I killed a man," the Earthquake said.

The girls got wide-eyed and looked at him with genuine alarm, all except the Amazon. Her expression didn't change at all. Covering a yawn with her right hand, she rolled her eyes and said:

"You killed a man."

"That's right," said the Earthquake.

"Do you mind, ladies, if we return to a more stimulating subject?" Bowman asked. "We were discussing the Greeks and their philosophy…"

"I see it all now," said the Amazon, who had obviously taken a humanities course or two. "You killed your father, solved the riddle of the sphinx, and married your mother."

"And you were hounded across the galaxies by the fates…" Wilma said.

"That's Orestes," said the Amazon.

"And you wanted to join the Foreign Legion," I said, "but you couldn't pass the physical, so you wound up in the Navy under an assumed name."

"Something like that," he said. "It was my mother's lover that I killed. He had some connections to the mob. I had to get out."

"O'Toole," Bowman said, "you're beginning to piss me off, just like always."

"You don't believe me, do you Bowman?"

"No, I don't. Give him another beer, Maggie. Maybe it'll keep him quiet."

Maggie was sitting next to the cooler, and she reached in, rattled around in the ice a bit, and drew out a frosty can, which she tossed to the Earthquake. He made no move to catch it, and it landed squarely in his belly.

"Oomph," he said. "Hey, watch what you're doing."

"That's a cold-blooded killer you're dealing with, Maggie," Bowman said.

"Kinda makes you want to treat me with more respect, don't it?" The Earthquake smiled and then giggled.

"Tell me about the Symposium," Maggie said to me.

"The what?" the Earthquake asked.

"Your little get-together to discuss philosophy," the Amazon said. "Maggie's been telling everyone about it. You'd think she was in the company of Socrates and Protagorous."

"What I found out," I said, "is that I don't know anything about philosophy. We've been reading *The Story of Philosophy*."

Maggie beamed. "Will Durant," she said. "I have a friend who read that. But she's one of those brainy types, you know."

"How about *Martin Eden*," I said. "Have you got it yet?"

She looked away.

"I got it," said the Amazon. "And I've been reading it. I wanted to see just what it is about this dog sled rider of the far north that fascinates you guys so much."

"Betty Ann is the family intellectual," said Maggie.

"And what did you find out?" I asked.

"I'll admit he was a hell of a man," she said. "If there really is such a man. I can't believe anyone could start from ground zero and educate himself in such a short time."

"Now that," said the Earthquake, "is exactly what I said about him. But Mill and Bowman are true believers."

"I'd like to be," said the Amazon. "I'd like to meet a man like that."

Bowman rolled open his eyes, looked up at her, and said, "You just did, baby." She smiled.

"Tell us some more about Plato and the Greeks," Maggie said.

"For one kiss," I said, "I'll tell you anything you want to know."

"Get out of my way, Wilma," she said.

Wilma ducked, and Maggie and I met directly over her. Her lips were on mine (peaches, ripe peaches), and her arm went around my neck and pulled me toward her.

"Hey," said Wilma. "I'm being crushed."

"She told you to get out of the way," said the Earthquake.

Wilma sort of backed up, then crawled to the other side of Maggie, putting two warm bodies between herself and Earthquake.

"Now, what about those Greeks?" Maggie whispered.

"They were intellectual athletes," I told her. "That doesn't mean they were smart boys who went in for sports; they were mind-jocks. They dashed around the universe at will, looking into dark corners."

"Did you figure that out all by yourself?" Maggie asked.

"Well," I admitted after a moment, "it was actually something I got from Mr. Stuart."

"Who is this Stuart?" Wilma asked. "You guys quote him like he was the Gospel. He must be the smartest man in the hemisphere."

"He's pretty smart, okay," Bowman said. "He owns a used bookstore in San Diego. He's the one who put us onto Will Durant."

"According to Durant," I said, "Aristotle invented logic. Think of it! Invented logic!"

"What were people doing before then?" the Earthquake asked. "Was every human on earth illogical until Aristotle showed up?"

"Most people are illogical even today," said Bowman.

"But not you," the Amazon said.

I said, "The Greeks were confident in their ability to come to proper solutions using nothing more than clear thinking. They were willing to follow their minds no matter where they took them."

"And where was that?" Wilma asked.

"Well," I said. "They had an atomic theory three hundred years before the birth of Christ. Some of them knew the world was round and that it orbited the sun. The absurd didn't bother them, so long as it was logically constructed."

"No pelican ever dies of old age," said the Earthquake.

Silence fell over the camp. I looked at Maggie, who looked at me, then I turned to look at Bowman, who for the first time in quite awhile actually lifted his head out of the Amazon's lap, and turned to look at the Earthquake.

"That's the craziest damned thing I ever heard," Bowman said.

"Pelicans do not die of old age," the Earthquake repeated.

"Did you read that somewhere?" Bowman asked.

"Nope. Never read a thing about pelicans. Don't know a thing about pelicans and don't give a damn." He took a long drink of beer. "But I know that it is impossible for a pelican to die of old age."

"What, pray tell, do they die of?" Wilma asked.

"Broken necks," said the Earthquake, "as any fool who uses proper logic can tell you."

"Trust O'Toole to bring us down to earth from whatever celestial peregrination we may be on," I said.

"I'm waiting to hear the rest of this," Bowman said.

"How do pelicans catch their food?" the Earthquake began. Then he answered himself. "They dive for it. They fly along, then suddenly they drop head first, hit the water like a rock, and come up with a fish. So it stands to reason that over time, as they get older, and as they lose elasticity and bone density, their necks get weaker and weaker. Then the day comes when they can't take the impact anymore. Bingo. Broken neck. Dead."

Silence again. Then Wilma and Maggie began to giggle. Then I joined them.

"O'Toole," Bowman said, "if I wind up in Bedlam, I'll find myself chained up next to you."

"Just following my logic wherever it goes," he said.

"I hate to admit it," I said, "but there's something to what he says. Not that pelicans die of broken necks, but…"

"Well," the Earthquake said, a bit pugnaciously, "show me where my logic is wrong."

We all sat there in silence, waiting for someone to speak up and refute an obvious absurdity.

"That's just silly," Wilma finally said.

"Then what's wrong with it," said the Earthquake.

"It's...Well, it's silly," she repeated.

"Break out the food," Bowman said. "O'Toole makes me hungry."

"Yeah," said the Earthquake. "What have we got? How about some sliced, charcoal-broiled sow snouts."

"Sick!" Maggie shouted.

"Brother Dave Gardner," the Amazon said. "And stewed tomatoes on light bread, so you have to lift and eat fast lest it fall through the crust."

"And they fell upon them," I said, "and consumed them with the gusto of a hound dog."

"Ah," said the Amazon. "You know Brother Dave."

"Love him," I said.

"Another Southern moron," said O'Toole.

We were sprawled all over a large blanket the girls had brought. The beer cooler was sitting on the sand with the food basket nearby. Bowman brought it over, threw back the lid, and we looked down at two chickens, roasted to a beautiful, golden brown. I do not exaggerate when I say that the Earthquake's eyes expanded measurably, that he licked his lips, and that he drooled slightly before saying in a husky, passionate tone, "Look at them chickens."

The girls had brought along other food than the chickens, but because of the Earthquake's comment, chicken became so central to the feast, in our minds at least, that for years afterward, if Bowman and I were eating together, and if chicken were on the menu, we would look at one another, lick our lips, and say, "Look at them chickens." This saying may turn out to be, in the long run, Earthquake O'Toole's most lasting verbal legacy, along with a variation on the quote that stands at the head of this chapter. He said it as we began tearing the chickens apart and handing the pieces around. The girls had brought plastic knives, forks, and spoons, but nothing that could actually be used to cut the chickens.

"Mary Alice, you dunce," the Amazon said.

"Oh, shut up, Betty Ann," Maggie responded.

"Here," said the Earthquake, ripping a chicken apart with his bare hands. "Let's not let a little oversight cause a family feud. Do you like white or dark meat?"

"White," I said. "How about you?"

"White," he said. "That's the problem with chickens. They don't have enough white meat on them."

I had managed to secure a chicken breast and was tearing into it, and washing it down with beer. There were lots of other people on the beach that day, but they all seemed far away, as if we were confined to a circle of light that they couldn't enter.

"Our education system is all fouled up," I said. "We don't really learn to think. We just cram a bunch of facts in our heads, then we take a piece of paper and wave it in front of people and say we're educated."

"And how would you do it, professor?" the Amazon asked.

"I think I'm pretty well-educated," Wilma said.

I said, "Plato's plan interests me. For the first ten years or so, the students did nothing but gymnastics. Developed their bodies and their coordination."

"But only the men," Maggie said. "The women stayed at home and cooked and sewed."

"Wrong," Bowman said.

"Wrong," I repeated. "Plato sent all the children to school, no matter what social class they came from, or who their parents were, or what sex they were."

"Pretty liberal for a guy who thanks God he wasn't born a woman," the Amazon said.

"He was looking for talent," I said, "real talent. And he knew it could be found anywhere, in any human. He wasn't willing to reject anyone at the outset for any reason."

"Okay," Wilma said. "So what came next?"

"Next came music. The first part of the education concentrated on the body. The second part concentrated on the spirit. Ergo: music. Finally they get around to philosophy."

"So now we have athletic, musical philosophers," said the Earthquake.

"Something like that," I said. "But there is a weeding out process going on. Some fall out along the way, can't keep up. Most people aren't suited for philosophy. They don't want the truth. They just want opinion. They go by the way side."

"What happens to them?" Maggie asked.

"Oh, they have their place in society," I said. "You can't have an entire society of philosophers. Who would..."

"Clean the toilets?" the Amazon said in the tone she reserved for her most cynical remarks. "They were a bunch of elitists, your Greeks."

"They believed in a well-ordered society," Bowman said. "They had sense enough to know that you don't put a suit on an ape and send him up to address parliament. Neither the ape nor parliament benefits."

"I can see where this is going," the Earthquake said. "The philosophers wind up in charge and everyone else has to shine their shoes and wash their clothes."

"The philosophers wind up in charge all right," I said. "But that doesn't mean that everyone else is a slave to them. But they are in charge of the government."

"Sounds like a tyranny," said Wilma.

"I thought the Greeks believed in democracy," Maggie said. "That's what one of my teachers said."

"Some of the Greeks believed in democracy," I said. "But Plato wasn't one of them."

"He hated democracy," Bowman said. "He thought it was mob rule, the worst form of government."

"Plato believed in an aristocracy," I said. "But it was an aristocracy of ability. Not one of birth."

"Any way you slice it," said the Earthquake, "I wind up shining your shoes, Mill. And I ain't gonna do it."

"Where does Nietzsche fit into all this?" asked the Amazon.

"I don't know much about him," I said.

"Your buddy Jack London talks about him all the time," she said.

"God is dead," Wilma said. "That's Nietzsche."

"That's scary," said Maggie. "That's kind of what I always think of when I think of philosophers. They leave you without a shred of anything to hold onto."

"Nah," I said.

"Nietzsche was sort of like Plato," Bowman said. "I've been reading Will Durant on him. He was an elitist."

"The superman," said the Amazon. "I can see why you like him, Bowman. You and Miller."

"Are you a superman, Miller?" Maggie asked, snuggling close to me.

"Pass me some of those grapes," I said.

"Here," she said. "Let me serve you, superman. Lie on your back, and I'll drop them in your mouth. I saw this movie once, and the women were doing that."

I felt like some sort of king, lying there under the sun with Maggie hovering over me, meat in one hand, beer in the other, one girl dropping grapes in my mouth and another fanning me. Wilma, obviously intent on avoiding the Earthquake, made sure to maneuver herself so that Maggie and I were between her and him, and pretty soon she got a piece of cardboard and began fanning herself with it.

"Hey, Wilma," I said, "how about turning some of that air on me."

She did for awhile, until she got tired of it, tossed the cardboard aside and lay flat with her chin on her folded hands.

I looked around, and sure enough Bowman and the Amazon had disappeared to somewhere, and I was left alone with two women, and a man who might as well not have been there so far as one of the women was concerned. This became something of a problem for me, interfering, as it did, with my scheme for getting Maggie alone.

Twilight was washing around us in purple and gold.

"Let's go down the beach by ourselves," I whispered to Maggie.

"We can't," she whispered back.

"Why not?" I asked. "Is there some rule against it."

"Wilma," she whispered.

"What about her?"

This conversation was being carried on mouth to ear.

"She's frightened to death of your buddy Earthquake," she said.

"Frightened?"

"Well, not exactly scared. But she doesn't want to be left alone with him. She's afraid he'll make a pass at her."

"I'm sure he will," I said. "So what? If she doesn't like it she can tell him to get lost."

"But he scares her."

"Frankly," I said, "I was figuring on making a pass at you."

"Go ahead," she said, and blew in my ear. "You don't scare me, not one little bit. And I won't tell you to get lost."

"Actually," I said, "I feel a little hampered, out here beneath God's blue sky with the whole world looking on."

"Well, if you were planning on getting my bathing suit off," she whispered, "you couldn't do that even if we were hiding under the bushes."

"Ah, the cruelty of it all," I said. "Here I am, young and vigorous. Maybe not wildly handsome, but certainly not ugly."

"You're very good-looking," she said.

"Then let's get over there under those bushes and at least take a chance that I can get your bathing suit off."

"Oh, Miller," she said. "Kiss me. There'll be time for other things."

Oh, Maggie, how wrong you were. This was our time, and there would never be another like it for us. We couldn't have known it, but this was the last day we would ever be together, though I talked to you on the telephone several times, and you wrote me at least one letter after I was aboard ship. I heard from someone whom I can't remember that you took up with a pre-law major at USC, but whether or not that's true, or, if it is, what came of the relationship, I couldn't say.

We drove home together later, full and happy, with the Earthquake forced to drive (it was his car), and Bowman and the Amazon up front with him. They weren't talking; they were kissing one another, and getting downright indecent, not at all troubled by the public around them. I was in the back seat with Maggie and Wilma. We sang together: Somewhere beyond the sea, somewhere waiting for me, my lover stands on golden sands and watches the ships that go sailing…Then Maggie threw herself on me and became very passionate, and Wilma was left to look out the window.

It was 1960. There was no Vietnam, no Watergate, no Monica Lewinski, no assassinations or burning cities. We were young, and the world abounded with poets and philosophers whose names were written in gold, and truth and beauty were ours for the taking.

Chapter 10

Kings of the Earth

Until philosophers are kings, or the kings and princes of this world have the spirit and power of philosophy, and wisdom and political leadership meet in the same man...cities will never cease from ill, nor the human race.

—Plato.

This guy Kennedy is a jerk deluxe. And Nixon is even worse. And the Democrats are up in Los Angeles getting ready to turn the country over to a bunch of Hottentots.

—The Diary of Earthquake O'Toole

Neither Bowman nor I are heavy drinkers. I suppose both of us are control freaks and get very nervous when we feel things slipping out of our hands. But on rare occasions we have been known to over indulge. This was one of those occasions, though neither of us planned it that way. We decided we hadn't brought enough beer, and were about to go and get some more, when Bowman, as if by magic, produced a bottle of Glen Livet 12.

"Ambrosia, my boy," he said.
"The water of life," I said.
"Here's to the Earthquake," he said, tilting the bottle upward.

He passed the bottle over, and I raised it so that the golden light of the dying sun bent through the green glass. I catch the sun in a green vial and drink it down. And now I have power over the elements; and now I have discovered all the ancient secrets of truth and beauty; and now I am a poet and lover of wisdom.

The problem of chickens and white meat begins to make sense, and I am ready to acknowledge that beneath the Earthquake's apparent stupidity, there was some sort of unnamed brilliance.

"Bowman, I realize for the first time just how dumb I am."

"Well, congratulations. You are now qualified to be executed with Socrates, the wisest man in Athens because he realizes he knows nothing. Here. Have a cigar."

"Ah, you thought of everything."

"Except how to light these in the face of a landward wind."

We huddled with our backs to the wind, wasted almost a book of matches, and finally managed to get one of the cigars lit. With that we lit the other. Now we were indeed lords of the earth, holding Promethean fire in one hand and Dionysian fire in the other. The cigar smoke ascended upward and was whipped away by the wind, *pneuma* to the Greeks, another word for spirit. We were awash in whatever dreams are made of; it was swirling all around us; and the Glen Livet metamorphosed from a fire in the throat, to a warmth in the belly, then finally to a pregnancy in the brain.

"I am about to give birth. All I need is a midwife."

"Allow me. I have presided over many a birth. Some were stillborn. Some were downright monstrous. And some were not without a certain wild, uncontrollable charm."

"Well," I said, "it suddenly seems to me that the one key ingredient that made the Greek Summer the unique experience it turned out to be was the Earthquake. No Earthquake, no nothing."

"This is surely one of my more monstrous pieces of midwifery," Bowman said. "In fact, spread your legs and open up your womb. This one is going back where it came from."

"Don't forget to reattach the umbilical cord."

"Will a simple square knot do?"

"Listen to me, my son. The Earthquake was the antithesis to our thesis. He was the opposite that defines a thing. Without him we fall into the fallacy of the suppressed correlative. And have you noticed the strange insightfulness of his diary entries. Maybe this country does need more white meat on chickens. Maybe the five cent cigar is passe. Speaking for myself, I would certainly rather have a good white-meat chicken in the White House than either Kennedy or Nixon."

"Brother, that's the truth," Bowman said. "Do you remember the Democratic Convention of sixty?"

"I hardly knew it was going on," I said. "Except for the Amazon. She was the political aficionada in our midst. She would show up at the pool every morning that week, red-eyed from watching television, screaming and weeping about the southern delegations. The Kennedy crowd was going to drive the money-changers out of the temple. Remember?"

"Yeah," Bowman said. "I remember."

He drew on his cigar and blew smoke upward into the sea wind.

He said, "Of all the things I can't figure out, forty years after the fact, the ongoing Kennedy phenomenon stands preeminent. I didn't like him at the time. I don't like him now. If Oswald hadn't shot him, he would be remembered as nothing more than a lecherous Bostonian who slid through Harvard on his bootlegging father's money. But the shots fired in Dallas were heard 'round the world. Now there he is, second only to Lincoln, who is second only to Jesus Christ. I believe we will see the day when the Lincoln Memorial will be altered. Jack Kennedy will be sitting on Lincoln's knee, playing Mortimer Snerd to the Great Emancipator's Edgar Bergen. Pass the bottle over, boy."

I did. And the years slid away, and behold there was the Amazon, stomping into the pool area with her dark glasses in her right hand and rubbing her eyes with her left.

"I cannot believe it," she said. "I simply cannot believe that a handful of unreconstructed southerners can hold an entire convention hostage."

Bowman was coiling up a hose on the south end of the pool, on a small patch of lawn behind the diving boards. The Earthquake was up on the north end, sitting with his feet dangling in the water, staring down as if he saw a mermaid motioning to him. Hopewell...I don't remember where he was. Probably out front talking on the telephone, or in the head. Chief Crouch was present, but only barely. He was in the office. He never came out of the office these days, a mere shell of the profane, hard-drinking, card-playing malcontent who had sounded general quarters and marched into the pool.

I was seated in a folding chair, leaning back against the main building just outside the door to the entrance area, and drinking in the marvelous, scented air.

It was nine-thirty in the morning, we were healthy and well-fed, and it would have been very difficult to have found better duty anywhere in the United States military. We had every reason to be happy, and I for one was. The Amazon, however, was not because the political climate in the country didn't suit her.

She replaced her glasses, came to where I sat, put her hands on her hips, and said, somewhat belligerently, "Have you been watching the Los Angeles convention?"

"Are you kidding me?" I said. "Maverick and the Alaskans. That's all I watch on TV, except when a Popeye cartoon is on. And sometimes I watch Mister Lucky, if Bowman is around."

"Of all the..." she began. "Oooh." She spat it out like overworked tobacco. She walked away, wandered about at the pool's edge, then came back.

"You and Bowman are philosophers," she said. "At least you claim to be."

"I claim nothing of the sort," I said. "I only claim an interest in philosophy."

"Well act interested then. We have got an entire group of people in this country disenfranchised because of their race, and those suh-thuhn gentlemen from Texas to Georgia are going to see to it that they stay that way. What was the War all about? That's what I'd like to know."

"What war would that be, Amazon?" I said. "The Second Punic War or the Peleponnesian War?"

"That war in which your revered ancestors seceded."

"Watch it, Yankee."

"You see," she said. "This is exactly what I mean. We have two countries. When are we going to get over this Rebel and Yankee business and live up to what we say we are?"

By this time Bowman had come strolling up. He put his arm around the Amazon's waist, reached over and kissed her on the cheek.

"My beauty," he said. "How like unto a rose at dawn thou art."

"Oh, stop it," she said, pushing him away.

"Loveable little cuss, ain't she?" I said.

"I'm sure she means well," Bowman said, and we both laughed.

The Amazon was having none of it. The country was in dire straits, and instead of fixing it, we were behaving like a couple of buffoons.

"You'll have to forgive your companion," I said. "Affectionate as she might have seemed on the beach during our recent outing, troubling news from the north has caused a transformation in her attitude. You were, of course, watching the Democratic Convention in Los Angeles last night. It came to you, complete with commentary, via the TV in your barracks."

"Actually," he said, "last night was my night to watch Mister Lucky, and..."

"Shut up," she said. "Shut up. That's enough. I don't want to hear anymore." And waving her hands like a down-home minstrel singer, she took off for the office to converse, I suppose, with Chief Crouch. I don't know what she hoped to learn from him, because she was utterly daft if she was thinking he had watched the Convention, but she went in there nonetheless.

And it was ten o"clock, and the doors were opened. Same song, as they say, forty-third verse. In came the mob, and we spent the day ogling the girls and reluctantly casting an occasional glance toward the rest of the swimmers.

If Bowman and I thought this was the end of the political conversation, we were to be sadly disappointed, because it turned out, much to my bewilderment and consternation, that the Chief had, in fact, watched the Convention, was keenly keeping an eye on it, knew the key players and the issues. And then, to make matters more entangled and baffling than ever, Earthquake O'Toole was not only watching, but had a point of view exactly the opposite of the one expressed by the Amazon. The Chief, so far as I remember, was sort of neutral. Bowman and I were sort of ignorant. But the Amazon and the Earthquake were passionate and ready to go to war.

"You want some illiterate sharecropper running the country? Is that what you want?"

I wasn't a direct party to this portion of the conversation; I only heard it as I sat on the mid-pool tower and the Amazon and the Earthquake were passing along behind me.

"Why don't you just say it," she replied. "It's the skin color you don't like."

"Okay," said the Earthquake. "I'll say it. I ain't turning this country over to a bunch of Hottentots."

"Better that than Estes Kefauver or that fool Johnson."

"Oh, mister lifeguard," a voice called. "Will you come and save me?"

It was a cute girl, about thirteen years old I would have said, splashing around with some friends right below the tower.

"Come back and drown in five years," I called down. "And I'll come save you."

"Oh, mister lifeguard," a falsetto voice called from behind me. It was Hopewell.

"Go ahead and drown," I shouted.

The political debate raged all day, around the pool, out front at the check-in counter, in the snack area where there were tables and chairs under large umbrellas, in the paved area where people lay side by side, smeared with various oils and baking under the California sun. And always it was the same two people, and only those two—the Amazon and the Earthquake. The irresistible force and the immovable object. The yin and the yang. The Rebel and the Yankee, except both of them were Yankees to my southern mind. The Earthquake was having the time of his life, picking away at the Amazon and enraging her with his (a term we now use, unknown at the time) political incorrectness. I doubt very much that he had a genuine political conviction; but the moment he found out how seriously the Amazon took her politics, how easily aroused she was, how passionately she believed in saving the world by voting right, and how certain she was that her way was the right way to vote—the moment the Earthquake realized all this, he was utterly delighted. He immediately became a right-wing reactionary.

"Why don't you just put Castro in the White House?" I heard him telling her at one point. "We'll plow up Highway three-ninety-five and plant sugar there. We'll call ourselves the People's Republic of California."

"*Ad hominem!*" she shouted. "That's what you people always do. You start losing the argument, so you degenerate to name calling. Just because I believe in justice for everybody, does that make me a communist?"

"No," he shouted back. "It only makes you goofy."

"*Ad hominem*! You can't get away with that, you chubby little puke."

"*Ad homie*-whatever, BAG."

"I'll knock your fat ass into next week," she said, drawing back her fist.

O'Toole took off, laughing, with her right behind him.

I blew my whistle. "Hey," I shouted. "No running in the pool area."

"Oh, bugger off," the Amazon shouted back.

"Look at the two of them," I told Bowman later that day. "The Amazon believes in the holy grail of universal love and brotherhood, and is willing to whip the Earthquake's butt to demonstrate it."

This turned out to be one of those days that wore on into the hours of deep twilight. The pool was finally closed, the last swimmer pushed out the front door, the last trash can emptied, the area hosed down. All of this was done by Hopewell, Bowman, and myself, with no help from the Chief (who never helped anyway, being exempt from manual labor by his rank and his delicate condition), and absolutely no help from the Earthquake and the Amazon, exempt because their country needed them to solve its political problems. They had retreated to the tables in the area at the south end, and Chief Crouch had joined them, and there they sat, swearing, and calling one another names. Actually, the Chief was neither swearing, nor was he calling anyone anything. He was drinking a Coke and putting in a comment from time to time. Bowman and Hopewell and I went down and joined them, and managed in a very short time to find out why my grandfather always said, "Never discuss religion or politics with anyone you want to keep as a friend."

If grandfather was right, then this was the perfect arena for a political discussion, because aside from Bowman and me, there were virtually no friends there, unless I include the Earthquake. According to him, we were the best friends he'd ever had, but at the time neither Bowman nor I thought of him in that way. Hopewell was a nice enough guy, but he was just another human shipwreck who washed up on the same island with us. The Chief was the Chief. No need to make anymore of it than that. And then, there was the Amazon.

What the Amazon was to us is difficult to determine these many years after our association. Bowman talked about her as if he loved her, but just as quickly he would talk about her as if she were the left tackle on the high school football team, or perhaps a tree or a fence post. To me, the Amazon was sort of like an older sister, one who always thought I was in the way, until she needed something. And after this day she seemed very remote, as if she had dropped off another planet, or moved in from some exotic neighborhood populated by eastern European refugees. I couldn't understand her then, because then she did not fit into any political category I had ever encountered.

Understand, this was a time of great political naivete. We had won the Second World War a scant fifteen years before, and my earliest memories were of men in uniforms and black-and-white newsreels of goose-stepping Nazis. Nuclear bombs had gone off over Japan, then hydrogen bombs in the Pacific, and Tail Gunner Joe McCarthy dragged a bunch of people up before the House Un-American Activities Committee and invited the nation to watch via television. Watch we did, and most of us agreed with the Senator, though many would deny it now.

Looking back at the Greek Summer is, in some ways, like looking across an impassable chasm of time, or like looking through a flawed telescope to a country on the far side of a river. We were compelled to cross the river, and the very act of crossing changed us, and we find now that we can never go back. Assassinations, and Vietnam, and Watergate changed us; and burning cities and sit-ins changed us; and we were changed by political action committees, and women burning bras, and people demanding to vote, and by women demanding the right to abortion. We were changed by McLuhan and Simone de Beauvoir, and by Betty Friedan and Kate Millet.

Today, the Amazon would seem rather ordinary, a person who would cause little more than a raised eyebrow, if that. But in the Summer of 1960, she sounded like a companion of the Hollywood Ten, and I hardly knew what to make of her. The Earthquake, however, did not appear to be the least bit troubled by her, or by anything she said, simply because he had no genuine commitment to either side of the discussion. If she had been on the right, he would have slipped over to the left, and the angrier she became, the more outrageous his position became. He pulled the whole thing off fairly well, for never once did he smile or do anything to indicate he wasn't absolutely serious; and he was argumentative, and loud, and red-faced, just as if he were a south Boston ward heeler haranguing for votes.

"You can't give ignorant people who can barely read the right to vote," he kept saying. "Tell her, Mill."

"How did I get into this?" I asked.

"Yes, mister elitist?" the Amazon asked. "How indeed. Plato and his philosopher kings, that's how you got into it. Well, I don't wish to live in Plato's vaunted Republic where a slave is a slave and proud of it."

"The Earthquake isn't talking about slavery," said Bowman. "How does slavery get into it. He's talking about the ability to understand issues..."

"I seriously doubt he knows what he's talking about," the Chief put in.

"Look," said the Earthquake, "the right to vote shouldn't be just handed out willy-nilly. I personally think that people ought to take tests and pass them before they can vote."

"That is just hare-brained," said the Amazon. "Do you know what that translates to? Just exactly what they have in the South right now—and what they're bound and determined to keep. You keep a man ignorant, then tell him he hasn't got enough sense to vote. Even Plato believed in educating everyone. Miller, you said so yourself."

"Yes," I said. "That he did. But Plato didn't believe everyone had some sort of God-given right to a position in government. That was something that could be determined only by his own aptitudes and abilities."

"*His* own aptitudes," said the Amazon. "What about *hers*?"

"Okay," I said. "I stand corrected."

"Women have periods once a month, and it messes up their heads. You can't have a woman running the country and fighting a menstrual headache at the same time." The Earthquake said this, leaning backward, sighting the Amazon down his stubby nose, and narrowing his eyes as if he were delivering an addendum to the Gettysburg Address.

The Amazon was enraged.

"He's ragging you, Amazon," Bowman said. "Can't you see he's just ragging you?"

"I'm as serious as a heart attack," said the Earthquake. "Women are hormonally unfit to govern. And the products of the African continent are unfit to govern. Hell, they can't even keep themselves clean."

"I've known plenty that were cleaner than a lot of whites I know," the Chief said. "Go over to the barracks right now and take a look. It ain't the Negro who needs to clean up. Put a uniform on him, and…"

"And you've got a baboon in a uniform," the Earthquake said. "Next thing you know we'll be letting apes and chimpanzees vote."

"You are too disgusting for words," said the Amazon. "I've already wasted too much time talking to you, you bog-trotting, shanty-Irish, bigot."

"Oh," said the Earthquake. "Now who's the bigot. Did you hear that, boys? Obviously the sainted Miss Greybow, of English extraction, has a problem with the Irish."

"Not the Irish," she said. "With one Irish bigot."

"It's all right, St. BAG. Don't bother to apologize. I recognize all the words. I've been hearing them all my short life, and I'll be telling Father Mulkayhee about it first thing in the morning. I'm sure he'll be saying a prayer for you."

"I've got a great idea," I said.

"I know your ideas," the Amazon said. "You want to save up your Confederate money and wait for the South to rise again."

"Amazon," I said, "you can't know my ideas unless you let me tell them to you. Would you be willing to do that?"

She snorted and looked away.

"Let's see if we can do what Socrates would have done," I said. "Let's figure out exactly what the problem is and see if we can address it with some intelligence, because right now you two are doing nothing but insulting one another."

"Ain't gonna be governed by a bunch of Hottentots," said the Earthquake.

"You *are* a Hottentot," said the Amazon.

"And you're a bag."

"That's enough," said the Chief, with as much ardor as he could muster up under the circumstances.

"Look," said Bowman, "let's agree that we want the best leaders we can get. Can we agree on that? Now, let's agree that a great leader has to have certain qualities. Can we agree on that?"

Heads nodded, faces scowled.

"Now," he said, as if he were addressing a kindergarten, "can we agree that talent and ability can crop up anywhere, man or woman, red, black, or white?"

"You may inform the ambassador from the Congo," the Earthquake said, trying his best to mimic Brer Possum, "that we's having chittlins for dinner."

"What do you care what we're having for dinner?" Hopewell said. "You'd eat the rear end out of a polecat if someone held it for you."

"All right," I said. "There's your proposition. Talent can be found anywhere."

The Earthquake went into a high falsetto. "Tell the ambassador that I can't see him. I have a splitting headache."

"This is impossible," said the Amazon. "I've wasted an entire day talking to you, and that's quite enough. But before I leave I'd just like to say that if you, Percival G. O'Toole, are representative of the white American male, give me Harry Belefonte any time."

And out she stomped, with the Earthquake calling after her, "Don't let the door hit you in the butt, Betty Ann." Then he fell back in his chair, laughing like Woody Woodpecker and wagging his head from side to side.

"Well, Earthquake," Hopewell said, "looks like you've ripped your drawers with her, and I mean for good."

"Ripped 'em the first day we met," the Earthquake replied. "Who cares? She's a castrated wrestler who can't figure out whether or not to pee standing up. Ain't that right, Bowman?"

"I like her all right," Bowman said.

"Her sister sure ain't a castrated wrestler," I said.

"Brother, I'll say," Hopewell said. "When you get tired of her, toss her my way."

"Let's get back to politics," Bowman said. "I hope you guys realize that we're a long way from Plato's vision. Look at Los Angeles and tell me if you see any philosophers there."

"I don't see any heading for Chicago either," said the Chief.

"Which means we wind up doing what we always do," said the Earthquake. "You pick the best of two bums and hope he doesn't screw things up beyond repair."

"Looks like the Democrats will nominate Kennedy for sure," said the Chief. "And my guess is the Republicans will run Nixon."

"Not Rockefeller?" Bowman asked.

"Nah," the Chief said. "Rockefeller ain't got a snowball's chance in hell. It'll be Kennedy and Nixon. Two ex-sailors."

"Boy, if that wouldn't be a pair to draw to," I said; and after a moment, when no one responded, "I keep thinking of Glaucon and Thrasymachus. We're no better than what they said. Might makes right. You do what you can get away with. Philosophers don't run things. You know who runs things? The man with the biggest club. That's the way it's always been. I guess that's the way it'll always be. But it looks like we'd come up with a better way."

"I hate to remind you guys of this," Hopewell said, "but that's exactly what the Earthquake said the first day we were all together."

Ignoring him, Bowman asked, "Who you voting for, Chief?"

"Kennedy," he said.

"How about you, Miller?"

"I'm nineteen, Bowman."[1]

"Yeah. I forgot."

"I knew a lot of guys who had their brains blown out when they were only seventeen," the Chief said. "It always seemed to me that they should have had some voice about who their leaders were. But what do I know? I'm a washed up drunk waiting to die."

"Kind of a morbid way to look at it," I said.

"How old are you?" Hopewell asked.

"Thirty-eight next month," he said. "If I live that long."

"Whadaya mean, if you live that long?" said the Earthquake. "Thirty-eight ain't all that old."

"I feel ninety," said the Chief. "I'd give my eye teeth for one good jolt of anything. But I gave Stanford my word."

Crickets were singing in the bushes, the sun was below the horizon, and a light wind had come up, sweeping down from the hills to the east. The Chief spoke, softly, more to himself it seemed that to us:

"I was nineteen when the Japs hit us at Pearl. I was on the Arizona. In fact, I should have been aboard, but I went ashore the night before and wound up passed out drunk in a Hotel Street whore house. I would have been court martialed for being AWOL in the face of the enemy. But in the confusion no one seemed to have missed me. I owe my life, such as it is, to booze. I've wished many times that I'd stayed sober and gone down with the ship. Ah, well, let's get the hell out of here. This place is depressing."

Right, and it was due to get even more depressing, and that in very short order.

---

1. In 1960, the voting age, nation-wide, was twenty-one.

Chapter 11

▼

The Good Guys Versus the Bad Guys

July 20, 1960. This is a hell of a note. The Amazon won't speak to me anymore, and Mill and Bowman think it's funny. But I don't think it is. I tried to smooth things over with her. Talk about being touchy. A little political discussion, and she wants to have my ass keel hauled. Took her a flower, and she told me to put it where the sun don't shine.

—The Diary of Earthquake O'Toole

The flower that O'Toole brought to the Amazon on that hot morning in July was about the sorriest excuse for a peace offering that I have ever seen. But I don't think it would have mattered if he had brought her orchids; the lady simply was not going to be mollified. She became an outspoken, vigorous Jack Kennedy partisan. Chief Crouch became a lukewarm supporter of Kennedy. Bowman and I were lukewarm about everything but ourselves. Hopewell was just lukewarm. As for the Earthquake, he sort of drew his head in as much as he could (it's a tough move when one doesn't possess a neck) and went about masquerading as a turtle.

But back to the flower.

We were walking to the pool that morning, fresh from a breakfast fit for hungry sailors, when the Earthquake suddenly stopped in his tracks. We crossed a paved area and passed in front of a quonset hut surrounded by scrubby grass that had been put there, no doubt, in a vain effort at beautification. In this scrubby green expanse, at a small spot where grass refused to grow, a weed of some species had sprung up. I call it a weed because I remember my botany teacher's definition: a weed is nothing but a flower no one wants; and no one wanted this flower. It was off-white, the leaves were ragged, and it drooped there in the morning sun as if begging for someone to put it out of its misery. Well, the Earthquake did just that.

"What are you doing with that thing?" Bowman asked.

"Wouldn't you like to know?" he said. He was holding it in front of him like a small boy taking a present to the teacher. Dirt was still clinging to its miserable little roots.

"I would like to know," Bowman said, "and that's why I'm asking."

"Well, if it's all the same to you," he answered, "I think I'll just let that be my secret. I've noticed that you are a cynical bastard, and I think I'll spare myself a morning dose of cynicism."

We went on our way.

When we got to the pool, we found the Amazon had already come in, and was in the office talking to Chief Crouch. Bowman, Hopewell and I headed for the locker room to get out of our dungarees and into something more becoming to the well-dressed lifeguard.

"Where is O'Toole?" Bowman asked, looking around.

"I think he went into the office," Hopewell said.

"Well, he'd better take a suit of armor with him," Bowman said, "because…" He stopped and his mouth dropped open. "He wouldn't have the guts," he said.

"To what?" I asked.

"I just realized why he picked that bedraggled weed. He got it for the Amazon."

Then we heard her, through concrete walls, around door jambs and between the joints in the overhead, her voice booming like a siege gun:

"Why you ignorant, fat moron…Take that thing and put it where the sun don't shine!"

And in a moment or two the Earthquake came in, looking beaten and confused, holding his sagging flower in one hand and his hat in the other.

"Lord have mercy," he said. "I feel like I've just been relieved of fifty-thousand years in purgatory."

"Earthquake," Hopewell said, "remind me never to send you to comfort bereaved relatives after a funeral."

"Have a little political discussion," said the Earthquake, "and someone comes after you with a battle axe. I was just having fun. Just pulling her leg a little."

Then he gritted his teeth, became grim and resolute, and flung his peace offering in a nearby waste basket. "Well she can sit on it and rotate," he said. "She's the battle axe around here. If she thinks I'm gonna crawl and grovel just to get on her good side, she's got another think coming."

"You never were on her good side anyway," Bowman said.

"I'm not even sure she has a good side," said the Earthquake.

"Kennedy's Irish," said Hopewell. "You're Irish. Maybe if he's elected he'll send you to Ireland as our good will ambassador."

"Or maybe to the Congo," I said.

"Yeah," said Bowman. "I hear they serve delicious chittlins over there."

Three of us laughed. The fourth did not. In fact, the Earthquake didn't laugh or smile that entire day so far as I remember; and for the rest of their time together, with a few exceptions, he and the Amazon communicated with one another by means of a go-between.

"Miller," she would say, "you may inform Satchel-Ass O'Toole that he is to clamber up onto the mid-pool tower and keep his eyes out for drowning children."

And the Earthquake: "Kindly give my compliments to Saint Bag, the Pious, and inform her that the Earthquake knows his job and can struggle along without her instructions."

"Brother O'Toole," I would say, "The Amazon, the Queen of Hearts in the great card deck of life, would be gratified if you would take the mid-pool tower. And Amazon, Archbishop O'Toole will see you answer before the Ecclesiastical Court unless you quit calling him Satchel-Ass."

The whole thing was hilarious, and I really thought that sooner or later they'd start laughing, and it would all be over. But it was a vain hope, I assure you. The funnier it got to the rest of us, the madder it made the Amazon and the Earthquake, until they finally quit speaking to one another—even through intermediaries. The Amazon posted the assignments in writing on the bulletin board in the reception area, and she and the Earthquake settled down to a long period of open hostility.

Now I say it was funny to the rest of us, but this truth has limited application because funny and fun, though verbally speaking they derive from the same root word, are not necessarily the same things. Day rolled into day, the hostility did not abate, and the funny ceased to be fun.

"I feel like I'm living in a village somewhere between Athens and Sparta," Bowman said one morning.

We had a day off, and we had gone—just the two of us—into San Diego to make a day of it. Our plans were to hit one of Vic Taney's gyms and pump a little iron, then get something to eat, then head for Mr. Stuart's book store to see what we might scare up, and finally wend our way to our favorite spot on the rocks above La Jolla Cove. By noon we had accomplished the first part of our plan, and we were sitting, pumped tight and feeling truly herculean, in a sandwich shop over tuna-on-rye and tall glasses of iced tea.

"That's a nice analogy, Bowman," I said. "Living in a village between Athens and Sparta. I'll have to remember that one."

We were looking through the shop's plate glass window onto the busy sidewalk outside where well-dressed men and women hurried along.

"There goes a really lovely analogy," Bowman said, indicating a girl in a tight skirt and high heels. "Take a look at the rack on that woman, son. Now if the Amazon and O'Toole were at war over something important, like that girl for instance, I could sort of accept it. But this political crap..."

"Ah, but you see, my friend, this political crap is very important to the Amazon. O'Toole can have fun with it, but the Amazon can't. She is a true believer. I mean, she really thinks that it makes some kind of difference who gets into office."

"And you don't?" Bowman asked.

"No," I said. "Do you?"

"Not really."

"Just last night I was reading in Book Six of *The Republic* how Socrates characterizes politicians. They're all scoundrels. But the sad thing is, I don't think they all start out to be that way. It's the system itself that corrupts them."

Bowman seemed only half there. He was listening, but clearly his mind was somewhere else.

"I'm thinking about asking for a transfer back to the squadron," he said when I asked him what the matter was.

"Are you out of your mind?" I said. "The best summer of your life; paradise regained; girls, sunshine and water; and you want to go back to an airplane hanger and get your knuckles skinned up tightening bolts?"

"Yeah, I know it sounds stupid, Mill," he said, "but this war between the Amazon and O'Toole is getting to me. Everyday the same old thing. Hostility you could cut with a knife. I'm sick of living in an armed camp."

"I'm not sure you can get transferred," I said. "We're only half way through the summer, and who are they gonna replace you with? Lifeguards don't exactly grow on trees you know."

"Okay," he said. "But those two are driving me out of my mind. Maybe I'll check in to sick bay and say I'm a head case. I'll spend the rest of the summer looking at Rorschach blots. Yes, Doctor, it's plain as day to me. That's a big monster, and that's a virgin he's gobbling up."

"Forget it, Bowman," I said. "You'd never pull it off. You're too normal. Now for the Earthquake, it would be no problem. I think he always treads a thin line between lunacy and…"

"Lunacy," Bowman put in. "Between lunacy and lunacy, which makes him a lunatic."

"Bowman, you're stuck. You've got at least another month and a half of lifeguarding, so you might as well make the best of it. Hell, we'll just isolate them and contain them. We'll put them in a corner together and let them go at it until one is standing and one is down and out."

"I wonder what it would take to get them to make peace," Bowman said.

"The Amazon has got to come off it," I said. "You've got to admit, lunatic or not, the Earthquake isn't the problem."

"Sorry, Mill, but I think he is precisely the problem."

"You really are in love with the Amazon," I said.

"Fifty-fifty," he said. "But O'Toole is the problem. Running off at the mouth like that. Do you think he's really serious about all that Hottentot stuff?"

"Fifty-fifty," I said.

"You know what I'd like to see?" He looked at me, as seriously as I've ever been looked at.

"So," I said. "Spit it out, boy."

"I'd like to see Chief Crouch leave and Chief Hawkins come in."

"Who is Chief Hawkins."

"Works in supply."

"Black?"

"So black that on a dark night he has to smile before you can see him. And very sharp, and not the kind to put up with any garbage from the Saint Louie flash."

"Well, he ain't coming, so forget it. Besides, I don't think it would make any difference, because I'm not sure that when it gets right down to it the Earthquake really cares. Look at what he said about women, but he manages to tolerate the Amazon telling him what to do."

"Yeah," Bowman said. "Just thinking out loud, Mill. You're right, Miller. Damn it! You're always right. We'll ride it out, lacerated but proud, holding our heads up like the true warriors we are."

"Drums beating," I said. "Ragged banners fluttering in the wind. Sound the charge, bugler. And the lean, locked ranks go roaring down to die."

"Our sandwiches are going stale."

I took a bite of mine, chewed, then said, mouth half full, "I still like your Athens and Sparta analogy. They hated each other, but when they were threatened by barbarians, the Persians, they came together for a common cause."

"The Amazon and O'Toole ain't got a common cause," Bowman said.

"Well, then, how about the Olympic games. They declared truces during the games so that every city could send its athletes to compete."

"We've got no Olympic games."

"Then one of them is taking the fall," I said. "And I don't think it's gonna be the Amazon. She is definitely not the loser type."

We finished our lunch, left, and walked four blocks south to Mr. Stuart's used book store.

"Well," Mr. Stuart said when we walked in, making the little bell over the front door tinkle. "And how are my two young Greeks today?"

"In the doldrums, Mr. Stuart," Bowman said. "Beaten about the head and shoulders. Bruises, contusions and lacerations. Fading fast. Start the violin music."

"What's the problem? And where, by the way, is your running mate?"

"He's one of the ones bruising, contusing and lacerating us," I said.

"I can't believe you boys have had a falling out," he said.

"We haven't," I said. "Not exactly."

Bowman explained the situation to him, while I stood by and put in an occasional comment.

"Bowman says it's like the Athenians and the Spartans," I said. "But that's about as far as we've gotten."

"What you need then is a common enemy," Mr. Stuart said.

"Yeah. Well, we got that far too," I said. "But that's about as far as we've gotten.

"No one they fear enough to get them to make common cause, huh?"

"Nope."

"Well," he said. "Think about it. By the way, have you boys read *Raintree County?*"

"Saw the movie," Bowman said. "Boy, that Eva Marie Saint causes me to think impure thoughts. She reminds me of Veronica Lake."

"I didn't see the movie," said Mr. Stuart. "I suppose she played Nell Gaither."

"Yes," I said. "But back to the book. Why should we read it?"

"A copy came in the other day," he said. "I immediately thought of you two."

"Civil War," Bowman said. "Man, we are living in the middle of one of those right now."

"This is more than a Civil War book. The Civil War is just the backdrop, the event behind the events. It's really a book about philosophers doing philosophy. It's about young men educating themselves by bouncing ideas off one another. Sort of like the Golden Age Greeks."

"Talked me into it," I said. "How much do you want for the book."

"Five dollars."

"Don't have it."

"Take the book and pay me later," he said. "If you don't like it, bring it back and pay me nothing. That's my special deal to a rare circle of my customers, which you boys have entered."

"Gosh, thanks, Mr. Stuart," I said.

He went off briefly and came back toting the book.

"Ross Lockridge," he said, handing me the book. "He never wrote another. His cousin wrote *The Snake Pit*. But he was obviously more philosophically inclined."

"That looks like about a thousand pages," Bowman said. "You'll be all Summer on that one."

"I wonder why he never wrote anything else," I said.

"Maybe that's all he had to say," Bowman said. "Margaret Mitchell never wrote anything after *Gone With the Wind*."

Mr. Stuart frowned and shook his head. "Lockridge suicided," he said. "So whether or not he had anything else to say, we'll never know. Anyway, read it. The search for the golden raintree is symbolic of man's search for the meaning of life."

"I got that from the movie," Bowman said. "Did you see the movie, Mill?"

"I saw it, but I didn't think much of it at the time."

"My guess is that the movie and the book have very little in common," said Mr. Stuart. "Except perhaps for Nell Gaither and Johnny Shawnesy. Shawnesy was a poet, a philosophers. And the Perfessor...I consider him one of the great creations of recent American fiction."

"Philosophy and war," I said. "Poetry and bloodshed. Maybe we ought to get the Amazon to read this one."

"The Amazon?" Mr. Stuart said.

"Lifeguard at the pool," Bowman said. "Beautiful, tall, built like Babe Zaharis, opinionated, mean as hell."

"And Bowman's in love with her," I said.

"And she and your buddy O'Toole are at war," Mr. Stuart said.

"That's it," Bowman said. "Political disagreement."

"Well," said Mr. Stuart. "I sort of like your Sparta and Athens bit. You know, during the Civil War someone, I don't remember who, tried to get Lincoln to settle the thing by starting a war with Spain or France, or one of those countries. I don't remember which one. Get us to unite against a common enemy, you know. He refused to do it. But it might have worked. It took the Spanish American War for us to really pull together again as a country."

We prowled around the bookstore for awhile then left, me toting *Raintree County* and Bowman, not to be outdone, having picked up *Atlas Shrugged*, another book about as thick as the Oxford English Dictionary.

"You'll be all summer and fall on that one," I said.

"Here's what we'll do," he said. "We'll go to the Cove. You go one direction, I'll go the other. When we get hungry, we get something to eat. Then we pick up some beer, head back to the Cove, and discuss what we've read."

"I love it when someone plans my life for me," I said, "particularly when it's someone who wants to leave a job as a lifeguard for a job as a mechanic."

"Just thinking, Mill. Good grief! Can't a man think anymore?"

But it wasn't a bad plan. It was better than anything I could come up with. So we did it.

Parenthetically, allow me to say that *Raintree County* and *Atlas Shrugged* were another two of the revelatory documents that made the Greek Summer what it turned out to be. I don't know how many people read either of these nowadays, though librarians assure me that Ayn Rand's books are checked out most of the time. I don't know that I would have cared to use either of them in the philosophy classes I taught at the university; neither book could be called philosophy in a formal sense; but I know what both books did for us, young and vulnerable as we might have been. It didn't take us two months to read them either. In about a week each of us had read his book and was trading out with the other, and for weeks thereafter, for years really, we discussed the ideas we found there.

I digress. But what is life, after all, without a little digression now and then?

While reading *Raintree County* at the Cove, and as I paused between chapters, or between thoughts, to consider what I had been reading, I came up with a plan to get the Amazon and the Earthquake to reconcile. Translated: I came up with a common enemy. Thus, Bowman and I knew we had struck the mother lode, when he, while reading *Atlas Shrugged*, came up with more or less the same idea. We saw it as clear as day, as clear as ever did Archimedes prior to his cry of, "*Eureka!*"

The common enemy was the United States Navy.

"How's the book going, Mill?" Bowman asked.

We had gone down to a hamburger place for a little sustenance.

"Great. It's like a history and philosophy lesson all rolled up into one. Talk about young Greeks! How's yours?"

"Let's put it this way, if the Amazon were anything like Dagny Taggert, wild horses couldn't drag me away from her."

"I know how to solve our problem," I said.

"So do I," he answered.

"We'll get the Navy after them."

"Exactly," he said. "How did you know?"

"It came to me in a flash. Give me a place to stand, and I will move the world."

"So how do you plan to get the Navy after them?"

"Well, we have to get Chief Crouch in on it; and Hopewell; and maybe even Commander Stanford."

"You had me with you up until now," he said. "Why do we have to get them in on it?"

"The way I see it is this. These two are bad for morale. Bad morale translates into non-attention. Non-attention translates into someone drowning and no one even noticing. We're a team, but you can't be a team when some of the members are pulling in opposite directions."

"Okay, I'm with you," Bowman said. "But I still don't see why Crouch and Stanford need to be in on it."

"How would you do it?"

"Real simple. An anonymous letter."

"An anonymous letter? A letter to who? Saying what?"

"Not to Chief Crouch," Bowman said. "I'm not even sure he can read at this point. We send it to Commander Stanford, and we make it from an irate mother."

"Bowman," I said, "for one of the clearest thinking guys I've ever known, you can be real hare-brained without half trying. An anonymous letter from an irate mother. And what is this letter going to say?"

"Something like this. I will never bring my children to your pool again, and I will urge all other parents to boycott the pool. My children were swimming there the other day, and one of them nearly drowned while this one fat lifeguard and the tall woman were arguing with each other. Either get rid of both of them, or…"

"Now just a minute, Bowman. Just a damn minute. That's all an absolute lie."

"Of course it is," he said. "That's just precisely the point. The two of them are accused of something they both know is a lie, and they have to pull together to defend themselves against it. Then we chime in and defend them, and by the time it's over, we're all friends again."

Something in the way I was looking at him made it obvious that I didn't like his solution.

"So give me your answer," he said.

"We go to the Chief and Commander Stanford, on the q.t., and we tell them what's going on. We make it clear that we don't want anything to happen to either O'Toole or the Amazon, but they're just about to drive us nuts. We get them to go along with us. They tell the Amazon that she's about to be fired, and they tell the Earthquake that he's on the raggedy edge of going back to the squadron."

"But for what reason?"

"There's been a complaint."

"A complaint by who? One of us? Now they pull together, but they hate our guts. How are we any better off?"

"No. They don't tell them who the complaint's from."

"So I have an anonymous letter, and you have an anonymous complaint. Both ways we use a lie for the greater good. How is your plan better than mine?"

It seems odd now, many years later and hundreds of miles away, thinking about the incident in the comfort of my study, an aging philosophy professor surrounded by the many books he has collected in his one-way trip through life; but odd as it may seem, it is the truth. The longer we talked, the more Bowman's plan made sense to me. In fact, it seemed a strategy worthy of Patton or MacArthur. I had only one concern.

"What if Stanford does nothing with the letter?" I asked. "What if he reads it, thinks it's from a crank, and just throws it away?"

"Think I hadn't thought of that, huh, Miller?" Bowman said, grinning in a most self-satisfied manner. "He ain't gonna throw it away because we're going to send a copy to our congressman."

"Nah." I shouted, waving my hands. "Nah!" throwing my half-eaten hamburger back on the plate. "You start to make some sense, then you deviate into silliness. You want to get a cast of thousands involved, including Congress?"

"Act like you've got some brains, Mill," he said. "We're not going to send anything to Congress. We're going to send the letter to Stanford, and down at the bottom we're going to show copies going to Congress, and whoever."

Of all the stupid things Bowman and I ever did—and we did many—this has to be ranked among the top five or six. It never occurred to either of us that our chessmen couldn't be manipulated about on life's great chessboard in our pre-planned manner, that having minds of their own they might go shooting off in an unforeseen direction.

Amazon, if you're out there and reading this, believe me, we never meant any harm. Earthquake, if you are at all aware of what's going on, believe me, we never meant any harm.

Oh, and to Chief Crouch and Commander Stanford and Mr. Greybow—sorry about that.

Chapter 12

▼

Epistole Adelphon

Paulos desmios Christou Iesou, kai Timotheos ho adelphos, Philemoni to agapeto kai sunergo hemon.

—Paul and Timothy to Philemon, ca. a.d. 66

I can't believe you have no better control over your lifeguards than to endanger a child's life like this.

—Bowman and Miller to Stanford, a.d. 1960

Something stinks around here, and it ain't the plumbing. I'm beginning to feel like I have unseen enemies, or an enemy. It must be the Amazon. Vicious, vindictive bitch! I leave her alone. Why can't she leave me alone?

—The Diary of Earthquake O'Toole

Perry Como used to have a variety show on television, way back when, and at one point he would sing songs that people had written in and requested. "Letters," an off camera chorus would sing, "letters, we get stacks and stacks of letters." And I'm sure they did. Como was a popular singer in his day. And I imagine that Congress, and the President, and the Pope, and Commander Stanford all got stacks and stacks of letters that summer. I don't believe, however that any of them got a letter that caused as much consternation in his own little world as did our letter to Commander Stanford.

After we had agreed on our plan and had returned to Miramar, we immediately began thinking of what we would say in our letter and how we would say it. We rejected the idea of a typewritten letter as too obviously contrived. We wanted actual cursive letters, made in actual ink, by an actual woman. We couldn't write the letter, of course; it would be too easy to spot our handwriting. In fact, we couldn't even tell someone else what to write; it would be too easy to pick up on our manner of speaking. Imagine an old Bowman-ism such as, "Why, that's the craziest damn thing I ever heard," getting slipped in there. The cops would come to us like homing pigeons. We got this friend of Bowman's, a girl he knew from college (name withheld in case the statute of limitations on chicanery hasn't yet expired), to do the writing, and we just gave her a general idea and let her put it into her own words. She wrote about three letters, each of them on lined notebook paper, before she came up with one that satisfied us. And at the bottom, after signing, "a well meaning dependent mother," she wrote, "P.S., I am sending a copy of this to my congressman, my senator, and to the local newspaper editor."

We put the letter into an envelope, also addressed by hand, and with no return address, and mailed it from the downtown post office. We swore our female conspirator to secrecy, telling her that the last person we knew of who had done something like this and talked about it had come down with a mysterious venereal disease.

What a plan! We were so proud of ourselves, without even bothering to wonder whether or not the letter would have the desired effect. Of course it would. Bowman said it would, and I agreed.

One thing I will say—we were partially right. The letter got swift action. As I remember it, we mailed the letter on a Friday evening. On Monday morning, Stanford showed up, spent an hour or so with Chief Crouch behind the closed office door, then came out looking grim and angry. In his right hand, clutched like it were a top secret plan to invade Romania, was our letter.

"This is it," said the Chief after Commander Stanford had left. "I'm taking to the bottle again if it harelips the governor. How much is a guy supposed to stand for?"

And the summonses began. One after another Stanford dragged us over to his office, trying to find out who the anonymous letter writer was. When I meekly suggested that we take the letter seriously by considering the possibility that it came from an irate mother, he simply erupted.

"Congress! Newspapers! Well, there's no doubt about who the guilty party is. It's that fat little bastard O'Toole."

"But sir, the letter says a woman and a fat lifeguard." I was being obsequious nearly to the groveling point. "Maybe Miss Greybow is the problem."

"Miss Greybow!" he shouted. "Miss Greybow!" We were in his office, behind closed doors. His voice vibrated the windows. "I'll have you know, Miller, that Miss Greybow got this job because her father is one of my closest friends. I have known the young lady all her life. When I say it was O'Toole, I mean it was O'Toole. And I don't need to be corrected by a seaman who's not dry behind the ears."

"No, sir," I mumbled.

"Now," he said. "Do you have any idea what's going on?"

"Well," I said. "All I know is that one evening we all got into this discussion about the convention in Los Angeles, and Miss Greybow and Earth…and O'Toole disagreed about Kennedy. The Ama…a…Miss Greybow really got mad, and they've been mad at each other ever since. But I don't know about this other stuff. I can't believe they almost let a kid drown."

"I talked to Chief Crouch," he said. "His brain's so embalmed he hardly knows what day it is. Hell, he's not even sure what a swimming pool is. Then I got Miss Greybow over here, and she left in tears. O'Toole is next. I'll get the facts out of him if I have to run him head first into the bulkhead."

I was glad, beyond measure, that O'Toole was the next one hauled up before the Commander, because it gave me a chance to talk to Bowman before he, Bowman, went over there. But it turned out I couldn't talk to him anyway. The Amazon had quit, cleaned out her locker, packed her few belongings, shot the finger in the general direction of O'Toole, and slamming her car door so hard that we could hear the sound all the way out to the high board, roared off in a cloud of dust, never to be seen by any of us again. Then O'Toole went over to Commander Stanford's office, and that left three of us to watch an olympic-size swimming pool and a chief petty officer who definitely needed watching. I sat on the mid-pool tower. Hopewell was down on the shallow end. Bowman walked the perimeter.

"Bowman, we need to talk," I told him as he passed by the tower.

"We damned sure do," he responded. But he had to keep moving.

"This ain't coming off the way I thought," I said as he passed me the second time.

"You wouldn't kid me now, would you?"

This is the way our conversation went, two or three sentences at a time as he passed the tower, and in between these snatches of conversation there were the usual episodes of whistle blowing and threats.

"Get that Coke out of the pool, kid."

"You lost your contact lens and want us to do what? Swim underwater and look for it? What are you, some kind of nut?"

"Bowman, the Commander and the Amazon's old man are friends, and…Hey, you, pull your trunks back up. This ain't a nudist colony."

"Her old man. You mean her father?"

"That's what he said."

"Great. I guess they were aboard the Yorktown together with Chief Crouch."

Well, guess what. It turned out that Luther Greybow had been aboard the Yorktown with Stanford and Crouch when the Japanese dive bombed it at the Coral Sea. We didn't know it at the time, and Bowman thought he was making a joke, but in the long run, it was anything but a joke. The Amazon had gotten the job at the pool on the basis of suck, pure and simple. It was not that she wasn't qualified, and not that she didn't do the job well; but none of that had figured in her being hired. Her father was a friend of the skipper, and Stanford had already demonstrated in Chief Crouch's case that friendship cut pretty deep with him.

"Bowman," I said later, in one of our passing exchanges, "if it comes out that we wrote that letter, we are on our way to the Russian Front."

"Or whatever Front the Navy uses," he said.

Two hours later the Earthquake came back, looking grim and beaten, like Sisyphus must have when he was first told what his eternal punishment would be. Hopewell, Bowman and I were starving, having had no lunch breaks, no breaks of any kind, and fighting down rising panic in that warm California sun.

Hopewell was next.

Chief Crouch brought sandwiches and cokes out to us.

"Lawsy me, Miss Scarlet," I said. "I ain't never birthed no baby."

Bowman wasn't amused. "If we get caught," he said, "you'll think Atlanta got off easy."

We made it through that day, though how we managed it is, along with where elephants go to die, one of the world's great mysteries. We shut down the pool. We locked the front doors and gathered in the office in darkening shadow and beatific silence. It was Chief Crouch who finally spoke.

"I'm done for," he said. His hands shook, and I knew right then that his days on the wagon were numbered.

"Why?" Bowman said. "You didn't do anything."

"None of us did anything," the Earthquake said.

"Miss Greybow thinks one of us did," the Chief said, and he looked right at the Earthquake. "So does Commander Stanford."

"Well, don't look at me," said the Earthquake. "I saw the letter. I sat right there in front of Commander Stanford and wrote out the letter for him. Part of it anyway. Just to show him that it's not my handwriting."

"It's more than that," said the Chief. "I never told any of you this. I was told to keep it quiet. But I'm gonna tell you now. Luther Greybow, Betty Ann's father, is an old friend of ours. He and Stanford and I were aboard ship together. He didn't want his daughter hanging around a bunch of sailors. He entrusted her to me. I was supposed to keep an eye on her."

It occurred to me that it's hard to keep an eye on anything when you're staring through a bottle of Jim Beam. But I said nothing.

"Stanford says he's having the letter dusted for finger prints," the Earthquake said.

I looked quickly to Bowman, then away. I don't know about him, but that news hit me like a strong emetic, and I swallowed hard to keep my meager lunch down.

It was Earthquake, bless his fat little heart, who dragged me back from the abyss by saying, "That's stupid, though. I touched the letter in Stanford's office. Had my hands all over it. Of course my finger prints are on it. What's that prove."

"Same here," I said.

"Yeah," Bowman said.

Hopewell said, "Let 'em dust. My finger prints damn sure ain't on it."

"Mine neither," said the Chief. "Stanford never even showed me the letter. Well, what the hell. We're now one lifeguard short, and we can't replace her this late in the game. I had three different ships shot out from under me in the Pacific, and that was fun and games compared with this. I'm ruined with Stanford and Greybow."

"Why are you?" Bowman asked. "So someone writes a crank letter. Why is that your fault?"

I finally found my voice, and in as persuasive a tone as I could muster said, "Stanford's making a mountain out of a mole hill. What's an anonymous letter? He should just treat it as some sort of sophomorish prank."

"He's a politician," said Crouch. "Always been that way. Doesn't want anything on his record that even looks like a blemish. A copy of the letter went to Congress and a local newspaper. It wouldn't mean a thing to me, but it does to him. And I can guarantee you that it'll mean something to Luther Greybow when his daughter comes in and tells him she was forced to resign…"

"That's a damn lie," said the Earthquake. "She wasn't forced to do anything. She just got mad and quit."

The Chief moaned and shook his head.

So there it was, a fiasco of the first water, created by two well-meaning fellows who had not yet experienced the truth of Robert Burns's line about mice and men, and how their plans often go haywire. Burns, of course, said it with more eloquence than I just did.

We left the pool that evening, all four of us walking together, and O'Toole doing all the talking. Hopewell seemed bored with life and with Stanford's political woes, thus demonstrating for all the world that either he had nothing to do with the offending letter or he was the world's coolest liar. Bowman and I tried to swagger along with a measure of Hopewell's confidence, but I for one was scared to death. The Earthquake—well, that's another story. He was neither quietly confident, nor was he fearfully subdued, he was obnoxiously angry.

"Tell me I wrote some stupid letter. Hell's fire! If I'd written the damn thing, I would have signed my name to it. Stanford and the Amazon's old man don't scare me any. Hell, I've got half a mind to write a letter to my congressman."

"Attaboy, Earthquake," Hopewell said. "Whatever you do, don't you dare have brains enough to lay low and let the thing blow over. Yessiree, Bob! Get out there and create an incident that will have 'em talking for years."

"Don't encourage him, Hopewell," I said.

"Why not?" Hopewell asked. "Retreat straight ahead, that's what my uncle used to say."

"Mine used to say," Bowman said, "that stupidity is its own reward."

"I'm writing my congressman," said the Earthquake.

"Earthquake," I said. "I don't recall ever hearing in history that someone figured out how to crucify himself. But I believe you're about to turn the trick—and pierce your own side while you're hanging up there."

"Ahhhh!" he snorted, waving toward me with utter disgust.

That night in the barracks, long after the lights were out and I had fallen into a fitful sleep (it must have been around two o'clock in the morning), someone shook me. It was Bowman.

"Mill," he whispered. "Wake up, Mill. We have to talk."

I had been having this goofy dream in which the Earthquake was hanging on a cross and the Amazon and Stanford were down at his feet shaking dice over his jock strap. "Just a sacrificial lamb," the Earthquake was saying. "Get me a typewriter and some paper. President Lincoln will hear about this."

"Go away, Bowman," I said. "Can't you see I'm in the midst of starting a new religion."

"Come on. Wake up."

"For crying out loud," I said, and threw back my blanket.

"Quiet. Let's go downstairs."

We walked through the darkness. Someone was snoring. Someone else snorted and shifted in his bunk. We crept downstairs to the lounge and sat on a couch that had needed re-upholstering long before we'd arrived at Miramar. I yawned, reached into my skivvies and scratched my privates.

"This is a helluva mess," Bowman said.

"We're not in any trouble," I said. "We can't be. No one knows who sent the letter, except for us and your friend. There's no way we can be tied to it."

"The question is, do we let the Earthquake take the fall?"

"Yeah, I know." I stuck up three fingers in the Boy Scout salute. "A scout is trustworthy, loyal, etcetera, etcetera."

"So what are we gonna do?"

"Lie like the good Boy Scouts we are and let him take the fall, I guess. Unless you have a better plan."

We sat in the darkness, dumb, breathing through our teeth.

"I can't do it, Mill," he finally said.

"We lied about the card game," I said.

"Yeah, and I didn't like that. But, that was to save our own asses when we were really guilty. We've got a buddy in the sling, and we know he's innocent."

"We're the only ones who'll ever know."

"That's just the problem. If no one ever knows, we will. I can't do it."

"I can't either," I said. "But I have a feeling there's no mercy in this particular court. We go in there and prostrate ourselves before the tribunal, and it's over the hill to the poor house."

"Then I guess that's the way it is. Dear Mom, I won't be home for Christmas for the next few years. I'm busting rocks on a Georgia chain gang. Your loving son, Bruce."

"Think, Bowman," I said. "There's got to be a way to resolve this short of ritual disembowelment."

"I'm waiting to hear what it is," he said.

"Look, we know that Congress and the newspapers aren't going to be around to check on us, because they don't know a thing about it. Right?"

"Right."

"So the main problem is that we've upset the Amazon, and she quit, and now Stanford and Crouch think they've let her old man down. Right."

"Right."

"So you and the Amazon have swapped several gallons of saliva. She's got to have some emotional attachment to you. Call her up and talk her into coming back, and maybe it'll go away."

"All right," he said. "I'll do it. First thing in the morning."

"But don't tell her we wrote the letter. That's our ace in the hole. We don't play that one until it's showdown time."

"But if it comes to it I'm confessing. I won't say you had anything to do with it. It was my idea after all."

"That is a definite 'no.' If you go, we both go."

"Tomorrow, I call the Amazon."

"Maybe I'll call Maggie. It can't hurt to grease all the wheels on the wagon."

At about nine o'clock the following morning, I called Maggie from the phone in the pool's reception area. A woman answered the phone.

"Ama...a, Betty Ann," I said.

"This is Mrs. Greybow."

"Is Maggie there, Mrs. Greybow?"

"Who?"

"Oh...a...Mary Alice?"

"I think she's still in bed...No, wait, here she is. Mary, telephone."

"Who is it?" a voice in the background asked.

"Doug Miller," I said, without waiting for Mrs. Greybow to ask me.

"Miller," said Mrs. Greybow. "I want you to know that Betty Ann cried herself to sleep last night."

"Give me the phone, mom," I heard Maggie say. Then, "Miller, I don't get any of this. Betty Ann and I were up half the night last night. I was just listening, you know. But what is happening? She thinks Earthquake wrote this crappy letter."

"It wasn't the Earthquake," I said.

"How do you know?"

I hesitated, realizing that I had almost given us away. "He says he didn't," I said. "And I believe him."

"I wouldn't believe anything he told me."

"Maggie," I said, "the Amazon is over-reacting to all this. I don't think anything will come of it at all."

"She says Commander Stanford is treating it like a major felony or something. And my dad is furious."

"Maggie...Aw, look, Maggie. The whole thing is just a misunderstanding. We need the Amazon to come back. And what about you and me? I never told you this, but I really am crazy about you."

"Miller," she said, "I think you and Bowman are about the two neatest guys I ever met. And Betty Ann really likes Bowman. I mean she really likes him. But she says she hopes she never sees either of you again."

"Let's get together," I said. "Just you and me. We can't let something this silly..."

"It's not silly to us."

"Maggie," I said. "Tonight. Pick me up and let's go somewhere."

"I can't, Miller. I'm going up to San Luis Obispo to stay with my aunt for the rest of the summer. Then I don't know what I'm going to do. I just got word that USC has accepted me for the fall semester."

I never felt lower.

"If Bowman calls the Amazon," I finally said, "will she talk to him?"

"I don't know," she said.

"He's gonna call her."

"Maybe she'll talk to him. She really likes him. She likes you too, but she loves Bowman."

"Will she talk to me?"

"I don't know."

"Is she awake?"

"Yes. But she's still in bed. Crying. There's a phone in our bedroom. Hang on a minute."

There was silence for what seemed an age, then static, then the receiver being lifted, and a groggy voice:

"Hello, Miller."

"Amazon," I said. "This business is killing me."

"What do you think it's done to me?"

"Ah, my sweetheart," I said. "My queen of hearts. Don't you realize that I might be your brother-in-law someday?"

"You and Mary Alice will forget each other by this time next year," she said.

"Well, I might be your husband, then."

"Wrong girl, wrong place, wrong time," she said.

"Listen," I said. "Bowman is just as upset as I am. He's gonna call you later. Talk to him, Amazon. Just talk to him."

"I'll talk to him," she said.

"I've got to go, my angel, my jewel in heaven's crown."

She chuckled. "Goodbye, Miller."

"Goodbye. But let's not let it be for long. Oh, and by the way, I know the Earthquake didn't write that letter."

"That means you know who did."

"I didn't say that. But I know it wasn't the Earthquake."

"Oh, Miller," she said, and she started crying and hung up.

About the time I was hanging up, Bowman wandered in from the men's locker room, looking as sad as I've seen him look.

"I called Maggie," I said.

"Oh," he said.

"I'm in love with her," I said.

"Oh," he said.

"I talked to the Amazon."

He said nothing, only looked at me. I couldn't tell if he were glad or angry.

"She wants to talk to you," I said.

"Okay," he said. "I'm gonna call her. But this is like walking out to the wall before a firing squad."

"This woman loves you, Bowman," I said. "Marry her, and I'll marry Maggie, and we'll all be one happy family."

"Keep spinning your dreams, Mill," he said. "One of these days, you'll spin us both right over a cliff."

"Well, I hope I'm dreaming right now," I said. "Because if this ain't a nightmare, I don't ever want to see one."

He didn't call until that evening after the pool had closed. He said he needed privacy, and that the phones at the pool were about as private as the evening newscast. There was a pay phone booth in the barracks, and he took a handful of coins, went into it, and stayed for over a hour, while I sat watching TV in the lounge.

When he came out, he said, "I'm going over to the base movie."

"The movie's already started," I said.

"So, I'll go in late. You coming?"

"Yeah," I said. "I guess so."

The movie was *The Apartment*. Jack Lemmon was good, but Shirley MacLaine wasn't my type, and the whole plot seemed contrived and silly to me. We got in about the time Fred MacMurray had started using Lemmon's apartment for his trysts with Shirley MacLaine, and I couldn't see what the big deal was because if

I'd been Lemmon, I'd have just told him to take a flying leap, even if he was my boss. At least I kept telling myself that's what I'd do, and I told Bowman the same thing after we left.

"Yeah," he said. "Too bad we missed the cartoon. I'll bet it was a Tom and Jerry."

"So what did the Amazon tell you?"

"It ain't what she told me. It's what I told her. I told her that I wrote the letter."

"Oh no you don't Bowman," I said. "No you don't. You're not buying the farm for this one. I said if one goes, we all go."

"So, call her up and tell her you were in on it with me."

"That's exactly what I'm gonna do. But right now I'm more interested in how she reacted to it."

"She said you told her that O'Toole didn't write the letter, and that she asked how you knew, and you got real uncommunicative and just said you knew, that was all."

"So now she knows how I knew. But now that she knows what we know, how does she feel about what we all know?"

"Not good. But at least she listened to me. I expected her to hang up on me. I tried to tell her what our plan was, how noble our motives were, all that cheap crap."

"And she listened."

"Yeah, she listened. Then I told her I loved her."

"Do you love her?"

"Not actually, but you know how women are. They like to hear that kind of stuff."

"I thought you were going to say something about all that cheap crap."

"I caught myself in mid-sentence."

"So is she coming back to the pool?"

"She said she wasn't. Said she couldn't work with the Earthquake anymore."

"But the Earthquake didn't write the letter."

"She just doesn't want to be around him."

"Well, Bowman," I said. "It looks to me like we are still in deep trouble. She'll call Stanford tomorrow and turn state's evidence…"

"She said she wouldn't. She said she knows we did it for what we thought were good reasons. Oh, and she said it was lucky I called and told her the truth. She was getting ready to hire a private eye…"

"Oh, my aching…You've gotta be kidding me. A private eye! Man, you'd think we tried to break into Fort Knox or something."

"Well, anyway, we'll see what happens."

We came to the street that ran between rows of barracks and terminated at the great, gray mess hall. Off in the distance the hangers were lighted up and pilots were logging night flight time.

"So what do you think?" I asked. "Are we dead or alive?"

"Right now," Bowman answered, "I'd say we're sort of in Never-never Land. Tomorrow, I guess we'll find out if we need an undertaker and six pall bearers."

Chapter 13

▼

Zoe Mou, Sas Agapo

We lay at night on the rocks at La Jolla Cove amid the litter of empty beer cans, two aging and only slightly bewildered philosophers, the immense, starry heavens stretching above us, laughing and singing songs about letters.

I sang, "Love Letters in the Sand."

"Thought I'd write and drop a line," Bowman began. I joined him. "The weather's good, the folks are fine, I'm in bed each night at nine. P.S., I love you."

"Love letters straight from the heart," I began. Bowman didn't know that one.

"It was in this movie," I said. "*Love Letters.* Jennifer Jones and Joseph Cotton. Sort of a Cyrano de Bergerac thing."

"I'm gonna sit right down and write myself a letter," Bowman began, and trailed off into a series of "La-la-las."

"Write me a letter," I sang, "send it by mail…"

"Send it in care of the Birmingham jail," Bowman responded.

"You know what I'd like to do," I said. "I'd like to look up the Amazon and Maggie."

"Miller," he said, "you're drunk."

"Of course I am," I said. "Do you think I'd come up with such a preposterous notion if I weren't. I'll tell you one thing," I said. "I'll bet you that to this very day, she'd like to see the two of us drawn and quartered."

"Well," said Bowman. "Everything was going fine until Earthquake O'Toole got into the mix."

"Got into it, nothing," I said. "He was never out of it."

"Yeah, but that lawsuit bit."

"You know," I said, "if we ever needed any proof of the power of the written word, the letter did it for us. Like I said that night coming home from the movies, you'd have thought we tried to break into Fort Knox."

"It was nip and tuck for awhile there," Bowman said. "I used to wake up in the morning and look around to see if I was surrounded by a posse. That damned O'Toole...We should have taken him out to sea and set him adrift. Talk about not knowing when to let well enough alone."

"I remember going into the pool that morning," I said, "and getting the news about the Amazon. Boy, it was like a weight off my shoulders—for about ten minutes."

The four of us came in together—all that was left now of the Starboard Section—and began our day as we always did, by changing into our bathing suits and going out to pool side. I dived into the pool and swam a quick two-hundred yards, then lay on the concrete at pool side and let the morning sunshine slant over me. Bowman was stretched in a beach chair under an umbrella reading *Raintree County*, which I had recently passed to him. The radio was on, Sam Cooke was singing, and Hopewell was dancing down on the shallow end and mouthing the words. The Earthquake was somewhere, sulking no doubt.

About the time I was feeling fairly decent, I heard voices across the pool, turned my head that direction and saw that Commander Stanford and Chief Crouch had come out of the reception area and were talking near the office. All at once Stanford began shaking his head, threw up his hands, turned on his heel and walked out.

"Bowman," Chief Crouch called, "come here."

What now, I thought. I lay back and closed my eyes, the fear coming back up in my throat. Crouch didn't sound angry, however, only a bit puzzled.

I heard low voices, and then Bowman: "The hell, you say! Why that the craziest damn thing I ever heard. Hey, Mill, bring your miserable self over here."

"If it's curtains, just tell me," I shouted back.

"Come here. Boy, if I ever get out of this chicken outfit I'm gonna get a job in a lunatic asylum."

I got up and walked around to where the two of them stood.

"Tell him, Chief," Bowman said.

"The mystery of the letter is cleared up," said the Chief. "Betty Ann Greybow called Stanford this morning and confessed that she sent the thing herself."

"Why, that's the craziest damn thing I ever heard," I said.

"That's my line," Bowman said.

I looked at Bowman. He looked at me.

Crouch, who hadn't the vaguest idea what was going on, said, "Okay. Well, I guess that clears that up."

"Why did she do it?" Bowman asked. I thought he meant, why did she confess to writing the letter, but Crouch obviously thought he meant (What else could he have thought, given his ignorance of what had gone on?), why did she write the letter?

"Women," the Chief said. "I'll never figure them out. She said she thought we weren't doing our jobs, and that bringing it to the attention of Stanford would kick us into line. Well, the doors open in thirty minutes. Everything ready?"

Bowman nodded.

Crouch went back into the office and left the two of us standing there.

"Bowman," I said.

"Miller," he replied.

"If you don't call her right now I will."

"I'll call her all right. Just as soon as I get a break."

"Is she coming back?"

"How would I know? Crouch didn't say she was."

"Well, if not," I said, "then here we are. The fabulous four. Left to fend for ourselves for the rest of a long, hot summer."

"I guess this means," he said, "that O'Toole is back in charge of our section."

"That makes me simply ecstatic," I said.

Bowman walked the perimeter of the pool for the first shift, which put him off duty at eleven o'clock, and he went immediately to the front desk. He would rather have called from the office, but that was the exclusive domain of Chief Crouch, and privacy there was out of the question. I had rotated through the two towers and was walking the perimeter before Bowman came into the pool area and climbed up on the mid-pool tower. When I walked past him, I said:

"So, what news do you bring, Hippocrates?"

"It's too crazy for words," he said. "I can't tell you now. It takes too long. But the Amazon is definitely not coming back."

And that is where matters stood all that day, until we had finally driven the last bathers and sun worshippers off the Acropolis and into the world below. Then we couldn't get rid of the Earthquake. He insisted on hanging around and airing his ongoing grievance against the Amazon, Commander Stanford, the Navy, and whatever Fates were in charge of his bewildering existence.

Bowman finally said, "Look, Earthquake, Mill and I need to talk in private."

"Oh, I'm not invited, huh?" the Earthquake said. "You two bums are probably in on it with her."

"Think what you want," Bowman said, "but Miller and I are leaving right now. We're going to the barracks, and we're gonna find a quiet corner, and we're going to talk together."

"Well, while you're talking," he said, "talk about this. This business doesn't end here. If that tall, athletic slut thinks she can defame the name of O'Toole and get away with it, she's got another think coming."

"What are you gonna do?" I asked. "Challenge her to a duel?"

"I'll do more than that. You'll see."

"Let's go, Mill," Bowman said.

We left, with the Earthquake trailing along after us, talking to himself about his good name, and his position in the Navy, and how he demanded the respect due a third-class petty officer and a defender of his country.

Over at the mess hall, we came in for a late supper. We were always late for supper when we were on duty, but the cooks all knew us, and took care of us, saving back some of the better stuff. It worked out well. The mob had always eaten and gone by the time we arrived, and we stuffed ourselves with chow which was good, but which we managed to constantly complain about. Hopewell was there ahead of us, the Earthquake was still tagging along, and the four of us loaded up the metal trays which are as much a part of Navy life as ships and ropes. We sat at the end of one of the long tables, reviewing the strange events of the day as much as we could. Hopewell and the Earthquake were, of course, in the dark about what had really happened, as were Chief Crouch and Commander Stanford.

Bowman and I finally excused ourselves and went off to look for a quiet corner, leaving Hopewell alone with the Earthquake. But not for long, I wager, because Hopewell wasn't the type to put up with too much nonsense, and the Earthquake was still complaining about how he had been slandered, and how that miserable, castrating slut hadn't heard the last of him.

Bowman and I walked back over to the pool and sat on a stone bench in the park across the street. It was dark and quiet, except for crickets and whatever other critters were screeching away out there. Bowman said that the crickets made more sense than most of the people he'd talked to that day.

"Would you like to fill me in on what you heard from the Amazon?" I said.

"It's not gonna make much sense to you," he said. "I'm still trying to figure it out myself. She said she realized that we—you and me—could get into a bunch of trouble about the letter. So she covered for us. The Navy can't do anything to her, and she doesn't intend to come back, so she…"

"So she becomes the sacrificial lamb instead of laying it on the Earthquake. Well, how noble and uplifting."

"You don't like it."

"I think it stinks. It's no different than if we'd let the Earthquake take the heat. Just a different person cast as the sacrifice. Brother, of all the slimy things I ever did in my life, this has got to be the lowest."

"I told her we weren't going to let her do it," Bowman said. "So she started crying again and went off into something about friendship and giving of oneself, and a lot of Sunday School stuff like that."

"Did you ever see *The Razor's Edge*?"

"Will you stop with the movies and books, Mill. This is serious."

"No, listen to me. This guy Larry is going to marry a lush named Sophie, and Isabel tries to stop him. So Somerset Maugham tells her she's wasting her time, because Larry is caught up in the most powerful emotion anyone can experience, self sacrifice, or something like that. Sounds to me like that's what our girl Friday is doing."

"Well, isn't that what we were doing?" Bowman said. "I almost felt decent. I was going to walk in there and confess, then walk out to the wall, heels together, no handkerchief if you please, and face the rifles. Down our hero goes into the dust, with a slight smile playing about his lips, and the old tri-color waving over him."

"You're a hopeless romantic."

"Me! What about you? *The Razor's Edge*. Well, play me hearts and flowers, maestro. You know what we really are? We're a couple of cowards, for all our hot-shot ideas and slick talk."

"All right. So we're a couple of cowards. But I'll keep it a secret if you will.

We sat in silence for awhile, Bowman leaning back against a tree under which the stone bench had been placed by some thoughtful sailor, me leaning forward, elbows on knees, hands folded, studying the ground between my feet.

"Does it occur to you," I finally said, "that we have painted ourselves into the old proverbial corner? Anything we do is gonna be wrong. If we confess, they shoot us and the Amazon hates us for not allowing her to play Saint Bernadette. If we don't confess, then we go through life knowing that when the chips were down, we showed yellow. And to make matters worse, there's another party to consider."

"Who's that?"

"The Earthquake."

"Oh, yeah. I forgot about him."

"Try to remember," I said. "Think real hard. It hasn't been thirty minutes ago that we heard him breathing out threats and slaughter. I don't know what he has in mind, but as of this moment he thinks the Amazon wrote the letter and tried to sting him on the deal."

"So what's the worst he could do?" Bowman asked. "He's gonna go around complaining for a few days, and when he realizes no one is listening, he'll finally shut up."

"Yeah. As Spencer Tracy said in *Inherit the Wind*, 'We can dare to hope.'"

"Okay, mister movie man. As Harry Morgan said in *Inherit the Wind*, 'I can do more than that.'"

"What are you gonna do, Judge Bowman?" I asked. "Find the Earthquake in contempt of court?"

"I don't know," he said, and we sat there in silence for another ten minutes or so.

"I'm going back to the barracks and going to bed," Bowman suddenly announced.

"If it's all the same to you," I said, "I believe I'll sleep under the bed tonight. Or maybe in the dumpster out at the curb."

"How about out in the sage brush?" Bowman said. "If we're lucky, a snake will come along and bite us."

"With our run of luck, even if it bit us it wouldn't be poisonous."

A snake bite would have been preferable to what we got.

The Earthquake met us at the barracks door. Actually, he was sitting out on the front steps enjoying the evening air and smiling magnificently.

"I knew you guys would be wandering in sooner or later," he said.

"Get out of the way, Earthquake," Bowman said. "I have a prior engagement with the sandman."

"How can you sleep at a time like this, Bowman?"

"Easy, Earthquake. Every time I see you, it makes me want to go into a coma."

"You'll think coma," said O'Toole. "I just got off the phone with a guy I know in San Diego, a legal expert. He says I've got a good case for libel against the Amazon."

Now Bowman and I had already gone up the steps, around the Earthquake, and were about to enter the front door. We did not enter the front door. I stopped and stood, if not like a block of stone, then enough like one that a distant observer might have thought I was. I leaned my head against the barracks wall, sort of like Charlie Brown leans against a tree when life has got him down, and stood, waiting for Bowman to say something, anything, for while something needed to be said, I had no idea what.

"Well," he said. "The jig's up."

I pushed away from the wall and turned around. Bowman had gone back to the steps and was sitting down beside the Earthquake.

"Now you listen to me, you pear-shaped, bald-headed moron," he said. "I don't know who you've been talking to, but if this is the advice he gave you, you'd better get yourself another legal expert. You've got no kind of libel case against the Amazon, because the Amazon didn't write the letter. Mill and I wrote it."

It was dark there on the porch, but even without light, I could have sworn I saw the blood draining from Earthquake's already pale face. He sat with his mouth opened, and for the first time I fully understood why he had been dubbed the Earthquake.

"Anyone home, Earthquake?" I asked.

"You rotten bastards," he said. "My buddies. Thanks, buddies."

"You think we don't feel rotten about it?" Bowman asked.

"Oh," said the Earthquake. "Okay. That makes everything cool. You write a letter that damn near gets me tarred and feathered, you leave me staked out like a piece of raw meat on an ant hill, but you feel rotten about it. How the hell do you think I feel?"

"Would it help any if I explain why we did it?" Bowman asked.

The Earthquake thought a minute, then turned to Bowman as if he were about to explain a rudimentary equation. "No," he said. "No, I don't think it would. As a matter of fact, I think it would make matters worse. I'm sure you both had my good at heart, and why quibble about these bamboo splinters under my finger nails."

"It's hopeless, Bowman," I said. "I'm going out and sleep with the snakes and scorpions."

And I did just that. Well, not exactly. I went back over to the pool alone, climbed the wall, and spent the night on an inflated air mattress some kid had left and had never come back to claim. It wouldn't have been bad sleeping, but the mattress was only about three feet wide, and I kept rolling off onto the concrete. I finally took it over to the lawn so that when I rolled off I wouldn't wind up with lacerations.

The sun came up the next morning, and there I lay, awake and fully clothed in standard Navy dungarees. I had taken off my shoes and socks and left them across the pool with my white hat, near the spot where I had originally alighted.

Why am I here, I wondered; and I immediately answered myself. I was here because I genuinely thought O'Toole was slightly unbalanced, and sleeping in the barracks with him just a few bunks over made me feel vulnerable, something like a naked Englishman at a DAR convention. Something like Hirohito at a gathering of the Pearl Harbor survivors. Something like...

I ran out of similes.

At about eight o'clock the Chief came in. He went straight to the office without even noticing me. About five minutes later he came out, went straight to one of the flower beds, reached behind a shrub, and came out with a bottle of something. It certainly wasn't coke. He had uncapped the bottle, raised it to his lips, and had taken a long swallow before he looked across the pool in the glare of the morning sun and saw me laying there on the air mattress. I had turned onto my side. I waved at him.

"Hell," he shouted. "I must be having d.t.'s again."

"Yeah, here I am, Chief," I said. "Your worst nightmare."

I got up, picked up the air mattress, and walked around the pool to where he stood with his bottle. The concrete was cool and refreshing on my feet.

"What are you doing here?" he asked.

"Spent the night here," I said. "There's a guy over at the barracks who wants to cut my throat."

"Want a drink?" he said, extending the bottle to me.

"Get outta here," I said. "Eight o'clock in the morning."

"It's never too early in the day to uphold Navy tradition," he said. Then he began to sing. "So ear-lye in the morning a sailor likes his bottle-o. Well a bottle of beer, and a bottle of gin, and a bottle of Irish whiskey-o..."

He had a pretty good voice.

"You gave Stanford your word that you would stay on the wagon," I said.

"I gave it my best shot," he said. "The more my mind cleared, the worse the world looked. Anyhow, I don't think Stanford and I are gonna be speaking to each other much. Luther Greybow neither. This letter business has got us all on the outs with one another. Greybow is pissed off at Stanford because his daughter got the old green weeny, and Stanford is pissed off at me because I was supposed to have seen it coming. Now I ask you, Miller, how could I have seen it coming? Hell, up until a few weeks ago, I couldn't see anything. The last thing I remember seeing before that was a kamikaze diving toward our bridge."

"I'm going swimming," I said. "See if I can wake up."

I went into the men's dressing room, stripped, got into the shower, and was just soaping up when Bowman walked in.

"Where have you been?" he asked. "I thought the snakes got you for sure."

"I slept over here last night," I said, shouting over the shower's noise. "On that abandoned air mattress Hopewell's always floating around on."

"Well, I'm going over to see Commander Stanford," he said. "Like right now. I'm gonna put this miserable business to rest once and for all. Are you coming?"

"I thought I was going swimming."

"I'm going to Stanford's office right now, before I succumb to logic and talk myself out of it."

"All right. Wait for me. Man, remind me never to skip breakfast again. I'm starving."

"Get a Snickers out of the candy machine."

We kept razors and toothbrushes in our lockers at the pool, since we used the showers there more than the ones in the barracks, and while I was shaving and brushing my teeth, Bowman hung around in a state of agitation, if not panic. I didn't blame him; I didn't like this confession business any more than he did.

"What do we do?" I asked him as we were walking from the pool over to the building which housed the administrative offices. "Boy, if I had been raised a Catholic, I'd know how to confess and stay alive afterwards."

"We tell the truth."

"And he kicks us out into the San Clemente Strait."

"I don't think so. I think he'll be glad to get the thing resolved."

"He thinks he's got it resolved. He thinks the Amazon wrote the damn thing."

"Yeah, but that won't last long. Earthquake got up this morning, having slept on things, and told me that us writing the letter changed absolutely nothing. The Amazon was the one who tried to tie it to him, and she's still guilty of malicious slander, and he's still gonna sue the bra off her ample chest. Those were his very words."

"Maybe we ought to just get a hit man and have him snuffed. I heard you can get a man killed in Mexico for about twenty-five dollars."

"That's expensive. I know sailors who'll do it for a bottle of bonded bourbon."

When we got to Commander Stanford's office, we wound up waiting for about thirty minutes. His secretary, a bespectacled Wave named Judy Calley, told us that he was busy with something, but Bowman assured me he hadn't showed up yet, that officers drifted in to work at their leisure. If this were true, his office must have had a back entrance, because he didn't come in through the front door. At about nine o'clock Judy's phone rang, she picked it up, said, "Yessir," hung up, and said, "Commander Stanford will see you."

"Kindly notify my next of kin," Bowman told her.

"And tell mom I loved her," I said.

She gave no indication that these comments amused her. She looked at us as if she knew we were guilty of something underhanded, but she couldn't quite put a label on it.

Inside, we both stood at a rigid attention.

"Stand at ease, men," Stanford said. "You're not guarding the tomb of the unknown soldier."

"Well...yessir," Bowman said. "We..."

"Yes, what is it? Believe it or not, I have other things to do."

"Well, sir," he said. "We came to admit that we wrote that letter. I know that the Ama...Betty Ann Greybow said she wrote it. But she didn't. She's just trying to cover for us."

I don't know what sort of reaction I was expecting from the Commander, but I know what I didn't expect. I didn't expect him to do what he did.

"Get back to attention," he said.

"Yessir," Bowman said; and up we popped, ramrod straight, heels clicking together, eyes fixed on the wall behind the desk. Much to my dismay, the picture on the wall at which I found myself staring was the famous one of the Arizona just after the Japanese bombs had hit it.

Commander Stanford had gotten up and walked to the windows behind his desk, and he stood there, his back to us, with his hands clasped behind him. From time to time he unclasped his hands and beat a fist into his open palm.

"You worthless horses asses," he finally said.

I cut my eyes over to Bowman. He was still looking straight ahead.

"I oughta shitcan the whole lot of you," Stanford said.

He turned around, walked around his desk, got right into Bowman's face, and said, his voice low and ominous, "Two days ago I couldn't find anyone at the swimming pool who even knew what a letter was. None of you could have even written the word letter, let alone a letter. Now I've got confessions rolling in from all and sundry. There's hardly a man in uniform who isn't eager to assure me of his guilt. Don't you relax a muscle, Miller!"

My nose had begun to itch, and I was wiggling it to try to get some relief.

Stanford walked back around his desk, sat down, and picked up a piece of paper. I think it was lined and three-hole punched, but it was hard to tell without turning my head to look directly at it, a move which would certainly have gotten me flogged, verbally if not physically.

"This letter came for me today," he said. "Not via the U.S. Mail. No. It was placed in a plain, unmarked envelope, no return address, and slipped under my office door. May I read it to you?"

We said nothing.

"I just asked you a question," Stanford roared. "Can I have the courtesy of a reply? May I read you this letter?"

"Yessir," Bowman said.

"We'd love to hear it, sir," I said.

"Thank you," the Commander said in a hostile whisper. He cleared his throat. "Deer Sur…That's d-e-e-r, like Bambi. And s-u-r. Deer Sur: I wish to cunfess (with a 'u') that I am the one hoo (with an aitch) committed the Jack-the-Ripper killings. Respectfully, Bruce Bowman. P.S., I was aded (no 'i' in aided) by my deer friend, Doug Miller, but I don't think he had his hart (no 'e' in heart) in it. P.S.S. I will not write my congressman becawse I think he is a pervert."

That was it. I couldn't hold it any longer. I exploded with a laugh that rattled the windows.

"You think this is funny, Miller?" Stanford shouted.

"Yessir," I said. "I guess you'll just have to court martial me, because I can't help it."

Then Bowman started laughing. Then salvation came from the most unexpected quarter: Stanford started laughing, and once we all got going, none of us could stop. Judy rapped on the office door, stuck her head inside, humorless as a tree, closed the door, and went back to whatever she'd been doing.

By the time we got ourselves under control and a certain measure of dignity returned to the proceedings, I felt better about things than I had in days.

Chapter 14

The Lords of the Ring

Amazed at the sight, he descended into the opening, where, among other marvels, he beheld a hollow brazen horse, having doors, at which he stooping in saw a dead body of stature, as appeared to him, more than human, and having nothing on but a gold ring; this he took from the finger of the dead and reascended.

—Plato, The Republic, Book II

Well, Mill and Bowman are at it again. I don't understand those guys. Are they for real? Mill thinks this latest stunt of theirs has proved Socrates right and Glaucon wrong. Me, I just think it proves they are both a little bit crazy, which I have thought all along. Unless there is some other reason for what they did. But, damn it, they are both great guys!

—The Diary of Earthquake O'Toole

I guess it was the letter incident, more than anything I can think of in retrospect, that made the Earthquake think of us as his best friends. He simply couldn't get it through his head that someone would confess to something if they didn't have to confess and if the confession might get them into trouble. But more of this later.

Bowman and I left Commander Stanford's office, after he had gotten control of himself, assumed the dignified pose he normally tried to maintain, and told us to get the hell out. If we were lucky, I thought, we had seen the last of him; he never came on the scene without spreading misery and gloom of some sort. Imagine my dismay when within thirty minutes of kicking us out of his office he showed up at the pool and got us all together at the deep end by the diving boards.

"This is it, Mill," Bowman whispered to me. "It's been nice knowing you."

"Maybe it's not goodbye, Bowman," I said. "We might get put in the same cell together."

We had changed into our bathing suits, and we were standing four-strong at attention. Attention is not an easy posture to assume, with a degree of dignity, when one is in a bathing suit, but we did our best. Chief Crouch stood in front of us, saluted the Commander, and said, "All present and accounted for, sir."

The Commander returned the salute.

"Men," said the Commander, "it's a rare thing in my experience when men do the right thing at the risk of causing themselves a great deal of trouble. Bowman and Miller have done the right thing. They confessed that they are the ones who wrote the letter that has caused us all the trouble. Now they didn't have to do this. No one would have known. But they weren't willing to have someone else be blamed for what they did. This is the sort of behavior that deserves commendation, and I think both of them should be publicly thanked. Their actions in writing the letter were foolish, and they know themselves that they shouldn't have done it. But I believe their motives were right, and their behavior in coming forward to take the blame is very refreshing. That's all. I know you have work to do. Keep a good watch on the pool."

The Chief saluted, Stanford returned the salute, and Stanford turned and left.

"All right," said the Chief. "Let's get this show on the road."

Note the informality. Not, "Section, ten-hut! Dismissed!" But rather, "All right, let's get this show on the road."

Strictly non-military, that was Chief Crouch. It made you sort of love him in spite of himself.

No one said much at first. There was little time to say anything, given the looming up of our opening hour and the impending influx of eager bathers. It wasn't really until after the pool had closed that evening that we had a chance to sit down and consider what had happened and the place to which we had been brought—or to which we had brought ourselves.

Hopewell was his usual disassociated, indifferent self, a man never, as I judged him, likely to come down with either hives or ulcers. Life rolled off him the way water rolled away from the bow of ship or wet earth rolled away from the plow. It wasn't that he was stupid or unconscious of what was going on around him, but rather that he was possessed of a magnificent indifference which immunized him against the cares plaguing normal men. He specialized in yawning and looking away to some point about ten degrees over whichever horizon he happened to be facing.

The Earthquake was of another spirit. Life to him was a great cafeteria in which one individual fed upon another, only to become a meal for another. One of his deepest convictions was that he had been wronged, not by some person, but by the invisible hand dealing out life's cards, and for this reason he was justified in doing what was necessary to even things out. He was eaten up, as Scott Fitzgerald confessed to being, by the smoldering hatred of the peasant.

Bowman and I were just a couple of simple dolts. We really believed all the Boy Scout things we had been taught, such as that honesty is always the best policy. To the Earthquake (and probably to Hopewell, as well), we were hopeless infants.

After the pool closed that evening, we went over to the mess hall to eat whatever agglomeration the cooks had foisted upon the fleet for that day. Trays were rattling and men were complaining, and a couple of mess cooks were swabbing the deck not far away.

"Damndest thing I ever saw," the Earthquake said. "Hopewell and I do nothing, and get nothing for our effort. Miller and Bowman screw us up like Hogan's goat on a bad day, and the Commander comes over and commends them. I ask you, is there any justice in the world?"

"You just don't get it, do you Earthquake?" Bowman said.

"Hell yes I get it," said the Earthquake. "Better than either of you guys do. If you want the world on a platter, be an asshole. Thrashy-whatsisname and Glaucon got it right. Socrates was an idiot."

"We couldn't let the Amazon take the blame for what we did," I said.

"Well, you were sure gonna let me take the blame."

"No we weren't," said Bowman.

"Oh, yeah?"

"Earthquake," he said, "I don't expect you to believe this. But you can believe what you want. Miller and I had already made up our minds to go over and tell Stanford the truth, even before the Amazon called in with her so-called confession."

Earthquake sat there for a moment, obviously at a loss for words. Then he turned to me. "Mill, is he lying to me?"

"He's telling you the truth, Earthquake. You don't think we're low enough to let you buy the rap for something we knew you didn't do."

"Aw, shut up," Earthquake said, and his voice broke a bit as he said it. He looked down at his tray, swallowed and coughed, and his shoulders started to shake.

"Earthquake, are you all right?" Hopewell asked.

Hopewell and Bowman were sitting on the opposite side of the table, across from the Earthquake and me. The Earthquake sort of swiveled to the side, fishing in his back pocket as he did, and he came out with a handkerchief and blew his nose, hard.

"Are you all right?" Hopewell asked again.

"Yeah," he said.

He returned his handkerchief to his pocket. He looked up, and I could see that he was crying.

"That's the nicest damn thing anyone ever did for me," he said. He was really having trouble getting the words out. I looked across at Bowman and Hopewell, and I could see both of them were at least as confused as I was.

Forty years later, when Bowman and I were discussing this incident, he asked me what I have asked myself many times: "What kind of jungle must that guy have come out of to say that was the nicest thing anyone had ever done for him? I didn't do it for him. I did it for me."

The evening the Earthquake said this, however, we didn't get a chance to explore the dark closets of his mind, because I had a sudden insight that took us off in another direction.

"Wow!" I said.

"What's up, Mill?" Hopewell asked.

"Wow!" I said.

"What is this?" said Hopewell, "A new language?"

"I just realized something," I said. "Bowman and I proved Socrates right and Glaucon wrong."

"Oh, my aching..." Hopewell let his head fall backward, and rolled it from side to side. "I gotta hand it to you guys. You're never too far from sandals and robes."

"Think about it," I said. "Think about the ring of Guy-jeez. Bowman and I had it on. We were invisible. Glaucon said you do what you can get away with. Well, we could have gotten away with this, but we didn't do it."

Bowman smiled. "You're right, Mill. By damn, you're absolutely right. We were home free. All we had to do was keep that ring turned around backwards."

By this time we had the old Earthquake back with us, suspicious and cynical. He had dried his eyes, squared his shoulders, and taken on that crafty look of an animal getting ready to lead the hounds up a blind alley. No more weeping in the confessional for him.

"I should have seen this coming," he said. "Okay, I appreciate what you guys did; but you don't need to think this qualifies you for a seat in the Vatican."

"Convene the Symposium," I said. "We have to talk about this. Who needs to sit in the Vatican? I'll be satisfied with a seat on the Acropolis with the Greeks."

"No, you don't," Hopewell said. "This philosophy business drives me nuts." He got up, took his tray and started off toward the galley. "Never prove anything," he was saying as he walked off. "Never know what's what. Just questions, questions, questions, and never any answers."

"Hey, you sailors move on out of here," the mess hall master-at-arms called to us. "We gotta shut this place down. Unless you were planning on staying all night and getting an early breakfast."

"What are we having for breakfast?" Bowman asked.

"Beans," one of the cooks shouted. "Navy beans."

"Maybe I'll just skip breakfast in the morning," Bowman said.

"You were hoping for eggs benedict?" said the master-at-arms.

We took our trays back to the galley, and left the mess hall, walking down toward the barracks. As we walked, the Earthquake spun out his theory about what had really been going on in Bowman's twisted soul, and in mine.

"You really confessed because you got caught," he said. "You weren't invisible. The ring of Guy-jeez is lost somewhere over in Greece."

"Who caught us?" I asked. "We were home free. But right is right and wrong is wrong. Just like Socrates said. Justice is one of those eternal things up in the world of ideas, and we had to do the right thing whether we could get away with doing wrong or not."

"No, you got caught," the Earthquake insisted.

"You keep saying that," Bowman said. "Well, who caught us?"

"Your conscience," said Earthquake.

At the barracks, we sank down on the grass. It was getting dark, and already a star was winking high up the heaven to the west.

"See, you two guys are at a real disadvantage. Somehow or another you got consciences. I got left out on that one."

"Behold our living mutant, Bowman," I said, pointing at the Earthquake. "What you and I were born with, he was born without. You said he was born lobotomized. Maybe he was."

"You're not born with a conscience," said the Earthquake. "Do you think a baby knows right from wrong? You gotta be taught. I'll bet around your house you had to apologize every time you broke wind."

"I'd be curious to know what you were taught, O'Toole," Bowman said. "You were raised by a bunch of Jesuits and nuns. Don't tell me they didn't teach you right from wrong."

"Confession," said the Earthquake. "Confession. Say a half-dozen Our Fathers, a dozen Hail Marys, and a Glory Be. I used to have such a long list at confession that I would write the thing down so I wouldn't forget anything. I'd go into the confessional with a flashlight so I could read it."

"Earthquake," Bowman said, "you are possibly the goofiest person I ever met or will ever meet."

"Well it's the truth," he insisted. "One night at Christmas, just before Midnight Mass, my flashlight batteries gave out, and there I was with a whole list of unconfessed sins that I couldn't remember. I took communion anyway. I'll admit I was a little scared. I thought I was gonna get it, from you know who." He pointed up to heaven.

"And what happened?" I asked.

"Nothing happened. Absolutely nothing. When I found out that I didn't have to worry about specifics, I started leaving my flashlight at home and just made sort of general confessions. I yelled at my aunt. I told Billy Horton I was gonna slap the silly shit out of him. That kind of stuff."

"You're a disgrace to the Church," Bowman said.

"Yeah, well what are you, you dirty Protestant heretic?"

"Yeah," Bowman said, "well, even I would know better than to take a flashlight into a confessional."

I laughed. "I gotta admit, Earthquake, every time I think I've heard it all, you come up with something so preposterous, so outrageous, that I'm left speechless."

"I never noticed you lacked for something to say," the Earthquake said. "Speechless. You guys? Don't make me laugh."

"Bowman," I said, then stopped and shrugged.

"Yep, I'll admit it's got me speechless," he said.

"Well," said the Earthquake. "If you guys are gonna get upset about a few lies in confession, I guess there's no need telling you about my Chinese girlfriend."

We waited.

"Well," I said. "Are you gonna tell us?"

"It was like this," he said. "She was deaf and blind."

"Stop right there, Earthquake," Bowman said. "Is this another one of those pelican things?"

"You wanna hear this or don't you?"

"I wanna hear," I said.

Bowman snorted and spat.

"She was deaf and blind," the Earthquake said. "She lived upstairs over this grocery around the corner from my uncle's place. Well, I happened to know that her bedroom was at the back of this dump apartment, and that you could get into it by climbing up a drain pipe that ran right down by her window. So one night I climbed up there. It must have been about midnight."

"This is sick," Bowman said. "I can see where it's going."

"Well, she was blind and deaf," the Earthquake said.

"You raped her?" I asked.

"If you wanna look at it that way," he answered.

"How the hell else could you look at it?"

"Oh, she liked it," said the Earthquake. "I'll admit that she fought a little at first. But she liked it. All that summer I climbed up the drain pipe. Then, the damndest thing, that fall she died. Someone said it was a heart attack."

"I sit here and talk to you for one reason," Bowman said. "I associate with you for only one reason. I know you're lying. You are the worst liar I ever met. But that you would even sit here and say something like that...Do you think that's cool?"

"I think it's the truth," Earthquake said. "I think I was invisible. It was like having the ring of Guy-jeez on. You do what you can get away with. Might makes right. And whether or not you two candy-ass college boys can understand it, that's how things work in the real world out there."

"I'm going up and read," Bowman said. "Mill, you can waste your time with this degenerate if you want to."

"You haven't heard the best part," Earthquake said.

Without turning around, Bowman said, "There's no best part where you're concerned, Earthquake. Just a bunch of filth spewed out of the fetid receptacle you possess in lieu of a mind."

"John Shawnesy said that," I proudly announced. "*Raintree County.*"

"An autopsy showed she was pregnant," Earthquake shouted.

"You're lying, Earthquake," I said, "and you know you are."

"But you've got to admit that it was a helluva story. Look at old Bowman. He'll worry about it all night. And anyway, I proved my point."

"Your point being..."

"The ring of Guy-jeez. You do what you can get away with."

"Which means that the only reason you didn't rape the Chinese girl is because you didn't get a chance—because she didn't exist. But if she had, you would have."

"Who knows? You wanna go over and catch a movie?"

"What's on?"

"*Anatomy of a Murder.*"

"I've seen it. But maybe you ought to go and find out about irresistible impulse."

"Believe I will." He hoisted himself up, walked away, and left me lying there alone, looking up at the stars that had begun to swarm like gnats against the blackness of infinity. For some reason, I began thinking of a story I had heard in Sunday School, about Abraham when he walked out one night on the dark hills of Judea, and heard the voice of God. Look up and count the stars if you can; so shall your seed be. I lay there waiting, I suppose, for a voice that never came. I dearly needed a revelation of some sort just then, a word from God, or maybe from Socrates, saying that Bowman and I were right, that we had done the right thing, that there was more to life than doing what you can get away with.

I thought of Mr. Stuart. He would know the answer. He was old, and wise, and well-read, and he would say...What would he say? He would say that truth is truth, and just men know the right thing and do it, not because they expect to get something in return, but because doing right is its own reward.

I went inside and found Bowman in the reading room. He looked up as I came in.

"Listen to this," he said. "This is the Perffessor in *Raintree County*. 'Human morality is a mere refinement of the social instinct, which we see also in some of the other animals. We're moral because it pays to be moral. But the really great problems of the Republic don't achieve moral solutions.' Who does that sound like?"

"Sounds to me like Percival G. O'Toole."

"Exactly. The boy's a genius in his own right. Unwashed. A trifle crude. But a pure genius."

I sank down on the far end of the couch Bowman occupied. "Tell me something," I said. "If he's such a genius, then why do I feel like taking a bath in a strong disinfectant after every conversation with him?"

Bowman closed his book. "Why do we hang around with him?" he asked.

"I guess just to see what he'll come out with next," I said. "I'll tell you the truth: I didn't even know people like him existed. But they must be common as dirt."

"I hope the hell not."

"We're off tomorrow," I said. "Let's go to town. We'll go to the gym, lift some weights, and go down and see Mr. Stuart."

We sat there a moment, wallowing in depression.

"We should be feeling great about now," Bowman finally said. "We did the right thing. Got commended by Stanford. Put the letter behind us."

"Along with the Amazon and Maggie," I said.

"We can patch that up," Bowman said. "I'll call her."

"But back to how we ought to be feeling. Sure, we did the right thing. Then the Earthquake dumps a pail of manure over us. Let's go talk to Mr. Stuart."

"Yeah," Bowman said. "Good idea."

I had no idea at the time (and I don't think Bowman did either) just how important Mr. Stuart had become to us. Young men are characteristically unsettled, proverbially wasteful of their youth and energy, ostensibly ignorant, and yet amazingly arrogant in their conviction that they possess truth as no one before them ever has. But now and then even young men come to forks in the road and don't know which direction to take.

The Earthquake was a fork in the road.

We could go the way of the Socratic Greeks, or we could go the way of the American street hustlers; and frankly, while the Greeks were more appealing, I had no answer for the street hustlers. It is easy to say there is such a thing as truth, and that it is forever graven on a white stone in that unseen, transcendent realm of the forms; to say that moral excellence never changes, that the wise and just man knows it and conforms his life to it no matter the cost. It is easy to say this, but when challenged by the O'Tooles of the world to prove it, or to shut up and admit that we all do what pays off, from the loftiest of ethicists right down to the lowest thief…Well, this is where Mr. Stuart was supposed to come to our rescue. He had become our confessor and counselor. We were Pinocchio trying to be real boys; he was Jiminy Cricket steering us around the rocks and shoals of life.

But Mr. Stuart would not be coming to our rescue, then or ever.

We got up the next morning, hit the mess hall, wolfed down some of the beans the cooks had promised us the night before. The Earthquake wanted to come along when we told him we were headed into San Diego, even offered to drive his car and pay for the gas himself. We told him we had plans that didn't include him.

"Go rape a blind woman," Bowman said.

"You damned guys can't take a joke," he said.

"The hell we can't," said Bowman. "We took you on didn't we?"

"It don't matter," he said. "I've got some business of my own to take care of."

We found out later just what his business was, and how he took care of it, but just then we put his "business" down to the usual inane babbling.

"See you later, Earthquake," I said. And we were off.

It was about nine o'clock that morning when we got off the bus in San Diego. We went through our standard routine, hit the gym, got nice and sweaty and pumped up, showered and dressed, then decided to go right to the book store and to get something to eat later. The downtown gym we worked out at was about a mile from Mr. Stuart's place, a brisk fifteen minute walk.

I knew something was wrong the minute we walked in the front door. There was a woman behind the counter, a woman we had never seen, and she looked simply terrible. She had on this old Mother Hubbard sort of a dress, and big glasses, and she had her hair tied up in a knot on the top of her head. But some of her hair didn't quite make it into the knot, and it was all over the place. She kept blowing her nose into this piece of Kleenex that had deteriorated into a soggy mess.

"We're closed," she said.

"Where's Mr. Stuart?" Bowman asked.

"Mr. Stuart passed away last night," she said, and blew her nose. "He had a heart attack. We took him to the hospital, but it was too..." She put her free hand to her forehead and started to cry.

We stood there like a couple of dummies.

"He died," she repeated. "We're closing the store."

I turned and started for the front door, and Bowman came after me.

"Wait!" the woman said. "Wait a minute, please."

I already had my hand on the door knob.

"Are you boys Bowman and Miller?" she asked.

We turned back.

"How did you know that?" Bowman asked.

"Milt told me about you. Last night. He knew he was dying. I kept telling him he would be fine, but..." She started to cry again.

"Milt Stuart," Bowman said. "I never knew his first name."

She got herself under control.

"Milt said that if anything happened to him, he wanted the store closed. We're going to auction off the stock next week. But Milt said if you boys came in, you were to have any of the philosophy books you want. So there they are. Take them."

"Are you Mrs. Stuart?" I asked.

"Miss Stuart," she said. "His sister. Milt wasn't married. His life was this shop."

"Miss Stuart," I began.

"Please," she said, "call me Emma."

"Well, sure, Emma," I said. "Look, this is terrible. We had no idea…"

"Your brother was sort of like a father to us," Bowman said. "He put us onto all this good philosophy stuff."

"Yes," she said. "He was like that. He was a very good man."

"I never knew a man who had read so many books," I said.

"It was his life. Our father was a friend of Jack London, you know."

"Your brother told us," Bowman said.

"Go on over there and take what you want," she said. "Milt would like that. Oh, one other thing. This is sort of strange, but Milt made me promise to tell you. He said you have a friend you call Earthquake."

"I guess he's a friend," Bowman said. "I think we're about through with him."

"He told me to tell you he hopes you will be kind to him. He said he's a lost soul, but that you two can help him if you will. He said you'll be rewarded for it later. Milt had a mystic streak in him."

"Earthquake is not an easy guy to be nice to," I said.

"But Milt wants you to try. Now go and get your books."

We each hauled a box of books out of Stuart's used book store that day. As I sit here writing, I look up at my book shelves and I see, without even turning my head, at least seven of Mr. Stuart's books. Augustine's *Confessions* is there, The Modern Library's *Nietzsche*, *The English Philosophers from Bacon to Mill*, Kierkegaard's *Either/Or*. I see Sartre's *Being and Nothingness*, but I am not sure if that came from Mr. Stuart or if I picked it up somewhere else.

When we returned to Miramar, I boxed my books up and sent them home. I knew I would never have time to read them as long as the Navy had the first claim to my life. Except, that is, for *Nietzsche*. That one I kept with me, carrying it aboard ship, off to Pearl Harbor, and all over Europe. I never heard the name Zarathustra without thinking of Mr. Stuart, and I never thought of Mr. Stuart without remembering the Earthquake, and without thinking of Glaucon, the ring of Gyges, and the possibility of a justice that transcends the world of the particulars. Mr. Stuart might have been able to clear all those knotty problems up for me, but he never got the chance.

Chapter 15

▼

A Cock for Asclepius

Crito, I owe a cock to Asclepius; will you remember to pay the debt?
—Plato, *Phaedo*

Mill and Bowman are really depressed about Mr. Stuart. Which I understand. I liked the old man too. It's a shame about him dying that way. But the boys act like they're mad at me about it, like it was my fault. Or maybe they're still mad about the Amazon and that crap about the Chinese girl.

—The Diary of Earthquake O'Toole

It was dark at the cove, but there was a strange sort of light that hung over everything. A wind had come up, and the air was getting cool.

In our drunkenness, we decided a quick swim would be a good idea. Wake us up. Clear our heads. Going to sleep was the last thing we wanted to do just then, with the enigma of Earthquake O'Toole still begging for some sort of solution. Of course, a wiser man would have asked us why, if we really wanted to think clearly about O'Toole and our relationship with him, we had consumed a case of beer and a pint of whiskey. So much for the silly notion that wisdom and old age go together.

We felt our way down the rocky path to the beach. The sand was warm and soft beneath our feet. The wind beat into our faces with the smell of salt and seaweed. The water was cool, the sea alive. It received us, bore us up in its arms, and we swam far out, turned, treading water, and looked back to the dark shoreline and the lights of town.

"Remember that time a skin diver got eaten by a shark right here in the cove," I said.

"Yeah," Bowman said. "That's a pleasant thought."

"The Earthquake said it was an insurance scam. Said Mutual of Whatever paid off, and the guy and his wife were living it up in Mexico."

"That character saw some underhanded plot behind every tree," Bowman said. "Anyway, thanks for the shark thing. You sure know how to put an end to life's simple pleasures."

"Which means you're going in."

"Damn right. Where are you going? Oahu?"

We swam back, walked the trail up to our sanctuary, and built a fire the way we did in the old days, a stupid thing to do up there with the wind blowing, but we figured there was nothing around us but solid rock, which wasn't apt to catch fire by any law of physics we knew.

"Thank God for driftwood," Bowman said. "There was always driftwood around. I wonder where it all comes from."

"It drifts in," I said.

"That, sir, was tautologically correct but empty of meaningful content."

"The definition of a tautology, sir," I said.

We got close to the fire and let it dry our wet skin.

"How many fires have we built on how many beaches?" Bowman said. "The hours we spent. The girls. Where did it all go?"

"The way of all flesh, my boy. We are as the sparks that fly upward into the night."

"The Earthquake certainly flew upward, didn't he. You know, we've still got his ashes here. What were we supposed to do with them?"

"Scatter them at the cove. But why be in a hurry? I kind of like having old Earthquake among us. It's sort of like old times. Except he's not here to say all that crazy stuff that used to drive you nuts."

"Drove us both nuts," Bowman said.

"Yeah, but I could usually tell when he was weaving us," I said. "You used to believe all that crazy stuff he talked."

"I came from a simple background, Mill, in which yea was yea and nay was nay. Not that we didn't know how to joke around my house, but every now and then we deviated into seriousness. The Earthquake lied from sunup to sundown, about everything, and if he got caught, he just giggled and went on to another lie."

"I thought he was lying about suing the Amazon," I said. "But it turned out he wasn't. And then, when he said he wasn't suing her, I thought he was lying again. And it turned out he wasn't."

"How can you possibly have any kind of friendship with someone like that?" Bowman asked.

"So why did we?" I asked.

"We didn't."

"Well, he hung around long enough. After you guys were discharged and you were going to school at L.A. State, he was still hanging around. There must have been something going on there. We must have conveyed something to him to indicate that he was a buddy, that we liked him."

"Two things I can think of, Mill. Only two. I keep coming back to them over and over. One was when we confessed to Stanford and took him off the hook for the letter."

"Which he wasn't on anyway, because the Amazon had already taken him off. No, my friend, we took the Amazon off the hook—for all the good it did."

"True. Very true. But that only shows you what a strange world the Earthquake lived in. Till I die, or slide into senility, whichever comes first, I'll never forget him crying in the mess hall and saying this was the nicest thing anyone had ever done for him."

"Okay. But you said there were two things. What was the other?"

"Other than the confession to Stanford, the only thing I can think of is that Mr. Stuart's dying wish was that we try to help the Earthquake. He's a lost soul. Those words kind of went into my brain in stereo."

"Well, we sure didn't make any promises to Mr. Stuart about that," I said.

"We didn't have to," Bowman said. "Sometimes someone asks you to do them a favor, and no matter what you say, you feel obligated to do it."

"Sometimes you feel obligated, even if they don't ask you. I don't know if I ever told you this, but I wrote to Emma Stuart for years. She had no other family. She went on living in San Diego for the rest of her life, taking care of her cats and worrying about life insurance premiums. Life insurance! As if she had anyone to leave anything to. And when she died...It's kinda weird. Kinda like what we're into now with the Earthquake. I got a letter saying she had left me something in her will."

"Why didn't you ever tell me about this?" Bowman asked.

"I don't know," I said. "I guess I should have."

"What did she leave you?"

"You'll never believe it. Listen to this one. She left me her favorite cat. Thomas Aquinas was his name. He came to us via railway express. My wife was allergic to cats, so he had to sleep in a storage shed in the backyard."

"Mill," Bowman said. "You are beginning to sound like the Earthquake. Look me in the eye and tell me this isn't some lie you're concocting."

"It's the truth, Bowman. So help me. That cat lived another ten years and finally died in the backyard, flat of his back with all four legs sticking up in the air. Like Snoopy asleep on the top of his dog house."

"Well the Earthquake died flat of his back," Bowman said. "With all four legs sticking up. Atop life's dog house, which he occupied his entire existence."

Bowman tossed another piece of driftwood on the fire, and the flames wavered up into the night.

"We're down to our last two beers," he said. "Shall we?"

"By all means," I said. "I'm already resolved to waking up tomorrow morning with the worst hangover of my life."

"We can't drink these, Mill," Bowman said.

"Why the hell not?" I asked. "Has Calvin Coolidge taken office again?"

"We have to pour them out. A libation."

"You're right again, Bowman. Where shall we pour them out?"

"Up there. Over the cliff and into the ocean."

We opened the beer, got up on unsteady legs, and walked across the rocks until we could walk no farther. There, thirty feet or so below us, waves were rushing in and pounding at the base of cliffs.

"To Jack London," Bowman said. We poured beer out, and down it went to join the eternal sea.

"To Socrates and the Greeks," I said.

"To Mr. Stuart and Emma."

"To the Earthquake."

"To the Amazon and Maggie."

"To Chief Crouch."

"To Hopewell and Commander Stanford."

We worked our way around the western hemisphere, mentioning everyone we thought deserved to be mentioned. Then we threw the empty cans out into the darkness, and out they went, and down and down, from litter to litter, world without end, amen.

"What about the Earthquake's ashes?" Bowman asked.

"I'm not ready for that yet," I said. "Let's hang onto him for a while longer."

We went back to the fire. Bowman sat. I lay on my belly with my chin propped on my hands.

"When I threw Earthquake out of my house after the baseball game thing," Bowman said, "I felt guilty for days. If I had believed Mr. Stuart could hear me, I would have apologized to him. But I just couldn't take that fat, bald-headed Irishman any longer."

"Well, it lasted that long anyway," I said. "To tell the truth, I thought it was over when we got back to the base and found out about the lawsuit."

"I could forgive him for that," Bowman said. "He tried to make it right, which wasn't an easy thing for an old street hustler like him to do. It was what he said to the Amazon that made me want to dump him. The only reason I didn't was because when the dust settled, I was madder at her than I was at him."

That the Earthquake said anything at all to the Amazon is passing strange, because the two of them had gone for weeks without any attempt at verbal communication, and had indicated that even looking at one another was only a shade preferable to physical abuse. Now, by George, without so much as a by-your-leave to Bowman and me, the Earthquake got on the phone and called her up.

Understand, we had no idea that he had written her a five page letter detailing his manifold grievances against her, not the least of which was the slanderous and malicious manner in which she had impugned his integrity. We didn't know that he had told her to line up her ducks, that he had a lawyer (he hinted that this was the guy Clarence Darrow consulted when he was in trouble), and that he was going to drag her into the hallowed halls where the blindfolded lady holds the scales, and have her whipped like a government mule. Nor did we know that he told her we were in his corner, cheering him on and urging him to take her for every penny ("That lying sack of horse shit," Bowman said, when he found out). We didn't know any of this. All we knew, at first, was that he was sitting on the front porch of the barracks when we came in from San Diego with our boxes and books, and that he seemed genuinely upset when we told him that Mr. Stuart had died. In fact, he started crying again, just like he did when he decided that our confessing we had written the letter was the nicest thing anyone had ever done for him.

He cried, got up and went into the barracks, and when he came out he said that he had something to do. That was it. We didn't see him until the next morning, and then we learned exactly what it was he had had to do, and what he had done.

We had a great breakfast that morning. The cooks had really outdone themselves. Omelets. Sausage. Biscuits. Coffee that tasted downright decent for a change.

"Brethren, this is what I call breakfast," I said.

The three of us—Bowman, O'Toole and I—were sitting at one of the tables near the front door. Hopewell was off the base, over-nighting with a girl he called Sweet Susie and whom he described as looking like something between Harlow and Monroe, but when I saw her for myself, one night at the enlisted men's club, she was more like W.C. Fields with a blonde wig. This was the second off day of our normal three day, port and starboard rotation, and I for one was looking forward to an entire day at the pool, with no kids to watch, no responsibilities to attend to, and nothing to do but read, gather the Symposium together, and throw ideas around. We might even, I thought, go over to the base gym and lift some weights, though we generally avoided that place. It was in the loft of what had once been a supply warehouse, and it was ratty in the extreme. As it turned out, we didn't lift weights, and we didn't convene the Symposium, and we ended the day just short of a general declaration of war. Bowman has since admitted that this is as close as he ever came to the actual commission of homicide.

We had finished our breakfast and pushed the trays to the center of the table. We were in the process of enjoying that final cup of coffee over which one lingers when one has no pressing engagements. I was about to outline the day's possibilities as I saw them. The Earthquake cut me off at the pass.

"I dropped my lawsuit against the Amazon," he said.

He was sitting next to Bowman. I was across the table from them.

"That was what I had to take care of last night. I called her up. I thought she seemed fairly civil. Well, at first anyway."

"Wait a minute, Earthquake," Bowman said. "Just wait one damned minute. Do you mean to sit there and tell me that you actually filed suit, in a court of law, against the Amazon?"

"Well," he said, "if you want to get technical, I didn't actually get that far with it. But I had all the paper work ready to go, and an attorney. Hell, don't sit there acting so surprised, Bowman, I told you about it."

"All you said," Bowman responded, "was that you had some shyster who said you had a good case for libel. Good grief! A school marm in McGuffy's primer could beat you on that one."

"Like hell she could," said the Earthquake. "But it doesn't matter now. It's all water under the bridge."

"Let's go back a few steps," I said. "You say that the Amazon was fairly civil about it at first. What was she at second?"

"We started arguing about the letter I wrote her..."

"You wrote her a letter." Bowman said, his voice rising.

"Good letter," said the Earthquake. "Good letter, if I do say so myself. Five pages long."

"Five pages," Bowman roared.

Men at the surrounding tables turned to look at us.

"You wrote a letter," said the Earthquake. "I wrote a letter. But after Mr. Stuart died, and with you guys confessing and all, I sort of felt bad about the whole thing. So I called her and..."

"Stop right there, Earthquake," I said. "What could you possibly have had to say that took five pages?"

"I had a lot of stuff to get off my chest," he said.

He looked from one of us to the other, then giggled. "I guess I said some stuff I shouldn't have said."

"I'm afraid to ask," I said. "But I'll ask. What did you say that you shouldn't have?"

He hesitated, giggled again, shrugged. "I said you and Bowman were behind me one-thousand percent. I guess that wasn't true, but I wanted to make her see how serious this thing was."

"And did you tell her last night that that part wasn't true?"

"Not exactly."

It was my turn to roar. "Not exactly!"

Men at the other tables turned to look at us again.

"You boys put a lid on it over there," the master-at-arms called.

"I was gonna tell her," Earthquake said. "But we started arguing, and..." He shrugged.

"You lying, no good, son-of-a-bitch," Bowman shouted, and he and Earthquake flew at each other and went to the deck, punching and gouging. It took the master-at-arms, two mess cooks, and two guys from the table behind us to get them separated. Then I rounded the table to the other side and got between them.

"I'll see you in your grave before sundown if it's the last thing I ever do," Bowman was screaming.

"You think you scare me, huh?" the Earthquake screamed back, red-faced and spitting out saliva with every word. "You don't scare me none."

Now the Navy didn't care if sailors got into fights, even though the Uniform Code of Military Conduct sanctions beating one another about the head and shoulders. The Navy cared about someone, anyone, causing trouble for the Navy, which this little spat did not. Besides, the master-at-arms and several of the cooks were friends of ours. So what might have resulted in a captain's mast, maybe even a summary court martial and time in the brig, resulted in nothing more than a highly profane tongue-lashing and an order to clean up the mess caused when several trays fell on the floor.

O'Toole said he didn't intend to clean up anything, that he was a third-class petty officer, and that there were plenty of mess cooks around to take care of it. Bowman, muttering threats under his breath, fell to and started picking up trays.

"All right, brother O'Toole," the master-at-arms said. "I'll see you up before the Old Man tomorrow, and you'd better have a good reason for making this mess, and for disobeying a direct order from a second-class petty officer." The master-at-arms emphasized the word "second," and pointed to the two stripes under his crow.

"Well, shit," the Earthquake said. "Gimme that swab."

I waited for the two of them outside. Bowman came first, jammed his hat on his head, and said, "I'm too pissed off to talk now, Mill. I'll see you later." He spat on the ground, smacked his fist into his left hand, and bolted off.

About that time the Earthquake emerged, blinking in the sunlight, and, of all things, went into that silly giggle of his. "Well, no harm done," he said.

"No harm done?" I said. "Are you nuts. You just got into a fight with a buddy who was willing to put it on the line to save your ass, and you stand there and say, 'No harm done.' Like hell there ain't no harm done."

"I've said it all along," the Earthquake said. "You boys take things too seriously. Ease up a little. Hell, no one got hurt."

"Earthquake," I said, "this may come to you as a shock, but the Amazon and Maggie are friends of ours. We like them. We more than just like them. This lawsuit business, and lying about us the way you did…We'll be lucky if either of them ever speak to us again."

We had started toward the barracks, hands jammed deep into our dungaree pockets, white hats tilted over the right eye the way the Navy likes to see them, the pride of Uncle Sam's fleet, and the darlings of our mothers's hearts.

"I'll tell you what, Earthquake," I said. "A friendship can survive only so many jolts, and I think this one has done it. We have to work together, but I don't think we're ever gonna be friends again."

"Oh," he said. "So you're taking Bowman's side?"

I stopped, turned toward him, hands on hips, and said, "What other side is there, Earthquake? You wanna tell me what your side of it is? I'd like, just for once, to see the world from your upside down, skewed, blurred, warped point of view."

The Earthquake had stopped to face me while I was raving at him, then he turned and walked on. I went after him.

"Come on now," I said. "Let me hear your side."

"There are always two sides, Mill," he said.

"You know how Bowman and I feel about those girls," I said. "You know it, and you deliberately jaked up what we had going. I believe you're still hot over Wilma Strupp. Hell's fire, man, we couldn't help it if she didn't dig your program."

"I don't want to talk about Wilma," he said. "I'm going to find Bowman and smooth things over."

"I'd leave Bowman alone right now if I were you," I said. "If it can be smoothed over—and that's a long shot—it needs a day or two to mellow."

This was putting it mildly. I went looking for Bowman, couldn't find him, took a book (I can't remember which one) and headed for the pool alone. It was fairly hot that day, and I went into the water as soon as I got there, and stayed submerged for most of the morning. Then I lay on the grass and let the sun dry me off. For some reason, there weren't a lot of people in the pool that day, which was fine with me. I talked to some of the other lifeguards, then dropped in to see Chief Crouch. He was drunker than I'd ever seen him. The Amazon had got it right: the man was an absolute detriment, a walking safety hazard. But fortunately he was too looped to walk, and he hated the sun too much to leave the office, so there he sat, obviously intent on drinking himself to death.

"I heard about the fight," he said.

"Pretty upsetting," I said.

"Nah," he said, waving his hand at me. "I've seen guys punch one another out in the morning and be out drinking together in the evening, best of pals."

"I don't think this one will come out that way," I said.

That was the end of the conversation. We had nothing more to say to one another. How he would ever make it to retirement was beyond me.

I left, walked to the far side of the pool, and propped myself up under the shade of one of our scrubby palms to read whatever book I had brought with me. I hadn't been reading long before I became aware of two tanned, hairy legs solidly planted in front of me. I looked up. There stood Bowman.

"It's over," he said.

"What's over?"

"Whatever I had going with the Amazon."

"You called her?"

"I wish to hell I hadn't," he said. "She took in after me like a biting sow. Ripped me a new one."

He sat down beside me. I closed the book.

"You told her the Earthquake lied," I said.

"Couldn't get a word in edgewise," he said. "My part of the conversation was one word, over and over. But. But. But. Man, I hope she comes down with hemorrhoids. I hope they revoke her work permit and send her back to Mongolia. And I hope they send the Earthquake with her and that she spends her life handcuffed to him."

"I don't know that Mongolia would let the Earthquake in," I said.

"You've got a point there. I don't care what Mr. Stuart said, I'm through with him."

"Well, speak of the devil," I said. "Look who just showed up."

"If it's the Earthquake, I'm leaving."

"It is the Earthquake, and he's heading our direction."

"See you around, Mill."

Bowman started to get up, but the Earthquake got to him while he was only half erect.

"Hold on there, Bowman. Wait a minute. Damn it, give me a chance to apologize."

"All right," Bowman said. He was now standing tall. "Okay, you apologized. Now for the rest of the summer you stay on your side of the pool, I'll stay on mine, and…and, you get the point."

"Dammit, Bowman," the Earthquake said. "Do you want me to grovel. I can grovel if you want me to. Look, you and Mill are the best friends I've ever had. Maybe you're the only friends I've ever had. Now, what I did was downright shitty, and I'm here to say I'm sorry."

The Earthquake stuck out his hand, and there stood Bowman, looking at it as if it were diseased. I was still sitting, watching, wondering what would happen next.

This incident, and what Earthquake O'Toole said about our being his best friends, is something we had forgotten with the passage of time. Actually, we remembered the incident, particularly the fight, and Earthquake's coming to apologize; it was the words we had forgotten. They came to us as we were reliving the Greek Summer at La Jolla Cove with the Earthquake's ashes resting in a plastic container between us.

Slowly, Bowman's hand reached out and took O'Toole's.

("Miller," he said to me later on, "if you ever tell anyone about this I'll kill you." I swore I wouldn't, but some oaths are apparently less sacred than others. Not only did I tell, I wrote it down in a book for all the world to see. Bowman read the book in rough draft, chuckled, and said, "It's all water under the bridge now, Mill.")

Then the Earthquake did an unheard of thing. He threw his arms around Bowman and hugged him, right there with the inhabited world looking on.

"All right, Earthquake. All right," Bowman said, and pushed him away.

"Let's go over to the EM Club tonight," Earthquake said. "Dinner's on me. I feel like the stone was just rolled away from my tomb."

Chapter 16

The Young Philadelphians

These boys are like brothers to me. I wish I could have grown up with them, instead of the bums on my block. I wish we could just hang around together. But I don't think they feel that way about it. I guess Mill and Bowman will always be friends, but I don't think they'll want me around after this summer.

—The Diary of Earthquake O'Toole

The EM Club was crammed to capacity that night, as usual, and the boys were all raring for action. The club was divided into two parts. The front room was a restaurant of sorts, where you could order food cooked, more or less, as you wanted it. Sometimes they had good steaks. Sometimes they were rotten. Sometimes, if you ordered medium rare, they came to you oozing blood. Sometimes, if you order well done, they came charred to a crisp. It all depended on who was doing the cooking.

Then, there was another room, the back room, where there was booze and live music. Sometimes the music was good, sometimes it was rotten. I'm beginning to hear an echo of myself. Sometimes life is good, sometimes it needs its tires retreaded.

The problem with the back room, as it concerned me, was that guys my age, that is under twenty-one, weren't supposed to be back there. But, like the music and the food, sometimes you could and sometimes you couldn't. It all depended on who was on duty. As a rule, sailors didn't care how old you were, as long as you were a sailor, but from time to time local law enforcement, or federal law enforcement, or whoever controlled things, got zealous and decided to be serious about protecting children like me, who were old enough to get their brains blown out but not old enough to get them beaten out in a barroom brawl.

We began the evening in the front room.

"What can we order?" Bowman asked.

"I said it was on me, didn't I?" the Earthquake said.

"Well, the steaks look good."

"I ain't Rockefeller, you know."

"Boy," said Bowman, "I saw that line coming. Can I get a baloney sandwich, Earthquake?"

"Get what you want, dammit!"

The steaks weren't too bad that evening, which meant that maybe everything else would be to our liking. There was a girl waiting tables who looked about eighteen years old. Bowman was trying to make time with her, and seemed about to succeed until the Earthquake pinched her on the butt. She yelled, a bouncer of some description came running, and what had looked like a promising evening almost came to a halt. The Earthquake, demonstrating a glibness of tongue rarely witnessed among the members of the sailing fraternity, talked his way right out of it.

"I know this looks bad," he said. "And I know you think I'm guilty of improper behavior. But the perpetrator was a man with a black mustache and long sideburns. A foreigner of some type. He was outside selling French postcards when we came in."

"Oh, Lord," Bowman moaned.

The bouncer started laughing. Then the waitress starting laughing.

"You keep your hands off the hired help, sailor," the bouncer said as he walked away.

"Good advice," the waitress said. "Now you other two guys might get away with a little feel here and there."

"What is this?" the Earthquake demanded. "Be cruel to fat Irishmen week?"

"Fat Irishmen I have no problem with," said the waitress, obviously a good woman with a come-back. "It's the concentration camp haircut, the sunburnt nose, and the goofy teeth I can't stand. Are you related to Curly of the Three Stooges by any chance?"

In response, the Earthquake went into a routine that is hard to describe verbally. It was a combination of Curly's gyrations, complete with sound effects.

"You are kinda cute," the waitress said. "In a disgusting sort of way." And then, to me, "Is he your mascot or something?"

"We don't even know him, lady," I said. "He was working with that foreigner outside, hustling French post cards, and he just followed us in."

"Hey, Pat," someone over near the kitchen called. "How about doing something to earn your pay."

She turned and gave the caller a very unlady-like hand sign. "Gotta go," she said.

This turned out to be one of those nights when moving from the front room to the back one was as easy as getting up and walking some twenty paces south. No one even acted like they had heard the term ID. We eased into one of the few vacant tables left, looked around for a waitress, and there was good old Pat. She looked a lot better in the darker room than she had out front, and as the night wore on she looked better and better.

"Set 'em up honey," the Earthquake said. "Start a tab and notify my next of kin."

"Who would that be?" Pat asked. "The baboon down at the zoo?"

Bowman and I roared.

"What are you doing back here," Bowman asked her. "Did you get tired of hauling steaks and potatoes around?"

"They got tired of me," she said. "Ran me out. I'm just filling in for a friend. Normally I'm a ballet instructor at a girl's finishing school."

"Where's your friend?" Bowman asked. "Or maybe two. We could make a three-some after hours."

"And who goes with Curly?" she asked, pointing at the Earthquake.

"One night with me," said the Earthquake, "and you'll never go back to these pretty boys again."

"Right," she said. And off she went to get the beer.

A country singer was wailing away on the low stage that took up about half the south wall. On a small dance floor, couples were oozing around without really going anywhere.

"I hate this shit-kicking music," said the Earthquake.

"Stick your fingers in your ears," Bowman said.

"A bright array of city lights as far as I can see," said the singer.

Pat returned with the beer. "Are you serious about me getting two other girls?" she asked.

"Hell, yes," Bowman said.

The singer wailed, "The cabarets and honky tonks their flashing arms invite a broken heart to lose itself behind those city lights."

"I hope you know what you're doing, Bowman," I said after Pat had gone off to wait another table. "There's no telling what she'll come up with."

"The last blind date I fixed you up with was Maggie," he said. "I didn't do too bad on that one, did I?"

"Not bad at all."

"Besides," he continued, "five beers from now, and whoever she comes up with will look like Theda Bara, Claudet Colbert, and Joan Crawford. Trust me on this, son."

"Well, I'll be damned!" a voice boomed. Making his way toward us through the smoky haze was our own Chief Crouch, dressed in civies which included a loud Hawaiian shirt; and hanging on his arm was a woman who utterly defies description. But I'll give it a go. She was about Earthquake's size, had on a dress that looked like something out of a Salvation Army grab bag, and had a face like a bare-knuckle prize fighter. If she had a tooth in her head, I don't know where she was hiding it.

"Fifty beers wouldn't improve that any," I whispered to Bowman.

"Seventy-five," Bowman said.

"The face that launched a thousand garbage trucks," I said.

The singer moaned, "Today I passed you on the street, and my heart fell at your feet, I caint hep it if I'm still in love with you."

"Mabel, meet the boys," the Chief said.

Introductions were made, and the Earthquake bounced up, bowed from the waist, and kissed the lady's hand.

"My, my," she said. "Aren't we gal-lahhnt."

"Join us," said the Earthquake.

"Don't mind if I do," said the Chief.

He dragged a couple of unoccupied chairs over from a nearby table, and there we were, as merry a group of mis-matched comrads as could have been imagined.

"Now this is the Navy," said the Chief. "Buddies out drinking together. I heard about the fight. Whad I tell ya, Miller. Flying fists in the morning, best of pals at night."

"Yeah," I said. "You live and learn."

"Hey, Hopewell's here somewhere," said the Chief. "There he is. Hey, Hopewell, come on over."

It was Hopewell all right, and Sweet Susie was with him, his imagined Harlow-Monroe. She was a few cuts above the Chief's sidekick, but that still left her down in life's bargain basement.

"Hey, guys," Hopewell shouted. "Come on over and meet the boys, honey. Here she is, Sweet Susie. Ain't she a peach?"

"More like a watermelon," Bowman whispered.

Sweet Susie seemed put out with the whole affair, but she allowed herself to be introduced, and we managed to find two more chairs, and the fun was underway.

"Remember," I said. "We're on duty tomorrow."

"Duty, hell," the Chief said. "I hate that damned swimming pool. Wish I could get back aboard ship."

"You're retiring pretty soon," Bowman said.

"Twenty-five days," said the Chief.

"We're gonna get married and move to Hi-wah-yah," said Mabel.

The Chief's weak laugh indicated that even in his drunkenness he had better sense than this.

"Well, congratulations, Chief," Hopewell said.

The rest of us mumbled similar things.

"Crazy arms that reach to hold somebody new," the singer screeched.

"Boy it's sure smokey in here," said the Earthquake. "Worse than the Western Front in the Spring offensive."

Pat came back to the table, and the Chief ordered up.

"Come on, boys," he said. "This round's on me."

"What's a good drink, Pat?" Bowman asked. "I don't mean this beer, but a real drink for real drinkers."

"Attaboy," said the Chief.

"We've got one called the pink squirrel," Pat said. "Comes in a big glass. You can't drink one and still be standing up."

"The hell you say," said Bowman. "Bring me one of 'em. Oh, and how about the girls?"

"I'm working on it," she said.

Earthquake, in the meantime, had gotten up and crossed the crowded room to where a girl was sitting by herself.

"What's this all about?" I asked no one in particular.

"That's a good looking girl," Hopewell said. "Surely old Earthquake..."

Before he finished the sentence the girl slapped the Earthquake hard, and back he came, swearing and holding his cheek.

"Well, you can't win 'em all, Earthquake," the Chief said.

"I doubt he can win any of 'em," Sweet Susie said.

"All I did was ask her to dance," said the Earthquake. "And she started in cussing like a sailor. Said to get away from her or she'd knock my so-and-so head off."

"Bet you told her where to get off, didn't you?" I said.

"Told her not to let her battleship mouth overload her tugboat ass."

"Hey, watch your language," said the Chief. "We've got ladies here."

"Why, Chief," Sweet Susie said, "it's a pleasure to meet a gentleman."

"Oh, he's a real gentleman all right," Mabel said.

The singer was running in high gear. "I don't know how on earth to find you. I don't know where on earth to start. I only know I'm here without you, and there's pins and needles in my heart."

"Hey, where are those drinks?" Hopewell asked. "A man could die of thirst around here."

"I think you've all had enough," Sweet Susie said.

"Just getting started, Sweet Susie," said Bowman. "Well, here she is now. Our little ambassatrix from the fountain head with my pink squirrel."

"Here it is," said Pat. "And be careful how you drink it. The girls are coming in, and I don't want to have to carry you out."

"Now you're talking," Bowman said. "Gimme my pink squirrel."

He took the tall glass—it looked like it held about a pint—raised it up, and said, "Here's to Jack London, and to all the boys that go down to the sea in ships."

"Well?" I said after he had taken a long drink.

"Tastes like pink lemonade. I don't think there's any alcohol in it at all."

Pat smiled and winked at me.

"Got me fixed up with a girl, huh, Pat?" I said.

She put a beer in front of me. "Got Bowman fixed up," she said. "You're going with me, honey."

"What about...," I jerked a thumb in Earthquake's direction.

"Yeah," she said. "But it wasn't easy. I told her he looked something like Orson Wells after a hard night on the town."

"I'm kinda pissed off," Bowman said. "I'm the one who did all the work, and you throw me over for this punk."

"You'll like her," Pat said. "She's an older woman. More your type. How's your pink squirrel?"

"Nothing to it," Bowman said, and took another long drink. "I think you're selling Koolaid with a pinch of hair oil in it and billing it as some mysterious elixir."

"Just wait," she said, and winked at me.

"I feel a dance coming on," the Chief said. "Come on, Mabel, let's show these kids how it's done."

"Come on, Susie," Hopewell said.

"I don't wanna," said Sweet Susie.

"Well do it anyway, you stupid slut," Hopewell said.

Pouting, Sweet Susie allowed herself to be led away to the dance floor.

"Here's one by Bob Wills and Tommy Duncan," the singer said. "Faded Love."

"If I ever saw two faded loves in my life," the Earthquake said, "that's them."

"Which two?" I asked.

"Take your pick," he answered.

The singer told out his grief: "As I read the letter that you wrote to me, it's you that I am dreaming of…"

"How's that pink squirrel coming, Bowman?" I asked, and turned to Bowman to find an empty chair. He was on the dance floor, cutting in on Chief Crouch. He danced a step or two with Mabel, then took off on his own, waltzing across the floor. Then he went into a sort of bunny hop, with his hands held up in front of him like paws.

"This is the latest craze," he said as he passed our table. "It's called the pink squirrel."

"Guess the Koolaid got the best of him," said the Earthquake.

Pat came along about that time, checking on the drinks.

"Looks like the pink squirrel got the best of him," she said.

"That's just what the Earthquake said," I told her. "Great minds, you know…" tapping the side of my head.

"Want another round?"

"Sure, why not. Put it on his tab."

"It's over the hill to the poor house," said the Earthquake.

By this time, Bowman had every dancer on the floor falling in with him, doing the pink squirrel in a sort of conga line around the floor.

"Hell, let's get in on it," said the Earthquake.

And up we jumped and fell in at the end of the line.

"Whooopeee," Bowman shouted. "I'm on a roll tonight."

The singer was singing something, but no one seemed to care, and, anyway, he couldn't be heard above the din.

The rest of the evening passed in a whirl of lights and noise. The girls Pat had lined us up with slid on stage at some point, and just then they seemed to be gorgeous, glittering creatures of the night. I have long since forgotten their names, and Earthquake didn't help me with his diary, as he did with Wilma Strupp. In fact, his entry for this episode, assuming I have got the right one, was two sentences long: "Hell of a party last night. Hell of a hangover the next morning."

Bowman's girl was a tall, dark citizen who looked something like Morticia of *Adam's Family* fame. I can't quite remember who the Earthquake wound up with, and I couldn't match her up with him the next morning, for reasons I will shortly reveal, but something tells me she fell on the lower end of the curve, somewhere between Mabel and Sweet Susie.

It's always a bit unsettling to wake up in the morning and have no clear recollection of what happened the night before. The last two things I distinctly remember were the fight that broke out over by the stage, shore patrol rushing in, a table overturned, and Chief Crouch saying, "Let's get the hell out of here before the paddy wagon comes."

"Where are we going?" someone asked.

"Over to my place," said the Chief.

The next thing I distinctly remember is someone either kicking me or hitting me in the side. It was Chief Crouch.

"Get up, Miller," he said. "Six o'clock. We're on duty in a couple of hours."

He was dressed in his uniform, looking no better and no worse than I had seen him a dozen times. Drinking himself into insensibility, then recovering after a couple of hours of sleep for another round was a style of life he had obviously cultivated for so long that it was, for him, child's play. (All right, so "child's play" is a hackneyed line. But give me a break, I've got a hangover here).

I started up, and fell back to the floor, looking up at a water-stained ceiling. My head felt like, well, fill in the blank.

"I'm done for, Chief," I said.

"Get up," he said. "Let's get cracking."

"Where's Bowman?"

"In the bedroom with some broad."

"Where's O'Toole?"

"Out in the front yard. The others are gone. Except for her."

"Her, who?"

"Her," said the Chief. "Right there."

I rolled my head to one side, and my nose hit another nose. It was good old Pat, out cold and snoring with her mouth open, looking as bad as I felt. Her breath was wretched, and mine must have been, because my mouth tasted as if I'd been gargling in a sewer.

"Get off the deck, Miller," the Chief said.

"All right, dammit! All right!"

I sat up. The room was moving. My insides were moving. Fortunately, I had all my body parts, and I was fully clothed, which meant I didn't have to leap what would have been an impossibly high hurdle, that of getting myself dressed.

"Here," said the Chief. "Drink this."

"Get it out of here," I said.

"Coffee. Drink it. I'm gonna get Bowman up."

"What about the girls?" I asked.

"Their car is here. Let 'em sleep. They can leave when they get ready."

I took the coffee mug, only because the Chief had it thrust in my face, and tried to get a sip or two down. It was a losing fight. I sat it on a nearby lamp table, got onto my hands and knees, and by a sheer exercise of the will got to my feet. I was about to cry. Pat was still out of it. I doubt an earthquake could have waked her.

And, speaking of Earthquake, we found him outside in a flower bed, covered with mud from head to foot, sleeping beside a bull dog, and with green paint on his shoes. Where the green paint came from, we didn't know. It remains one of the many mysteries we have never solved, and never will. But the Earthquake certainly let us know how he felt about it.

"Thirty dollar shoes," he said. "Florsheims. Ruined. Thanks, pals. The least you could have done after all the money I spent was to keep me out of the paint bucket."

"What paint bucket?" said the Chief. "I ain't got a bucket of green paint. Besides, them ain't Florsheims. Buster Browns, I'd say. His dog, Tige, lives in 'em."

"He was sleeping with Tige," Bowman said.

"Very funny," said the Earthquake.

That was about as close as we came to humor that morning. The Chief drove us to Miramar, the wounded troops back from the front, in need of convalescence and rest, in need of anything but what we had waiting. At the pool, we hit the shower, Earthquake fully clothed. He later hung his wet clothes over the concrete wall outside. He threw the shoes away.

At ten o'clock, the mob descended on us. I donned a pith helmet and a sweat shirt, put on sunshades, and sat on the mid-pool tower in a barely conscious state. Hopewell was down at the shallow end, brooding because Sweet Susie had given him the gate last night. Apparently the stupid slut comment had gone a little over the edge of what she found acceptable, or maybe she didn't like his low-class friends. Bowman and I agreed that he was well rid of her, but of course we said nothing of the sort to him, assuring him that she would come to her senses one of these days when it was too late, and that she would come crawling on her knees to beg him to come back.

Bowman, as it turned out, remembered less of what happened last night than I did. He denied, and denies to this day, inventing the newest dance craze, the pink squirrel, said it would be completely out of character for him to hop around a dance floor like a drunk, oversized rodent. But he showed a great curiosity about the girl he was with, and pressed me to think hard about it and give him a description.

"Well," I said, "Do you remember the Chief's girl, Mabel?"

"Oh no!" he said. "Say it ain't true."

"Well, you woke up with her this morning," I said. "What did she look like?"

"She had her back turned to me," he said, "and I didn't have guts enough to look. But if that damned Pat fixed me up with Mabel's sister, I'm going back over there tonight with a meat axe."

"Just kidding, Bowman," I said. "Just kidding. She was more like that singer that played Peter Gunn's girl friend."

"You don't say," he responded, brightening up considerably. "Well, maybe we'd better look her up again."

"I think I'd leave it alone if I were you," I said.

We rocked along until mid-afternoon, and by that time our youthful bodies had triumphed over the abuse we had heaped on them, and we were ready to go back for another round. Fortunately, we were broke and unable to do anything until the next payday, and by that time other concerns occupied our attention. The night's festivities had done one positive thing for us. From then on, until the summer ended and we all broke up, Bowman and the Earthquake and I were reasonably good friends. Surviving a war of that calibre must have a bonding effect on the combatants. But I'm not sure the Earthquake ever really forgave us for the green paint on his shoes.

Chapter 17

To the Chief, Ave Atque Vale

Prian himself
Was first to order the man to be set free
From his manacles and shackles and spoke to him
With friendliness: 'Whoever you are, forget
The Greeks – they have all gone from here.'

—Vergil, *The Aeneid*

The fire was down to embers by now, and Bowman and I were about down to embers, too. It was dark on the rocks above the cove, very dark, and there was nothing left to drink. We still hadn't dispensed the Earthquake's ashes, and neither of us had the ability to drive back to the motel.

"We'll just stay here tonight," Bowman said. "We'll get rid of the Earthquake in the morning, then we'll get the hell outta here."

"It's not very comfortable on this rock," I said.

"You're getting old, Mill," he said. "I've seen you sleep under tables, on floors, on a concrete sidewalk once."

"Yeah," I said, "but I was young and foolish then."

"Now we're both old and foolish, I suppose. Foolish enough to sleep drunk on bare rock, and old enough not to like it."

"You make it sound as if we haven't learned much over the past forty or so years."

"I don't guess we have," Bowman said after a bit. "Maybe we've collected a few facts here and there. I think I can render a plausible explanation of *The Republic* and a fairly plausible explanation of *Zarathustra*. I still don't understand Hegel."

"I think I understand him sometimes," I said. "But then someone comes along and proves conclusively that I don't and never did. I think I understand you, Bowman. I think you're fairly transparent. I thought I understood the Earthquake. But we've been out here all night, and I have yet to understand why he thought of us as his best friends. Think about it. Out of his entire life, he was with us no more than four, maybe five, months. And he leaves us all his worldly belongings."

"I doubt that he was ever close to anyone," Bowman said. "Our crazy parties, the Symposium, that may be as close to intimacy with another human as he ever got."

"Kind of pitiful when you think about it."

"Yeah, but don't get me onto another guilt trip," Bowman said. "Especially over the Earthquake. That's a waste of time. I don't care how rotten your childhood was, at some point you have to step up to the plate and take your cuts. He never did."

"But I'll tell you what," I said. "After you guys had that fight, and after the blowout at the EM club, I believe O'Toole would have given us the shirt off his back. I don't know why, but for some reason those were like epic events for him."

"I'd sort of like to have been a mouse in a corner at some of the parties in Olympus," Bowman said. "I'll bet that the myth-makers have sold us a bill of goods. I'll bet they were really nothing more than what we went through together many times."

"Do you suppose Aphrodite looked no better than Pat?"

"Probably didn't look as good," Bowman said. "Probably looked about like the Chief's girl, Mabel. She came to your birthday party, didn't she?"

"Came!" I said, and chuckled. "She crashed the damn thing. She wasn't even invited. Remember, the Chief was trying to get rid of her, her and that crap about getting married and moving to Hi-wah-yah."

"Come to think of it," Bowman said, "she wasn't at the Chief's retirement."

"She wasn't invited to that either," I said. "One of the Marines, that guy who used to do full gainers off the low board, told me she tried to get through the front gate, and they ran her off."

"I don't think the Chief would have known her if she'd been there," Bowman said. "I doubt he even knew what was happening."

"Probably not."

"Kinda weird, almost cosmic, him retiring on your twentieth birthday."

"The whole retirement was kinda weird," I said. "I didn't even think he was gonna show up. Imagine being AWOL for your retirement."

"He wouldn't have showed up if we hadn't gone to get him."

The retirement ceremony for Chief Crouch was set for ten o'clock in the morning, and Commander Stanford had planned a big gala out on the parade ground, with drums, trumpets, full dress uniforms, sort of like a triumphal recessional for a Roman general. Getting the Chief out the door with a measure of honor and dignity had become an obsession with Stanford, a debt he owed for services rendered, and he was determined to see it go off without a hitch. Imagine his consternation when we looked around at eight o'clock and the Chief was missing.

The pool was closed till noon that day. We had placed a sign on the glass front doors stating that all the pool personnel were on orders to an official exercise, and that we would be up and running as soon as we could get back. But, of course, with no guest of honor, the whole gala would be sort of pointless. Bowman called Stanford. Stanford was enraged, wanted to know if we had any idea where he could be, and said he was holding us personally responsible to find him and get him there.

"I'm getting tired of being held responsible for that lush," said the Earthquake.

Hopewell said, "You've got your hands full with yourself, don't you Earthquake?"

There we were, togged out in dress blues on a day that promised to be hot and humid, and ordered to comb San Diego and adjoining sub-divisions to find a man who obviously didn't want to be found.

I called the jails, both county and city. Nothing.

I called the hospitals. Nothing there either.

I called the shore patrol. As it turned out, they knew him and knew him well. He was one of their most consistent customers, but they said they hadn't seen him and had no idea where he might be.

Finally, I called his home. The phone rang something like fifteen times, it came off the hook, there was a muffled sound which might have come from a human, then a crash.

"He's at home," I said. "Let's go get him. Get your car, Earthquake."

"I'm not sure I remember where he lives," Bowman said. "We weren't exactly in the best of condition when we were over there."

"I know where he lives," Hopewell said.

So off we went, the four members of the truncated starboard section, dashing south on Highway 395, into the Lemon Grove area, and out to the frame house that when viewed sober left me wondering why, given a choice, the Chief would not rather have lived in a tent. The bulldog O'Toole had slept with was still there, laying like a sack of trash in the flower bed. He opened his eyes when we got out of the car and slammed the doors, said "Wuff," and went back to sleep. As it turned out, he was at least as eloquent as the Chief.

Up on the front porch, Bowman banged on the door. "Chief," he shouted, "get your drunken ass out here."

"Is the door unlocked?" I asked.

He tried it. It was.

We went inside and found the Chief, passed out in the front room, with the telephone receiver resting on his chest where he had probably dropped it after I'd called.

"Let's go, Chief," Bowman said. "A cast of thousands is waiting for your arrival."

"Omphlaagahblah," said the Chief.

"I didn't know he spoke Chinese," Hopewell said.

"Let's get some coffee down him," I said. "I owe him this one."

The Earthquake and I went out to the kitchen. It was an absolute wreck. The trash can in the corner was running over. There were empty beer cans and vodka bottles all over the floor, and there was a mess in the sink that I won't bother to talk about. Over in one corner, a mouse was gnawing on a crust of something, as unconcerned as if we were a part of his family. A variety of insects who shared the house with the Chief were out for strolls up and down the walls and under piles of refuse.

"Boy," the Earthquake said, "I hope we can find some coffee in here." He started going through the cupboards.

"I hope he's got running water," I said.

"Here's some instant," said the Earthquake.

"I hope this stove works," I said.

We managed to brew up a strong cup of instant coffee, took it back to the front room, only to find that the Chief was absent; Bowman and Hopewell had him in the bathroom, naked, in a tub of cold water, and he was fighting and swearing like a man possessed.

"You might as well settle down, Chief," Hopewell said. "Cause like it or not, you're going to your retirement looking half way civilized."

"Have you got the coffee?" Bowman asked.

I thrust the mug in the Chief's face.

"Ppraggamfuf," the Chief said.

"I guess that was Chinese," said Bowman.

"Swahili," Hopewell said. "I recognize it from a Tarzan movie I saw once."

"Where are his uniforms?" Bowman asked.

"What are his uniforms?" I asked. "How would I know what a Chief wears? What's the uniform of the day for a Chief?"

"Must be khaki," said the Earthquake. "This time of year it's always khaki for them as wear the hat."

"Get in the closets and see what you can come up with," Bowman said. "And look for some shoes and socks. And his hat. Hell's bells, we've gotta shave him. He looks like a lumber jack."

"Get outta there, Chief," Hopewell said.

The Earthquake and I went off to look for something to dress the Chief in.

We found one uniform, cleaned and pressed, hanging in one of the bedroom closets. So far, so good. We could find no clean shirts, no ties, no belts. He had socks and underwear mingled indiscriminately in the top drawer of a bureau. The other three drawers were empty. We found a pair of red and green suspenders.

Bowman and Hopewell, in the meantime, had gotten part of a cup of coffee down him and were struggling to get him shaved. When the Earthquake and I returned to the bathroom, they had the Chief flat on the floor between the toilet and the tub with Hopewell holding his head and Bowman sitting across his chest.

"Boy, this must be the world's dullest razor blade," Hopewell said. "Look at this grungy mother. He must have been using it to clean the head with."

"Ain't you gonna use some lather?" the Earthquake asked.

"Couldn't find any," Bowman said.

"Use some soap," I said.

"To hell with it," said Bowman.

"Ooooooow," the Chief howled. "You no good sons-of-bitches."

"Glad to see you back to your mother tongue, Chief," said Hopewell.

Bowman sang: "To feel sharp every time you shave, to look sharp and be on the ball, just be sharp, use Gillette blue blades for the cleanest, smoothest shave of all."

"How about this one," Hopewell said. "The wolf is shaved so slick and trim, Red Riding Hood is chasing him. Berma Shave."

"You bums are having a great time presiding over our execution," the Earthquake said.

The final results were not pretty, but we didn't have much to work with. The Chief's face and neck were nicked and cut, and covered with bits of toilet paper Hopewell and Bowman had patched him with. We couldn't find a toothbrush, and toothpaste was, of course, out of the question, so we made him gargle with Old Spice, on the theory that nothing could have smelled worse than his breath did just then. He cursed us at first, but after he had got a taste, he seized the Old Spice bottle and polished off about half of it before Bowman could get it away from him.

But the rotten shave, the bad breath, even the fact that he could barely stand up and had only an elementary grasp of the English language, were all problems we could probably have worked around if we could only have got him dressed properly. The cleaned and pressed uniform turned out to be one he was obviously getting ready to take to a tailor. The crotch was ripped out of it. The zipper was broken. A button was off the coat. The right leg had a hole about the size of a dime in it, probably the result of an uncontrolled cigarette.

"He's gotta have other uniforms around here," Bowman said. "He was always fairly neat looking at the pool."

"Well, you find 'em," the Earthquake said. "It's nine-fifteen, the clock's ticking, and Stanford wants him out on the parade ground at ten o'clock."

"Balls," Bowman muttered.

"Okay, boys, let's get him up and running," Hopewell said.

After we had dressed him, we stood him in the front room for final inspection. Bowman had him under one arm, Hopewell had him under the other, and I was behind him to keep him from falling backward. His socks were argyles, one red and one green. His shoes were the most decent part of the whole ensemble. His pants, held together in the front by a safety pin, were held up by red and green suspenders. But this wasn't too bad, because he had his uniform coat, which we also hoped would hang low enough to hide his torn crotch. His hat. Well, we couldn't find his khaki hat, so we had to use a white one. His tie was the worst part of the whole deal. It was multicolored, with a picture of Mickey Mouse, and the words, "Souvenir of Disney Land."

"This is the worst damned mess I've ever seen in my life," Bowman said.

"Well, it's nine-thirty," said the Earthquake. "We'll either produce him in thirty minutes, on the parade ground and ready to be mustered out of the Navy, or you'll see an even worse mess than this—like us splattered all over Stanford's windshield."

"Let's go," Hopewell said.

"Look on the bright side," I said. "Stanford just said for us to go and get him. He didn't say what condition he's supposed to be in."

"Your innocence is refreshing, Mill," Bowman said.

"Spxzzftss," said the Chief.

I have noticed that successful living is frequently a matter of taking problems as they come, working through them, putting them behind one, and going forward. But never, never, should one say, or even think, that things couldn't possibly get worse, because there is a great, cosmic plot unfolding, guided by those entities well known to our friends the Greeks, and they love to prove that no matter how bad things seem, they can get a lot worse.

Take Chief Crouch's retirement for example.

Okay, so he looked like a trick-or-treater in a bad costume; so he couldn't speak clearly and could stand only with assistance from three people; so he had no idea what was happening and gave no indication that he cared; so his face looked like he had been in an axe fight and every one but him had had an axe; so he smelled like a cheap barbershop. I still think we could have gotten through the ceremony with no more than a few raised eyebrows if the press and TV reporters hadn't showed up.

But Commander Stanford had only himself to blame for that one. Yes, we dressed the Chief and shaved him, but Stanford—politician and publicity hound that he was—put him on display before the news-hungry American public.

Now, on to the painful conclusion of the incident.

We got back to the base, with the Chief sitting semi-comatose in the back seat between Hopewell and myself, and through the front gate only because the two Marines on duty knew us from the pool and knew the Chief (We hadn't thought to look for his identification or a liberty card.). We drove as close to the grinder (Navy parlance for the parade ground) as we could get, which still put us a good city block from the place where the ceremony would be.

"There's no way the Chief is gonna walk from here to there," I said.

People were already filling up the review stand. The band was playing a Sousa number, and the flags were out and undulating in the mild, warm wind.

"I've got a blanket in the trunk," said the Earthquake.

"Hell, why not," Bowman said.

We took the blanket, laid the Chief on it, and each of us got at one corner.

"Up we go boys," Hopewell said.

"Man," said the Earthquake, "this bastard is heavy."

"Now you know how a corpsman feels," Bowman said.

We manhandled the Chief about one hundred and fifty yards to where a Marine color guard stood at a rigid attention. They were in dress blues, one holding the American flag, one holding the Navy flag, and two with gleaming rifles flanking them.

"Where the hell is he supposed to go?" Bowman asked.

"How the hell am I supposed to know," the Marine nearest us whispered through clenched teeth.

And then we saw them, over by the reviewing stand, the TV cameras being pushed around by real live human beings who, we could only assume, intended to broadcast the proceedings.

"I'm getting a real sick feeling," said the Earthquake.

A voice said, "Who are you guys?"

We turned, and there stood a tall man in civilian clothes who looked like he might at one time have played on the interior line for Notre Dame. He had on thick glasses, his hair was cut short, and he had on a Veterans of Foreign Wars hat. He clearly was of the Chief's generation rather than ours.

"We've got the Chief here," Bowman said. "Who are you?"

"Luther Greybow," he said. "Now, who are you?"

"We're just four humble sailors, sir," Bowman said. "What are we suppose to do with the Chief?"

He looked down at the man flat of his back at our feet.

"My aching ass," he said. "Where is Mel Stanford? Does he know Jim Crouch is in this condition?"

"I don't know, sir," Bowman said.

Suddenly, Luther Greybow looked up from Chief Crouch to us, letting his eyes run over us, grim and angry.

"Are you men lifeguards?" he asked.

"Not us," said the Earthquake. "We work at the golf course."

He later said what all of us were thinking, that if Mr. Greybow had known we were the ones who had caused the Amazon such grief, he would have torn us all limb from limb.

"We gotta go over there," I said, pointing to where the rest of Special Services were standing as a unit at parade rest.

"Hold on just a damn minute," said Luther Greybow. "We can't just leave him on the ground here."

"What shall we do with him?" Bowman asked.

"The plans were that he and Mel and I were to march behind the color guard, down to the reviewing stand, and take the salute from the station commander. Then there was supposed to be some short speeches, then…Are you sure you're not the lifeguards?"

"No sir," Bowman said.

"I don't even know how to swim," said the Earthquake.

Then it happened, as it must have sooner or later. Commander Stanford materialized as if by magic, coming toward us from the direction of the reviewing stand, looking magnificent in dress uniform, his chest covered with ribbons.

"What the hell is this, Mel?" Luther Greybow said. "And who the hell are these guys?"

"Four of the lifeguards I sent to get Jim back here."

"Oh, don't even know how to swim huh?" Luther Greybow said to the Earthquake. "Are you Bowman?"

"That's Bowman," said the Earthquake; and to Commander Stanford, raising a feeble salute, "Please, sir, may we be excused."

"What the hell are we gonna do, Luther," Stanford said.

"Maybe he could sit on the reviewing stand with the brass," said Luther Greybow.

"No," Stanford said. "He's gotta march up there with us. Hell, the newspapers are covering it. All about the three of us, old buddies from the war and all that, heroes who saved the country."

"May we be excused, sir?" said the Earthquake.

"Yes," Stanford shouted. "Get over there with your unit."

We never obeyed any command quicker. I tried to hide in the middle of the formation, which wasn't easy given that the men had marched onto the parade ground in formation, and that they were already standing at parade rest. We finally had to be satisfied with forming a rank all our own, at the rear, with vague plans to run like hell the minute the order to dismiss was given.

I don't know what Commander Stanford thought when he finally realized that the Chief's uniform was a disaster. What I *did* see was Stanford running to the reviewing stand, talking like a man possessed to another man in the uniform of a chief petty officer, and the other chief taking off his tie, handing over his hat, and fading away into the crowd. Then Luther Greybow and Stanford bent over the chief, still flat of his back on the blanket, and when they got Chief Crouch up he looked half decent, except for the pieces of toilet paper stuck all over his face. Greybow and Stanford started picking them off and throwing them away like they were strange insects of some sort. And all the while Stanford, red-faced and grimacing, was talking to the Chief; and the Chief's head was rolling around, and he seemed to be trying to understand something coming at him in a language he never heard.

"They'll play hell on getting him up to that reviewing stand on two feet," I whispered to Bowman.

Bowman started snickering, which got me started, then Hopewell. The Earthquake kept his composure.

The band began playing the "Star Spangled Banner."

"Ten-hut!" a bosun barked.

I cut my eyes over toward the color guard. Stanford and Luther Greybow had hauled the Chief up and were standing at attention, the Chief's arms over their shoulders, their inside arms around his back. He was hanging between them like a wet sheet on a sagging clothes line.

"Order arms," barked the bosun.

The band began "Anchor's Aweigh," and the color guard started east, passing before the sailors in dress blues standing at attention. And, wonder of wonders, the three old comrades in arms followed right along behind them, in accordance with the plan someone had worked out under the innocent assumption that any fool could follow plans. Maybe any fool could, but Chief Crouch could not. Stanford and Greybow still had his arms over their shoulders, and behind, each of them was holding him by the seat of his trousers. His feet were moving, not exactly in time with the music, and he looked like a bicycle rider whose feet had come off the pedals and were beating thin air.

Actually, the whole thing came off fairly well. The Chief didn't have to say anything (whoever did the planning may have been an innocent, but wasn't completely stupid), and the arms over the shoulders was interpreted by those on the reviewing stand as a gesture of affection between these men who had gone through the rigors of combat together. Even the TV and newspaper coverage was sympathetic. The closest any of the newsmen came to criticizing the way the Chief walked was a TV reporter who thought that the Chief was nursing an old war wound. I think Stanford fed him that line.

After the ceremony was over, Special Services had to pass in review as a unit before the brass on the reviewing stand. When we came down that grinder and the bosun ordered eyes right, I realized we were also passing in review before Commander Stanford and Luther Greybow, who were still holding up Chief

Crouch. I could have been imagining it, but it seemed to me that Stanford was looking right at me the entire time.

"Ready, front," ordered the bosun. We kept on marching, out to the edge of the parade ground, were halted, and the bosun called, "Dismissed."

We, that is the members of the starboard lifeguard section, scattered like a covey of quail. We had to go back to the pool, of course, but each of us seemed bent on taking a different path to get there.

Over in the men's dressing room we came together, and the Earthquake began to immediately voice the unasked for opinion that we were being victimized for the misdeeds of others. This was true, of course, but just then it didn't seem to make much difference.

"Who the hell put us in charge of Crouch, anyway?" said the Earthquake. "Hell, the way I see it we ought to get medals for even being able to get him out there."

"It's water under the bridge," Bowman said. "Let's get outta these blues, into bathing suits, and open the pool. Did you see all those cars out front?"

"I guess the Earthquake's in charge again," Hopewell said.

"We'll all be busted back to recruit seamen before the day's out," said the Earthquake. "Who'll have seniority then?"

"If we don't get this pool opened up," Bowman said, "Stanford will create a new rank for us: recruit seaman emeritus, or something like that."

The pool opened that day, but not because of our zeal and dedication to duty. Charley Long, radarman second class and head of the port section, came in just as I was unlacing my shoes, and said, "Stanford wants to see the entire starboard section in his office—now. We're gonna take over for you till you get back—if you get back. He's over there climbing the walls."

"Hell of a note if you ask me," said Billy Wood, one of the port section lifeguards who had followed Charley Long in. "I had some plans."

"I had some plans, too," said the Earthquake. "They had something to do with living to be twenty-two."

"This damned pool is turning out to be the bane of my existence," Bowman said. "I was never in trouble a day in my life. Eagle Scout. Passed the plate in Sunday School. Helped old ladies across the street. Now, every time I turn around I get dragged up in front of Stanford."

Over we went to the office of Commander Melvin Stanford, where we sat in chairs outside his office, while Judy the Wave typed away and acted as if we were part of the furniture. Finally her phone rang. She picked it up, said, "Yessir," and hung up. "Go right in fellows," she said, her lips warping into a smile of sorts. "The Commander is simply dying to see you."

Like soldiers heading up to the Russian Front, we single-filed it into Stanford's sanctuary. He was sitting at his desk. Luther Greybow, VFW hat over one knee, was sitting in the corner. The silence was—dare I say it?—deafening.

"You miserable shitbirds," Stanford said.

He was about to say something else, when his eyes began to blink, he began to cough, his face skewed to one side, and he flushed as red as a sunburned swimmer on a California beach.

"Mel!" Luther Greybow shouted, and leaped to his side. "Judy! Judy, get in here!"

We stood there for a moment, and then, because we didn't know what else to do, we did a right face, single-filed it back out, and kept going until we got to the swimming pool.

"I guess we should have tried to help him," Bowman said.

"I ain't a corpsman," said the Earthquake.

"I wonder what's gonna happen now," I said.

Chapter 18

▼

The Party

We are throwing Mill a party tonight, at Charley Long's place in Escondido. He'll be twenty years old. Still too young to drink legally. When I think of all the beer we've bought for that guy this summer, I can't believe we're not in jail for contributing to the delinquency.

—The Diary of Earthquake O'Toole

This must seem a strange chapter title to anyone who has read this book so far, because we were involved in parties of various sorts all that summer. Yes, but this was *the* party, the final one, the only one that really deserves the definite article, the one to be remembered by all who were present, an epic unto itself about which Plato might have written. The only problem he would have had would have been in trying to get any solid philosophical content out of it. What did it all finally mean, anyway? Perhaps I could aid him a bit. Life is one big party, to which all are invited at divine gunpoint, and each is forced to find his or her own meaning in it. It's a legend looking for a poet; a great, cosmic happening in search of a high priest and priestess; a script written out in the forgotten language of the gods waiting to be unriddled by the charismatic translator.

Sorry, Greeks, that's the best I can do.

Charley Long was the section leader of the port section, as I have already explained, and a man about whom I have had little to say. In fact, apart from passing references I have said nothing at all about the five sailors in the port section. This is not because they were unimportant, but because we saw little of them that summer. When we were on, they were off, and vice versa.

My birthday fell on Labor Day that year, as it often did. School was starting, and in many cases had already started. The summer was effectively over. The pool would be closing down in about a week, but already the good looking girls were gone, and we were left with dependent wives who were bored to tears and had nothing better to do than come out, sit around, and imagine that they were as attractive as they had been when they married the men who had ceased to be attractive.

Charley Long's party was for my birthday. At least he said it was. It was also a sort of farewell bash with the emphasis on bash.

Charley lived up the highway in Escondido, in a quiet house, in a tree-lined suburb, where civilized people did civilized things, where Ozzie Nelson came out to get the newspaper and waved pleasantly to Ward Cleaver, who was out with a hose watering his flowers. Charley lived here because he was the most civilized of the lifeguards, a married man with four children, a mortgage, two cats, Wheaties the breakfast of champions in the cupboard, and a fairly decent Ford sitting on the drive. Charley had a secret, of course. Occasionally he beat the crap out of his wife, and she occasionally threatened to have him locked up, and they finally went to divorce court where she accused him of cruelty, both mental and physical, and of other unmentionable things.

His response: she's frigid.

But all this was in the future. At the time of my party they were only arguing loudly and breaking a dish now and then.

Charley's wife was Angeline, a small, dark woman of Latin extraction, who had been good looking once, but who had begun sliding down hill long before any of us knew her. She had the tired, haggard look of a woman driven to distraction by four kids and a husband who wouldn't take the trash out and left the toilet lid up. But Angeline had this thing for me. I don't know how to explain it, because I never gave her any encouragement. She simply wasn't my type, even if she hadn't been married to a friend. I had, she told someone, character.

"Ha!" the Earthquake said when he learned of this. "He's got character all right. Every time he walks into a room someone says, 'Here comes that character.'"

An unnecessary reflection, I assure you.

The party was Angeline's idea. She came out to the pool one day, with all four kids in tow, and caught me while I was walking the perimeter.

"We're going to give you a birthday party, Miller," she said.

"That's swell, Angie," I said.

"Your birthday's on Labor Day. It'll be perfect."

"It's a lot of trouble to go to Angie," I said. "We could all just head for the beach and…"

"No, we're gonna have it at our place. I need a little excitement."

"That woman has the hots for you, Mill," Bowman told me later.

"How do you figure?"

"Look at the way she looks at you. Every time she's out here she manages to get as close to you as she can."

"She can forget it," I said. "Besides, I think you're dreaming. She's just friendly."

"Yeah, friendly. Friendly like a sex-starved, frustrated housewife."

It was certainly not your standard birthday party, with hats, noise-makers, and pin the tail on the donkey. No one brought any presents, and no one brought a cake. It was just a convenient way to put an end to the summer, slide over into the fall, and behave like a bunch of out-patients. In fact, several days before the party, while the Chief was nominally still in the Navy, Charley Long came around taking up contributions to buy the requisite refreshments.

The evening of the party there was a general exodus up Highway 395 to the suburbs. I don't know what you had to do to get an invitation to the party, but I suspect you had to be alive, human, and ambulatory. Miramar Naval Air Station must have been deserted that evening, except for those at flight quarters and their supporting personnel.

Angeline, to her credit, did try to create a sort of birthday party atmosphere. She had some helium filled balloons floating around, crepe paper streamers of various colors hanging from tree limbs in the backyard, and a sign written out on a long piece of butcher's paper and hanging between two trees: Happy 20th, Miller. Beer was iced down in tubs. Two long, folding tables, covered with butcher's paper, were set up in front of the sign, and the revelers could take their pick of potato chips, corn chips, and several kinds of dip.

"Looks good," Bowman said, when we came through the house to the backyard and out sliding glass doors onto the small patio. "What more could you ask for?"

"Music," the Earthquake said.

"No sooner said than done," said Charley Long.

He brought out a large radio, plugged it into an extension cord he had run from a kitchen outlet and out a back window, and the party was on. The radio was tuned to the same twenty-four hour station we always had playing at the pool.

Bowman had brought a brown paper bag with him. In it were three one ounce shot glasses and three quart bottles of Bull Dog Ale, a drink that is no longer on the market but was a favorite of sailors in that simple time.

"Why the shot glasses?" someone asked.

"I've got a plan," Bowman said. "A guy back home told me that if you drink a shot of beer every minute, within thirty minutes you won't be able to walk. That's my plan."

"That won't work," one of the revelers said.

"Hell it won't," said another. "Think about it. In thirty minutes you put down a quart of beer. In two hours you put away a gallon."

"Who's gonna keep time?"

"Who's gonna do the drinking?"

"Me and Mill and the Earthquake," Bowman said. He set up the shot glasses, opened the bottle, poured.

The three of us stood with shot glasses raised high.

"To my good buddy, Mill," Bowman said. "May he survive the evening and go on to greater and better things."

We tossed off the drinks.

"This ain't gonna work," Earthquake said.

"Keep at it," someone said.

"Hey, guys," a voice boomed.

It was Hopewell, and who should he be dragging with him but Sweet Susie, a woman we thought we had seen the last of after the EM club dance.

"Sweet Susie," I said, and threw my arms around her.

"Get away, Miller," she said, pushing me back.

"I can't help it if my emotions run away with me," I said. "I'm glad to see you. Hopewell said you had drop kicked him out for good."

"He came back on his knees," she said.

"Like hell I did," Hopewell said.

"Well, watch it, buddy," she said. "You're still on probation."

"Time," Bowman said. And the three of us tossed off our second ounce.

Bowman had put himself in a bad situation: if we were to carry out his experiment, someone had to keep time and keep the glasses filled. I must say, he showed remarkable self-discipline this evening.

"This ain't gonna work," the Earthquake said.

"Two ounces ain't gonna make anyone drunk," said Bowman. "Let's keep at it."

"Yeah, remember the pink squirrel," I said.

"What the hell are you guys doing with the shot glasses?" Hopewell asked.

Bowman explained it to him, then called, "Time."

Down went the third ounce.

"This ain't gonna work," said the Earthquake.

"Well I'll be skinned and stretched on a board," Bowman said. "Look who just walked in."

It was the Chief, up and navigating as if he were ready for the Olympic trials. He had his bulldog, the Earthquake's sleeping companion, on a leash.

"Chief," I said. "I didn't know you were still alive."

"No thanks to you sons-of-bitches," he said. "Dressing me up in that Mickey Mouse crap..."

"Wuff," said his bull dog.

"Aw, now you're not gonna hold that against us, are you, Chief?" Hopewell said.

"What's that dog's name?" the Earthquake asked. "We've never actually been introduced."

"Bullet," said the Chief.

"Bullet?" said Hopewell. "That tub of lard?"

"How about Lightning then," said the Chief.

"Time," Bowman said.

Four ounces, under the belt.

The backyard was filling up with people, most of whom I had never seen. Several of Charley Long's neighbors showed up, but this did not include Ozzie Nelson and Ward Cleaver.

The Chief worked his way through the mob and over to a lawn chair near one of the tubs of beer. Here he sank down, his faithful bull dog at his side, and prepared for a pleasant evening among his former associates. He was in for a rude awakening, but he couldn't have known this. He found a metal bowl, or maybe he brought it with him, and poured some beer in it for his bull dog.

"That beer ain't good for that dog?" someone said.

"He loves it," said the Chief.

Indeed, he seemed to have a real taste for beer. He lapped up what the Chief poured for him, said, "Wuff," and peed on a nearby bush.

"That dog is gross," Sweet Susie said.

"You mean old Bullet," said Hopewell.

"I'm renaming him," said the Earthquake. "From now on you are to be known as Lard."

"How about Sir Lard," I said. "Sounds more English."

"Excellent suggestion," someone said. "Here's to Sir Lard."

"Time," Bowman said.

Charley Long brought one of his neighbors over and introduced him as Pete Moss. Pete had his wife Lulu with him. They had both got an early start on the partying and were red-faced and wobbly.

"It is my understanding, sir," Pete Moss said to me, "that you are an accomplished quoter of Shakespeare."

"I like Shakespeare," I said. "But let's get something cleared up right now. Your name isn't really Pete Moss, is it?"

"Peter Paul Moss, yes indeed."

"Glad to meet you," said a drunk. "I'm Manure Pile Jones."

"I resent that, sir," Pete Moss said.

But the drunk had already wandered away.

"Can you quote Shakespeare?" Lulu Moss asked me.

"I fool around at it," I said.

"No one can quote Shakespeare better than my wife," said Pete Moss.

"No one," said Lulu.

"Well draw your iambic pentameter," I said. "And as he plucked his cursed steel away, mark how the blood of Caesar followed, as rushing out of doors to be resolved, whether Brutus knocked or no."

"Child's play," she said.

"Hey, Bowman," said Earthquake. "This woman thinks she can out quote Mill."

"That's the craziest damned thing I ever heard," Bowman said. "No one can out quote Mill. Oh, hell, time, time. I let it go three seconds too long."

"That ain't no damned way to drink beer," said the Chief.

"Wuff," Sir Lard said.

"Aw, wuff yourself," Charley Long said.

"Tomorrow and tomorrow and tomorrow creeps in this petty pace from day to day," Lulu Moss said. "And to the last syl-labubble of recorded time all our yester, yester, have lighted fools the way to deathy dusters."

"Is this a wuff in my hand," I said, "the wuff toward my wuff? Come let me wuff thee."

The Earthquake was down on the ground with Sir Lard, rubbing noses with him. "Some relationships can never be tarnished by the passage of fickle time," he said.

"All right, boys, move back and give me some room," a woman said. It was Judy, Commander Stanford's secretary. "I heard through the grapevine that there were some serious drinkers in this place. Happy birthday, Miller. I expect this will be your last."

"Hey, boys," I said. "It's Judy. And looking good, I might add. I don't think that Wave uniform does much for you. What dam of lances brought thee forth to jest at the dawn with death?"

"What he means is, what are you doing slumming with us bums?" Hopewell said. "If Stanford finds out, it's back to Hoboken, New Jersey, for you."

"Sandusky, Ohio," she said. "Stanford's in the hospital. You boys finally did him in. He had a stroke right there, and they hauled him out on a stretcher. Gimme a beer."

"You know, Mill," Bowman said. "You're right about this woman. She looks damned good as a civilian."

"What time is it, Bowman?" I asked.

"Oh, yeah. Time. How many is that?"

"I lost count."

"Get up off the ground, Earthquake," Bowman said. "Leave that damned dog alone."

"This dog is the love of my life," Earthquake said. "And, I might add, a helluva sight better than that barker you lined me up with at the EM Club."

"You feel anything yet, Mill?" Bowman asked.

"I feel pretty good," I said.

"It's working! It's working!"

"Come here, Miller," Judy said. She grabbed me and kissed me. "I always liked you guys," she said.

"Well, then, where's mine?" Bowman asked.

"Right here," she said, and kissed Bowman. "Stanford's gone and I'm coming out of the closet. No more Miss Goody Two Shoes. Hey, by the way, you guys got orders today. You're getting your muscle-bound asses outta Miramar. Too bad. But I guess my loss is some Yokosuka whore's gain."

"Where are we going?" Bowman asked.

"Yeah, where?" the Earthquake boomed and tried his best to bounce up from the ground. He fell back, sat on top of Sir Lard, and banged his head on the arm of the lawn chair Chief Crouch occupied.

"Just Bowman and O'Toole," Judy said. "And I don't know where you're going. They called over from personnel about sixteen hundred and said they had orders in for you."

"You're going to sea sure as hell," said the Chief.

"Why sea?" the Earthquake asked. He had, by now, managed to achieve an upright position, albeit on shaky legs.

"Cause it's the Navy, Earthquake," Hopewell said.

"We're airdales," said the Earthquake.

"Did you ever hear of aircraft carriers?" asked the Chief.

"I don't want sea duty," said the Earthquake. "I'll apply for a hardship discharge."

"I'll take sea duty," Bowman said. "If it's good enough for Jack London, it's good enough for me."

"Yeah, well with my luck," said the Earthquake, "they're cutting me orders for the Caine, or the Bounty. Or that damned thing London wrote about in the *Sea Lion*."

"That's *Sea Wolf*, Earthquake," I said. "The Ghost. Captain Wolf Larsen. You'll love him, Earthquake. A real intellectual."

"Well, Miller, you're not going anywhere," Judy said. "And I think you and I are going to get to know each other real well."

That prospect wasn't entirely displeasing, for the Judy I saw standing before me was not the Judy I had seen in Commander Stanford's office, with horn-rimmed glasses and stenographer's notebook, staring at us as if we were diseased. This Judy had shed the glasses (probably in favor of contact lenses), had on a low cut dress that emphasized her cleavage, and had let her hair down, both literally and figuratively. Her lips were soft and full, she kissed like a professional, and if she had told the truth, she was ready and waiting for me to hop on whatever train she was riding.

Like so many of my plans, this one never materialized. I know part of the reason; the whole story I can only guess at. The part I know casts Angeline Long in the starring role. I don't know where Charley was by this time. People kept coming in and leaving, the noise level was rising, as was the intoxication level, and things were sliding toward bedlam. Bowman was still calling, "Time," and we were still tossing down one ounce shots of Bull Dog Ale, though we had long since lost count of how many we had put away. Chief Crouch and Sir Lard were still drinking together. Sir Lard was now up in the lawn chair and the Chief was on the ground.

It must have been about this time that Angeline Long came around and found Judy hanging all over me. I don't know why Angeline thought she had been appointed to exercise the prerogatives of motherhood where I was concerned. Maybe Bowman was right; maybe she had the hots for me and felt herself out of the competition with the younger, unattached Wave in the field. Maybe she was drunk. Whatever the cause, she walked up to Judy, hands on hips, and told her to get her hands off me.

"Who are you?" Judy demanded. "The hall monitor?"

"Can't you see that he's drunk?"

"They're all drunk," Judy said, "and I'm working on joining them."

"You leave him alone," Angeline said, and pushed Judy backward.

This was not a good thing to do. Judy came back at her with a sound somewhere between a snarl and a shriek. They wrestled one another around the patio, fell on one of the unoccupied lawn chairs and smashed it down level to the ground, got up, fell over a retaining wall into a flower bed, and were finally separated somewhere between the rose bush and the rhododendrons. Angeline had a bloody nose, and Judy's blouse was ripped, exposing a lovely left breast.

Someone dragged Angeline, kicking and screaming, into the house, while Judy simply stood there smirking, outwardly as serene as the Venus de Milo, covering her exposed breast with one hand, and brushing back her hair with the other.

"Who the hell is that bitch?" she asked.

"That's your gracious hostess," Bowman said.

"Here," I said, shucking out of my t-shirt. "You'd better put this on."

"Miller," she said, "you've got great pecs."

"So do you, honey," I said.

"Time," Bowman said. "Where the hell is the Earthquake?"

"Gimme something to drink," Judy said.

With Angeline out of the picture, presumably in the house nursing her wounds and leaving me to the world's wickedness, things got back to the abnormal, which on this evening was normal. But not for long. Of all people, Mabel showed up. She wasn't invited, of course, but neither were most of the others. She came in crying, looking for the Chief, and found him on the ground beside Sir Lard.

"Hey, Chief," Bowman said, "here's Mabel. Got your tickets to Hi-wah-yah, Mabel?"

"What have they done to you, sweetheart?" Mabel said, and got down on her hands and knees beside the Chief.

I never saw anyone sober up so quickly.

"How did you get here?" he asked. "Where did she come from? Get your fat ass away from me."

"Don't talk that way, honey," she said.

Judy and I left the crowd and began dancing on the lawn to a slow song that was blaring from the radio. Somewhere over the noise I could hear shouting, but I paid it little attention since there had been shouting all night. Then the shouting gave way to whoops and loud laughter, and I distinctly heard Bowman say, "Better look for a hack saw."

"Wonder what happened?" I whispered in Judy's ear.

"Who cares," she said.

"Hey, Mill," Bowman shouted. "Hey, come on over here. Mabel handcuffed herself to the Chief."

"Maybe a cold chisel," someone said.

"Hell, leave them alone," someone replied.

"Where'd she get those handcuffs?" another demanded.

"I got 'em in a pawn shop down on Market Street," Mabel said.

Judy, togged out in my t-shirt, had begun laughing and couldn't stop. Everyone was laughing. Everyone, that is, but the Chief and Mabel. He was raging and swearing, and she looked like she was on the verge of tears, as if she couldn't quite comprehend what had upset him. They were on the ground, ringed in by drunk, laughing people, and she kept telling him how much she loved him and how the cuffs were a symbol of their unity.

"Symbol, my ass," the Chief said. "Either get the key and get these damn things off, or I'll amputate your arm at the elbow."

Hopewell and Sweet Susie had reappeared, and Hopewell pointed out that cutting off Mabel's arm wouldn't help—the Chief would still be handcuffed to a bloody stump.

"Then I'll cut off my own," the Chief said. "Just see if I don't. I'll take it off right there. Get the key, Mabel, before I knock out all two of your teeth."

"I threw the key away, honey bunch," she said.

"Anyone got some dynamite?" Bowman asked.

"Where did Charley Long go?" someone asked. "Maybe he's got some tools in his garage that would work."

Several of the boys went out to rummage through the trunks of their cars, and one came back with what looked like a cold chisel and a small sledge hammer.

"Just put it right there and start hammering," said the Chief.

"That won't work," said the guy with the hammer. "We're gonna have to get on something hard."

They moved over to the patio, followed by a growing number of well-meaning drunks.

"All right," said the guy with the hammer. "Both of you lay down right there and stretch out your arms."

"I ain't gonna do it," Mabel said. "I'm gonna stay chained up to my Chief. Just like a chain," she began to sing, "bound to my heart…"

"I ain't your Chief," Crouch replied. "And you'll either do what the man says, or I'll cut your throat."

"I ain't gonna," she said.

Several drunks wrestled her to the ground, and one of them forced her arm down and sat on it.

"Ready?" said the guy with the hammer. "Here goes."

He set the cold chisel on the chain between the two cuffs, took a mighty swing, missed the chisel and knocked a hole the size of a soft ball in the patio.

"Let's go back and dance," Judy said.

"Let's just sit over there and drink some beer." I indicated a relatively unoccupied part of the yard where a wooden bench was sitting beneath a tree.

"Sure," she said.

"Hey, Mill," Bowman called. He had detached himself from the mob and was coming toward us. He had a girl with him.

"We're going over there," I said. "Where's Charley Long?"

"He and the Earthquake and some of the others left. Said they were going to Tijuana. Meet Ginger," he said.

Ginger looked like someone named Ginger ought to look, which means she was a poor man's Ginger Rogers, with blond hair and long legs.

"I'm Doug Miller. This is Judy."

"Oh, it's your party," she said.

"Yeah, if you want to look at it that way. We're going over there. To tell you the truth, I don't feel very good."

Judy put her hand on my cheek. "What's the matter."

"Well," I said, "besides not being able to walk a straight line, I must have drunk a gallon of beer, one ounce at a time."

A great shout went up from the crowd back on the patio.

"The Chief must have just been freed," Judy said.

Free he was. The last I ever saw of Chief Crouch, he was up and running for the house, dragging his bulldog behind him. The last I ever saw of Mabel, she was being carried, a drunk on each limb, toward the flattened lawn chair the Chief and Sir Lard had occupied. This was the last I ever saw of most of the crowd that came to help me celebrate my twentieth birthday without knowing who or what I was, without even knowing the host and hostess—sort of like the mob that went out to Jay Gatsby's place on Long Island.

Actually, I never saw Angeline Long again, but I heard more about her than I ever wanted to from Charley. According to him, the house was a total wreck the next day, and Angeline took the kids and moved in with her mother. When he came back from Tijuana, sometime the following afternoon, she had left him a brief letter informing him that he would be hearing from her lawyer.

"Now ain't that just like a broad," Charley said. "It was her idea to throw the party. Then she blames me for the results. So, go and figure."

I assumed that the party was merely the final stage of a malignancy that had been eating away at their connubial relationship for a long time, but I said nothing.

The party was the last of a lot of things. The summer was over. The pool was shutting down. Bowman and the Earthquake were under orders to go somewhere else. And Judy, for reasons I never quite understood, didn't turn out to be the red hot lover I had anticipated. As Robert Frost said, "Nothing gold can stay."

Chapter 19

▼

Breaking Up is Hard to Do

And first of all Aristophanes dropped, and then, when the day was already dawning, Agathon. Socrates, when he had put them to sleep, rose to depart, Aristodemus, as his manner was, following him. At the Lyceum he took a bath and passed the day as usual; and when evening came he retired to rest at his own home.

—*The Symposium* of Plato

The last thing Bowman and I talked about that evening, lying on the rocks above the Cove with the stars above us and our fire a bed of glowing embers, was the breakup.

"It's funny," he said, "how little it meant to me at the time. I was excited about going to sea. And I only had a few months left on my enlistment. It wasn't until later, when I looked back at the Greek Summer, that I realized that I had lived through one of the most important times of my life."

"The thing that strikes me about it," I said, "is how abruptly it all ended. I guess that's the way it should have been, because it all started abruptly. One day I walked into the pool, you were there, and off we went to get the Earthquake out of jail. One day I walked into the pool and you guys were cleaning out your lockers, and it was over."

"You know, you're right," Bowman said. "There was no build up to the Greek Summer, and when it ended, it didn't slow down and peter out. It just stopped."

"Labor Day. The Chief retired. I turned twenty. No more Greek Summer."

"So what did we get from it?" Bowman asked.

"I got one of my best friends and a direction for my whole life," I said.

"I got a trench coat, a plastic container with ashes in it, and several hangovers," said Bowman. "And I got a best friend, too, and an avocation which I have pursued almost as avidly as you have."

"And memories light the corners of our minds," I said. "Misty, watercolored memories of the Earthquake, and the way we were."

"I'll never forget the day after the Party," Bowman said. "Judy personally walked over from Stanford's office to bring us our orders."

"Yep. I remember. The amazing transformation of the night before was reversed. She was back to being the old Judy, and for no good reason. She and I might have made sweet music together."

"Women, Mill," Bowman said. "I love 'em, but I'll never understand 'em."

Actually, Bowman and I had left the party with Judy, and with Ginger, and I, for one, had high plans for what remained of the evening. The problem was that Ginger did not, that Judy was driving and kept saying she had to be up and on duty at eight o'clock tomorrow; and, to make matters worse, Bowman and I were feeling the full effects of two quarts of Bulldog Ale consumed one ounce at a time. At some point—presumably at her home—Ginger got out. Judy drove us back and deposited us at the front door of our barracks; and off she went, still wearing my t-shirt under which one of her breasts flopped about in an unruly fashion. She brought the shirt back to me the next morning, neatly folded, with Bowman's and the Earthquake's orders.

Hopewell and I, heads throbbing, were checking the chemicals and adding chlorine to the water. I don't know why. The pool was closing for the season, and when it opened the following spring, we would be scattered all over the globe. But duty called, even unnecessary duty, and we rose to the occasion.

Bowman and the Earthquake, taking advantage of their third-class status were sitting in Chief Crouch's former office drinking coffee and trying to get into focus.

And in came Judy.

I smiled when I saw her, and waved.

She smiled, weakly, and waved back.

"Where are Bowman and O'Toole?" she asked.

"There," I said, pointing to the office.

Hopewell and I finished our task and headed for the office. Judy waited and met me at the door.

"Here's your t-shirt, Miller," she said. "I feel awful."

"You look great," I said. "But I'll admit that I liked you better last night."

"About last night, Miller…Look, that wasn't me. I just don't act like that."

"There was nothing wrong about the way you acted," I said. "That screwy Angeline Long is the one who ought to be apologizing."

"I've got claw marks on my boob," she said, touching at her left breast.

"I feel like I've got claw marks on my brain," I said.

"I felt so damned good about Stanford leaving," she said. "I started drinking as soon as I got off duty. I was flying high by the time I got to the party. Never again. I can't imagine what you must think of me."

"I think you need to get rid of those glasses, get a uniform cut low in front, and keep up the drinking," I said. "And, by the way, what brings you among us? I've never seen you at the pool."

"I wanted to bring your shirt to you—and these." She was carrying a large manila envelope. "Orders for your buddies. Then I gotta get back. Lieutenant Crawford is covering for Stanford, and I think he'll be even harder to deal with. Academy man. Real grade-A horse shit."

About this time Bowman and the Earthquake crept out of the office and into the sunlight.

"Here, guys," Judy said. She handed the envelope to Bowman. "You're going to the Bennington, Bowman. O'Toole, you're going over to North Island."

"Well," the Earthquake said. "At least it ain't sea duty."

"Wrong," Judy said. "Your squadron is heading for West Pac aboard the Hornet next month. Have fun."

"Fun," said the Earthquake. "Riding a stinking ship over to some slant-eyed republic, and you tell me to have fun."

"Be miserable, then," Judy said. "Either way, I'll sit here pecking on my Remington-Rand and taking down stupid messages in short hand. I gotta go."

"I'll walk you out," I said.

At the glass front doors we stopped.

"Judy," I said, "let's not let last night be our last one. I had a great time, even if I can't remember half of it."

"Call me," she said.

"By the way, when the pool closes down, where am I going?"

"You're going over to the golf course."

"You're kidding."

"Nope. From saving lives to patching greens. It's a hell of a way to fight a war if you ask me."

I kissed her. She smiled. "Call me," she said.

When I got back to the office, Bowman was on the phone with Prebble, his yeoman buddy in personnel who had helped him when he was trying to prove that Chief Crouch was never aboard the Yorktown.

"Here's how it is," he said after he'd hung up. "We can get a thirty-day leave if we want it. That's how it works when you transfer."

"Are you gonna take it?" the Earthquake asked.

"Yeah. Are you?"

"I don't know. What's to go home to? My Aunt and Uncle."

"Your mother, Earthquake," I said.

"To hell with her," the Earthquake said. "I hope she's locked up in a psycho ward where she belongs."

"I'm taking the leave," said Bowman. "Thirty days in Brookville, Ohio."

"I guess I'll take the leave," the Earthquake said. "I think I'll go to Vegas. I've got a system I want to try out on roulette. If it works, I'll be stinking rich and go AWOL and never see this place or any of you bums again."

"What about you, Hopewell?" Bowman asked.

"Back to the squadron," Hopewell said.

"Mill?"

"Judy says I'm going over to the golf course."

"The golf course," said the Earthquake. "What kind of deal is that? Join the Navy and chip onto the fourth green."

"Let's get outta these bathing suits," Bowman said. "I don't even know why we put them on. I'm heading to personnel to put in a leave request."

"I think I'll take a week of leave myself," Hopewell said. "Think I'll try to patch things up with Sweet Susie. She kicked me out again last night."

"I don't see much hope for the two of you," Bowman said. "Every time you go out with her, she says she never wants to see you again."

"It's the company I keep," Hopewell said. "You guys ain't house-broken, and she thinks that birds of a feather flock together. But…well, look at me. Am I that kind of guy? Why, I might be your family physician."

"You might be my local bookie," said the Earthquake.

We all walked back to the men's locker room together, and the boys started cleaning out their lockers. It didn't take them long. Bowman had an AWOL bag, and asserted his anal-retentive personality by folding his gear neatly and packing it away as if he were going to stand inspection when he got back to the barracks. The Earthquake dumped all his belongings in a pile on a sweat shirt, and tied it up into a bundle. Anal-retentive he was not. Hopewell, too, had an AWOL bag, and gathered up his belongings in a way that suggested he was neither an Earthquake nor a Bowman, but a hybrid somewhere between the two.

The handshaking began.

"You're a hell of a good bunch of guys," Hopewell said. "I never understood any of you, but I had a great time trying. Hell, I guess I didn't even try."

"Take care of yourself, buddy," I told him.

"Yeah. You, too."

The Earthquake started to shake my hand, then he hesitated, threw his arms around me, and hugged me as if I were a blood brother.

"Nothing will ever be the same, Mill," he said. "It'll never be like this again. This has been the greatest time of my life."

"It's been good," I said. "Better than anything I ever expected out of the Navy. I wonder if they would just keep me around as a permanent life guard."

"Fat chance," Bowman said.

"Yeah," I said, shaking his hand. "Well, you be careful out on the Bennington, pal. If you drop a bar of soap in the shower, don't bend over to pick it up whatever you do."

They all laughed.

"See you at the barracks later on," Bowman said. "Maybe we'll do something tonight. Last fling together, all that sort of thing."

"I'm about flung out after last night," I said. "But, hell yes. You've got it. One last fling."

After the boys left, I sat alone in that big, empty enclosure, with that big, empty pool stretched out beneath a gray sky. A light rain began to fall, pitting the pool's surface and whispering on the trees and flowers in the flower beds around the perimeter. I lowered the umbrellas on the tables, took them down and put them in storage. There was nothing left to do. I sat alone in the reception area, looking out the glass doors to the park where we had sat and discussed the Greek philosophers. Away in the distance, cars were passing by on 395, their windshield wipers beating back and forth, their lights probing into the mist.

The Earthquake was right: it would never be like this again.

That evening, after chow, Bowman and the Earthquake and I piled into Earthquake's car and headed for La Jolla. Bowman and I hadn't planned for the Earthquake to come along, but it was his car, and he wanted to come, and we didn't know how to tell him he couldn't. We took beer and a half-pint of Cutty Sark and walked up to a place on the rocks overlooking the Cove. None of us knew it at the time, but this was the very place where, over forty years in the future, Bowman and I would sit with the Earthquake's ashes, and read his diary, and try to understand the man with whom we had absolutely nothing in common, and who thought of us as his best friends.

The evening air, cooled by the rain, blew in from the Pacific. There was still a light mist. We wore pullovers. Bowman and I had on sneakers. The Earthquake was shod in the old, worn thongs he had schlepped himself around the pool in all summer. None of us had thought to bring anything to sit on, so we sat on bare rock. None of us had thought to bring anything to put empty cans in, so as we drank the beers we tossed the empty containers over the cliff into the ocean until we finally wound up with an empty paper bag and the cardboard containers the beer had come in. We tossed these over the cliff into the ocean. Bowman had brought cigars. We lit them with difficulty because of our unprotected position in the wind. We passed the Cutty Sark around, sipping from the bottle.

"I can get an early out," Bowman said. "Prebble told me today."

"How are you doing that?" Earthquake wanted to know.

"I'm gonna enroll at San Diego J.C. for the spring semester. My discharge date is in next April. But the Navy will let me go early to go to school."

"I'll be damned," said the Earthquake.

"Are you gonna do it?" I asked.

"Yeah," Bowman said. "Yeah, I am. I was one hell of a poor excuse for a student when I went up to Bowling Green. But I think I can handle it now. I did okay in the philosophy course."

"Any idea what you'll major in?" I asked.

"Think I'll be a teacher, Mill," he said.

"You'll be good at that," I said. "What are you gonna teach? I don't see you working with elementary school students."

"I don't see you working with high school students," said the Earthquake. "In fact, I don't see you teaching at all. I see you in a brokerage firm hustling stocks and bonds."

"Nah," Bowman said. "It's funny, when the summer began I was actually reading books on the stock market. I was intent on becoming a millionaire. It's all different now."

"What's different?" asked the Earthquake.

"The world. The world doesn't look the same to me. Mr. Stuart and his philosophy books, and the Symposium, and all the time we spent talking about the Greeks and London and Nietzsche—it changed me."

"Philosophy," I said. "You should teach philosophy."

"Nope," he said. "I don't want to do that. I don't want philosophy to be a professional thing, a job I have to do. I always want it to be something I do for pure pleasure."

"What about you, Earthquake?" I asked.

"I'm thinking about getting an early out," he said.

"Since when?" Bowman asked.

"Since just now," he said. "I didn't know you could do that. Maybe I'll get into San Diego J.C."

"That did it," Bowman said. "I'm going up to USC."

"Just kidding, Bowman," the Earthquake said. "But not about going to school. I'm tired of living a mediocre existence. I'm gonna get busy, bear down, be somebody. The way I figure it, if I really study, I should have no problem getting on the dean's honor roll. Then I pledge a good fraternity, start wearing shirts with button-down collars. Then, I go out for athletics."

"Like what?" I asked.

"I'm thinking track and field," he said. "I think I'd be good in the pole vault."

"That's the craziest damned thing I ever heard, Earthquake," Bowman said. "Look at yourself, Humpty Dumpty muscles himself over the bar at fifteen feet."

"Yeah, you hide and watch me."

"Have you ever pole vaulted?" I asked.

"No," he said, after a moment of silence. "But I knew a guy once who was built a lot like me. He was a great pole vaulter, and he said I ought to be good at it."

"Earthquake," Bowman said, "where is this all leading?"

The Earthquake took a pull at the Cutty Sark bottle, handed it over to me, and said with great solemnity, "I'm gonna work toward a Rhodes Scholarship."

It was dark enough that I couldn't see Bowman's face clearly, but I'm sure he was as dumbfounded as I was. Finally he said, "Why not just cut to the chase, Earthquake?"

"What do you mean?"

"Just run for the presidency and cut out all the preliminary crap."

I said, "I'll vote for you."

"Hail to the Chief," Bowman said.

"Why, hell yes," said the Earthquake.

"All right," Bowman said. "Returning from Never-Never-Land, what are you gonna do, Mill?"

"I don't know," I said. "I don't get out of his majesty's Navy until February of '63. I guess I'll work on the golf course and do my time."

"But then what?"

"I'd like to go to Europe," I said. "I'd sort of like to do some writing. Maybe I'll write a book about us and this summer."

"You need to get back in school," Bowman said.

"He's right, Mill," said the Earthquake. "I see you in a toga and sandals, students sitting around you, a Greek temple in the background, talking about the Ring of Guy-jeez and all that junk about the forms."

"Who knows," I said. "Pass the Cutty Sark, son. The golden fire is beginning to run around my brain."

Bowman handed the bottle over.

"You still going to Vegas, Earthquake?" I asked.

"You bums laugh all you want," he said, "but I've got a system that's bound to work. I could break the bank."

Bowman sang, "I'm the man who broke the bank at Monte Carlo."

"You don't put your money on numbers," said the Earthquake. "You go to the table and watch until you see one of the colors—say red—come up three times running. Then you put your money on black. Play the law of averages. If it hits red again, you double what you just lost and put it on black."

"Well, a fourth grade school marm could tell you that you can't break the bank that way." Bowman said. "That just brings you back even."

"I haven't exactly got the thing worked out yet."

We sat silently for awhile, puffing cigars, passing the bottle around.

"Where's the Bennington now?" I asked Bowman.

"She's at North Island," he said. "She sails for West Pac in two weeks."

"You'll be on leave."

"They'll fly me out. I'll pick her up in Hawaii."

"Man," I said. "I wish I was going with you."

"I wish you were, too."

"The Hornet's bound for the Taiwan Strait when she sails," said the Earthquake. "I guess I'll just go with her."

"What about Vegas?" I asked.

"I can save that," he said. "I'll muster out in six months, and they'll pay me off. Then I'll have some real cash to spend. By then I'll have my system worked out."

"What about the early out for school?" I asked.

"Next fall is soon enough," he said.

"I saw that line coming," said Bowman. "If you actually go to school and actually get a degree in anything, Earthquake, then I'll start listening to you. Forget the pole vaulting and the Rhodes Scholarship."

"It's always good to know that your buddies believe in you," the Earthquake replied. "That's what I like about you, Bowman. You always know how to encourage a guy."

"Remember, Earthquake," said Bowman, "that you're among friends now. You can save all the crap for your non-existent constituents. You're on a one-way trip to skid row, and the sooner you get there, the better."

For a non-prophet, Bowman was pretty good.

The rain had begun to thicken, and we were about to break it up and head for cover, when we noticed a light bobbing on the trail below us and coming closer. It was a cop. He had on a bright, yellow slicker and a rain protector over his hat.

"What are you guys doing?" he asked.

"Just sitting here talking," said Bowman.

He looked at the three of us as if to say he knew we were up to no good, if he could only figure out what sort of no good we were up to.

"It's raining," said the cop.

"It was only misting a little when we came up here," Bowman said. "We were getting ready to leave."

"You boys in the service."

"Navy," Bowman said.

"Let's see some ID."

I reached for mine. Bowman reached for his. The Earthquake was not prepared to suffer any further affront to his dignity, and thus simply sat there with his arms crossed.

"What's the problem with you, buddy?" the cop asked.

"My problem is," said the Earthquake, "that I am an American citizen being harassed by a jack-booted thug. You think I don't know the law. I don't have to show you a damn thing."

"Oh, Lord," Bowman whispered.

"Hey, Wendell," the cop called back in the direction he'd come from. "Come on up here."

In less than a minute there were two cops where there had shortly before been only one.

"See this fellow?" said the first cop. "He knows the law."

"Ain't that wonderful," said the second. "I love talking to guys who know the law."

"Officer," Bowman said, "I want you to know that I don't subscribe to a thing he just said. You wanted to see our ID. More than happy to oblige. Now, if it's all right, we'd like to be moving along."

"Maybe it's all right. Maybe it ain't," said the first cop. "Have you boys been drinking?"

"We had a couple of beers," Bowman said.

"He's only twenty," said the cop, pointing at me. "And just barely that. You been drinking, boy?"

"Not me, officer," I said. "I was just here with them."

I have no idea where my conversation with the cop might have led; perhaps to walking a straight line (which it is doubtful I could have done) and a subsequent trip to the city jail. But good old Earthquake, may his memory be blessed, began asserting his rights again, and the two cops turned their attention from me and back to him.

"Harassment," he said. "Pure, unprovoked harassment. We've already put up with this longer than we should. If you're gonna arrest us, arrest us."

"Shut up, O'Toole," said Bowman.

"You want us to arrest you?" the first cop asked.

"What's the charge?"

"Suspicion of public drunkenness for a start. And, buddy, you're under arrest right now."

"Like hell I am," said the Earthquake.

He lay down flat on his back and wouldn't budge.

"Get up," said the second cop.

"Make me," the Earthquake said.

"Add resisting arrest to the first charge," said the first cop.

"O'Toole," Bowman said.

The two cops jumped on the Earthquake, rolled him over, and slapped handcuffs on him.

The last time I ever saw Earthquake O'Toole, the two cops were dragging him off in the rain and he was shouting and carrying on about his rights.

"Well," Bowman said. "I guess Thrasymachus got it part way right anyway. The problem with the Earthquake is he can't figure out that they've got a bigger club than he does."

"The problem with us," I said, "is that we're stuck in La Jolla in the rain, miles from Miramar and with no way to get back. It's his car."

"He threw the ignition key under the front floor mat," Bowman said. "Let's get the hell outta here."

"Do you think we oughta try to bail him out?" I asked, after we were in Earthquake's car and heading home.

"Remember what I told you the last time we went to bail him out of jail, Mill? Let him stay there awhile. By the time he gets out, the Hornet will be in the Taiwan Strait. Talked himself right onto the chain gang."

"What do you suppose is ever gonna happen to that guy?" I asked.

"He's not going to Oxford on a Rhodes Scholarship, I can tell you that for sure."

"He's not going to the Olympics as a pole vaulter either."

"Nor, is he going to break the bank at Monte Carlo. Maybe he'll wind up running scams on old ladies, or shaking down drunks in Balboa Square."

"Mr. Stuart wanted us to look out for him."

"Mill, there's only so much a human can do. If the Earthquake is bound and determined to self-destruct, I don't intend to get in his way. Hell, son, he'll kill us all."

"Drive north, son," I said. "Drive north. Let's get to the barracks."

Chapter 20

Deja Vu, All Over Again

I must have slept well on the rocks that night. The last thing I remember is talking about the Earthquake being hauled off to jail. The next thing I remember is being waked up by something nudging me in the side, and there, standing over me and looking down, was a cop.

Impossible, I thought. I wondered, if only for a moment, if I had slipped backward in time and was confronting the same guy who had chased us off this spot forty years ago.

"What the hell is going on here?" the cop demanded.

I shook my head and blinked in the bright sunlight. I was staring straight up at the sky, and the cop, who was partially blocking my view of that beautiful, blue expanse, did not look happy.

"What are you doing?" the cop insisted.

"Just getting a little sleep, officer."

"Out here! On these rocks!"

"We were saying goodbye to an old friend," I said.

"We? What do you mean, we?"

"Bowman and me."

"Who is Bowman?"

"Him," I said, rolling in the direction Bowman had been the last time I'd seen him.

There was no one there.

"Look at this place," said the cop. "Look at all these empty cans. I'm tired of you bums littering up this place."

By this time I had sat up and had begun to look around me. We had, indeed, trashed things out. Beer cans and empty sacks were strewn over an area of perhaps 100 square feet.

"Officer," I said, "this is not what it appears to be. We are not…"

"Who is this 'we' you keep talking about?"

"Bowman and I. He was here last night. I don't know where he went."

"Okay. What about you and Bowman?"

"We are two retired philosophy teachers."

"Yeah. Right. And I'm Mata Hari."

"We came up here last night because a friend of ours died, and we were just reliving some of the old times. Look. I'll clean all this up. I just wonder where Bowman is."

"I'm kinda wondering that myself," said the cop. "Maybe he went where all the pink elephants and little green men live."

"Hey, Mill," Bowman called. He was coming up from the beach down below.

"Here he is," I said. And to Bowman: "Where have you been?"

"Went down for a quick swim," he said. "Clear up the old head."

"How about clearing up this mess," the cop said.

"Bowman," I said, "allow me to present officer…a…"

"Wilson," said the cop. "I'm walking down to the beach. When I come back up here, I want this mess cleaned up and you two out of here."

"I almost told him we had a right to be there," Bowman told me later on. "Then I remembered what happened to the Earthquake when he started standing on his rights."

We were glad to move out. It took us all of five minutes to get all the trash up and into a waste barrel about fifty feet to the east, and to get on our way back to our motel. Anything we had brought up with us, and which we wanted to keep, we had scooped into a large plastic bag in which we had carried up the beer, and this I toted over my shoulder like Santa Claus.

"Wouldn't it have been the living end," I said, "if this affair had ended with us getting arrested? Wherever he is, the Earthquake would have got the last laugh on us."

"You'll note that we didn't start telling that cop all about our rights," Bowman said. "Rights? Who needs 'em. I didn't want to be up there any longer anyway."

"It's the first time I've been at the Cove since that night we went up there with the Earthquake," I said. "We'll probably never go back again."

"Probably not."

At the motel, we got our gear together and prepared to vacate.

"That bed sure looks good," I said. "No more nights on rocks for this kid."

"No more overnight stays at places like this for me, "Bowman said. "Good grief. I could rent the Taj Mahal cheaper."

We checked out, got on the road, started north up the coast, and had travelled about fifty miles when I discovered the thing we had failed to do. It seems utterly stupid now, looking back at it, and I'm sure all good Freudians would be delighted to explain what was really going on in the deep recesses of our minds, but we were still carrying the Earthquake's ashes with us.

"This is just plain goofy," I said. "How could we not have done this? What's the matter with us?"

"I guess our brains have started to calcify," Bowman said.

"We'd better go back."

"Nah," he said. "Let's just pull over in Newport beach and throw him off the end of a pier."

"We can't do that."

"Why not? He'll never know."

"Yeah, but you will. Remember Tommy Lee Jones in *Lonesome Dove*?"

"Yeah. You had to remind me of that, didn't you, Miller? It was one of my favorite movies. Well I'm not going back now. So it's either off a pier in Newport Beach, or off a pier in Santa Monica, or off the rocks at Malibu. Or maybe just into a garbage can in my kitchen and out to a landfill."

"You'd throw your buddy into a garbage can?"

"No, probably not. But you've just brought up our unsolved mystery. The Earthquake was not, is not, will never be, our buddy. And why in hell he ever thought of us as his best friends is still beyond me."

"Wait a minute!" I said. I was pawing through the plastic bag that contained the ashes.

"What now?" Bowman asked.

"The Earthquake's diary. We haven't got it. We have your trench coat, my bag of marbles, *Martin Eden* and *The Republic*, and the ashes, but no diary. We must have left it at the cove."

"We probably threw it away by accident when we were cleaning up," Bowman said.

"We've gotta go back, Bowman," I said. "That diary is the only record we have of the Greek Summer."

"Turn around, drive back nearly seventy miles, paw through a trash can, and come up—if we're lucky—with a..."

"Wait a minute," I said. "I know where it is. I stuck it in my grip. It's in the trunk."

"Okay. So much for that. Which leaves us with the ashes."

"So what are we gonna do with them?"

"We'll think of something," Bowman said.

We rode on in silence for a long while. Frankly, I was exhausted, much as I had been when I had arrived in Los Angeles two days ago. Drinking all night and falling asleep on solid rock is not the sort of thing an aging philosopher should be doing. I was glad Bowman was driving. I let my head fall back against the seat and closed my eyes.

Finally Bowman said, "I have something to confess to you. And if you ever tell anyone this I'll have to deny it. I didn't forget the Earthquake's ashes. I kept 'em on purpose."

Without opening my eyes I said, "And the purpose was?"

He didn't answer immediately. I opened my eyes, sat up, looked over at him.

"I'm not sure," he said. After another long silence he said, "I'm giving the Earthquake's diary to you. It's nothing to me. It's more important to you. But I don't know why."

"And I don't know why you kept his ashes," I said. "And neither do you."

"Look," he said, "this plot is thickening fast. Why the Earthquake thought we were his best friends is something we'll never know for sure. But after last night, all the talk and remembering, I'm not sure he wasn't one of ours."

"Now," I said, "I'm doomed to spend the rest of my life trying to figure that one out. You threw him out of your house. You admit that we had absolutely nothing in common. There wasn't one thing about him, looking back as honestly as I can, that I can say I admired. He had no redeeming qualities whatever. Except maybe..."

"Except maybe a peculiar loyalty to us," Bowman said.

"He used people," I said.

"Everyone uses people," Bowman replied. "You and I use each other. But a friend sticks by his friends. And I really think there was nothing, and I mean nothing, that fat, bald-headed little Irishman wouldn't have done for us. Now, I ask you, Mill, what is a friend anyway?"

"Well," I said, "for starters, a friend is someone you like. I never was sure how much I liked the Earthquake. He lied every time he opened his mouth. He'd steal anything he could get his hands on."

"But do you know of anyone who has given us more genuine amusement over the years? Think of it. We say the Greek Summer was one of the most important times of our lives. And what would that summer have been without the Earthquake? He made the summer, as much as Socrates and Jack London made it. Things he said are chiseled in my mind like letters on a marble monument. That crazy thing about the pelicans."

"And the Rhodes Scholarship," I said.

"And that feud he and the Amazon got into."

"And pole vaulting. And breaking the bank at Las Vegas."

"The Earthquake's ashes are going home with me," Bowman said. "I've got a fancy urn I got in Singapore. That's where they're going. And I'll set them up on the mantle, and if anyone asks, I'll say, 'That's the final resting place of Earthquake O'Toole, one of my best friends.'"

Thus, we come to the final irony. Bowman threw the Earthquake out of his house, said he never wanted to see him again, and what is left of Earthquake O'Toole is at home with Bowman for good.

*   *   *   *

About three months after this, on a day in which rain fell from morning until evening, I got a call from Bowman. He was on his way back to Ohio and had arranged to stop over for a couple of hours in Oklahoma City. I drove out to the airport to meet him. I found him in one of the lounges, wearing the Earthquake's trench coat and looking like Bulldog Drummond.

"What are you drinking?" I asked.

"Glen Livet," he said.

"Miss," I called to a waitress. "One more Glen Livet for me, if you please."

The time passed all too quickly, as good times always do. After we had caught up on all the minor things—how are the kids, and so on—he said, "You might be interested to know that I've been in touch with the Amazon."

"You're kidding," I said. "Where did you find her?"

"There was nothing to it," he said. "I remembered where she lived, got in touch with the alumni association of the nearest high school, and bingo. They knew exactly where she was. In fact, she's still in San Diego. A retired teacher."

"Was she glad to hear from you?"

"Glad! She about peed her pants. She asked about you. She said Maggie is in Minneapolis, married to an insurance salesman."

"And what about her? Married?"

"Nope. Divorced. When I get back to Malibu I'm gonna call her. Take her out to dinner."

"I wonder if she's as good looking as she was forty years ago."

"Who is?"

"Some look better than others. But it won't matter. You'll have a great time together. Give her my regards."

"Sure. And, by the way, here's to Jack London."

We raised our glasses, finished off our whiskey, got up, and walked together down to the gate.

The End

0-595-29767-6

Printed in the United States
1450600004B/262-267